ACCLAIM FOR THE LATE LADY

"Another winner. . . . *THE LATE LADY* is a sure thing for all Bone fans or anyone with a taste for British mysteries."

—*Booklist*

"Fascinating characters, an intriguing plot, and sharp detecting. . . . An amazing tale unfolds and Bone is as interesting as ever."

—*Oklahoma City Sunday Oklahoman*

Jake Marsh: Renowned for his book-turned-TV series, *The Late Lady,* he was happy to play the role of the hard-drinking author—but his shock when Kingsley's body was found seemed genuine enough. . . .

Fenny Marsh: Jake Marsh's second wife had been good friends with his first, Kingsley. Plain but talented, she was secure enough to be on easy terms with Morgan Carradine, star of *The Late Lady,* even though the beautiful actress was Jake's current mistress. . . .

"A fine mystery distinguished by complex, intriguing family relationships. . . . This is a literate, finely tuned story."

—*Publishers Weekly*

"Nice sense of place and an attractive, Dalgleish-like hero."

—*Philadelphia Inquirer*

Ysobel Marsh: From her own suite of rooms on the first floor, Jake's doting mother had an excellent view of the household's comings and goings. . . .
Paul Lackland: Fenny's young business partner had grand schemes for expanding her home-based designer clothing enterprise. It irritated him no end that she would not listen to reason. . . .
Chris Thorne: He was Ravenna's uncle, so Kingsley's arrogant brother was still welcome at the Marsh house—or, at any rate, tolerated. . . .

Charlotte Bone: Bone tried not to let his sixteen-year-old daughter's taste in boys worry him. But he could not see the charm of a skinny specimen with bleached white hair and earrings, who had spent a night with Ravenna Marsh—and therefore become a murder suspect. . . .

Grizel Shaw: Bone's no-nonsense Scots girlfriend was a science teacher at Charlotte's school. When Bone finally proposed, he was surprised to learn that Charlotte, too, had been hoping he would. . . .

Books by Susannah Stacey

Goodbye, Nanny Gray
A Knife at the Opera
Body of Opinion
Grave Responsibility
The Late Lady

Published by POCKET BOOKS

THE
LATE LADY

SUSANNAH STACEY

POCKET BOOKS
New York   London   Toronto   Sydney   Tokyo   Singapore

This book is a work of fiction. Names, characters, places, and incidents either are products of the author's imagination or are used fictitiously. Any resemblance to actual events or locales or persons, living or dead, is entirely coincidental.

POCKET BOOKS, a division of Simon & Schuster Inc.
1230 Avenue of the Americas, New York, NY 10020

Copyright © 1992 by Jill Staynes and Margaret Storey

Originally published in Great Britain in 1992 by Random Century Group

ISBN: 0-671-73895-X

First Pocket Books Paperback printing April 1994

10 9 8 7 6 5 4 3 2 1

POCKET and colophon are registered trademarks of Simon & Schuster Inc.

Cover art by Mark Hess

Printed in the U.S.A.

THE
LATE LADY

1

The cry came again, agonized, waking the reluctant echoes. Then once more it rose, the cry of a soul in Hell despairing at eternity, and sank into the shocked silence.

"Those *bloody* peacocks. Just why do you have to keep them?"

"So that I can hear you say 'those *bloody* peacocks' and do that dear little jump sitting down. They've got out again, though. I agree they are too near the house and I'll send Anna down with the feed and a screwdriver to fix their gate." Fenny, leaning on the back of her husband's chair, rubbed her cheek on his. He bore the caress, but jabbed at the block of paper in front of him.

"I'm writing, for God's sake."

"You're not. You're only thinking about it. You've been thinking about it for hours now and it's all but lunch time. That's what I came to tell you."

"I don't want lunch."

"Then you can come and not have it in half an hour. I wouldn't bother you, old love, if you were actually engaged in any of the processes of writing, but I do know the difference. Christopher and Paul will be here pretty soon."

As the door shut behind his wife, Jake recognized belatedly the warning in her last remark: guests. He made a face at the writing pad and, outside the window, the peacock trailed long skirts across the lawn and screamed in triumph. A damned soul, thought Jake, seeing his mortal foe in the flames beside him. He liked this thought enough to bend sideways and scribble it on the jotting pad next to his jar of pens.

He returned to the manuscript before him, read it through, crossed out four words, then two sentences, then tore it off, crumpled it between his hands and, taking careful aim, shied it into the wastepaper bin he deliberately kept on the far side of the room. So much for a morning's work. The peacock commented. He stared sourly at the peacocks.

Foxes came regularly out of the surrounding woods to raid the dustbins. Why couldn't they make a medieval feast of it—treat themselves to a peacock takeaway?

For once, he knew what the trouble with his writing was; with an idea in his head that he wanted to explore, which perhaps was a book, he had to produce ideas for a new series instead. Television was money, independence; books weren't. At least, *his* books weren't.

Upstairs, Fenny shut the door of her workroom with a sigh, and leaned against it, studying the pattern of scraps pinned to the corkboard on the opposite wall. It was nearly right. Perhaps she should alter the design altogether, since the shades weren't blending—give up the idea of Grandmother's Garden and put some stars among the hexagons, definitely change it. No time now, though, for Morgan's jacket must be finished. She sat down quickly in her working chair before she could start to play with her design, and took the jacket on her knee. Guests! She didn't need them today. She knew Paul would be a nuisance because he would talk business, and to her mind a business partner should know when to let well alone. Chris, now: in China they would have had a special formal title by which she could address the brother of a husband's first wife. Formality would help. She

2

never knew how to talk to him and she couldn't think why he came. She'd told him Ravenna was still abroad, but he'd said he wasn't coming to see his niece; and she lacked the nerve to say: Then why on earth are you coming?

For a moment, while she feather-stitched in golden silk, the room's order and peace took hold of her. She relaxed and became absorbed in the rhythm of stitching.

A tap at the door heralded Anna herself, her thin face flushed, wisps of fine dark hair portending an early dissolve of the bun twisted on top of her head. She had smears of flour on her apron and on the side of her nose.

"I'm sorry to disturb you."

"You know you're about the only person who doesn't. Anything wrong? Dom being a pest? Getting in your hair?"

Anna put a hand to her hair and, feeling its imminent collapse, pulled the pins out and swirled the bun up again. She spoke through a hairpin as she stabilized the construction. "No. Dom's with Ysobel watching cartoons . . . I wanted to ask, do I have to go to the fête? I'd much rather stay here this afternoon and help you. I could do the pressing."

"Anna dear, I'd love it if only you could; I need a hand, but I need you more at the fête. If I didn't have to finish this jacket for Morgan, I'd go myself and it'd be all right. They expect Jake to go, and if he goes, someone must keep Dom happy or Jake will spend the whole time enjoying himself with Dom instead of socializing."

"Of course I'll go, then. But I thought Ysobel said she'd look after Dom?"

Fenny gave a little shrug. "Ysobel is not feeling so well after all. She thinks the fête would be too much for her."

Anna, smoothing back tendrils of hair from her face, made her hair seem quite *poudrée,* but the eighteenth-century look stopped there. She wore striped shorts under her apron. "I thought Ysobel was a bit keen on her lady-of-the-manor stunt, Famous Author's Mother."

Fenny grimaced at the jacket as her hand whipped to and

fro. "Well, today she's settled for the uncomplaining invalid. The moment she heard I wasn't going she said she wouldn't either. God, I'm a cat, and she's a jewel among mothers-in-law, but she's *there*. If only she had a proper granny flat and wasn't so interested in everyone's movements . . . I'd like to walk down my own front stairs and out of my own front door without knowing her door was open and that she expected me to look in and say where I was off to."

"She's not a bit like a mother-in-law, so slim and chic. People with a heart condition aren't usually slim. And her room's so lovely . . . I found her scissors, by the way, down the back of her sofa like before, and I brought yours back."

"I saw. Thanks. She can get up the stairs when she wants to. She'll spoil the blade with her paper-cutting. Did her package come from Durrants?"

"No post today. Mrs. Price brought her an American magazine with an article about Jake, though."

"Thank goodness. That'll please her. It's awfully touching, those scrapbooks, though Jake can't bear them."

"I'll leave Ysobel's tea on the trolley for her. D'you think you'll get that jacket finished in time?"

"Got to. Morgan's to wear it on Tuesday night."

"Will it be like an ad for you, her wearing it on TV? People asking where she got it, and wanting one too? It is gorgeous."

"I hope not. I've got all I can cope with as it is."

"Don't you mind Morgan coming here? Honestly? If I were you I'd hate her coming to this house. Jake shouldn't ask her here."

"He didn't. *I* did. I like her. She's a cool sort of person, so I don't know if she likes me or not, but she keeps the rules. And she needn't worry, anyway. I'm no competition."

"You're his wife."

"And just as well for me. Not much chance as a mistress. You tell me, Anna, how many men can you count on the fingers of one hand who've had a dog for a mistress?"

"George Henry Lewes," said Anna promptly.

Fenny sat up, her hands stilled. "Fast answer," she said admiringly. "Who is George Henry Lewes?"

"Was. George Eliot's lover."

"Oh my God. Yes. I suppose I'm a slight improvement on George Eliot, though I believe she was adorable when animated. She looked like a horse in ringlets, didn't she? With top Mensa-rating."

"A bad century for looking pretty. If you weren't, those obligatory ringlets were an awful handicap. Like putting frills on a ham."

"Elizabeth Barrett Browning looked like a curly-eared spaniel." Fenny threaded up her needle, turned the jacket, and started on the next seam. "Suppose Robert Browning muddled her and Flush? They both lay on a sofa and gooped at people between curls. Though probably Flush didn't wear a crinoline."

Anna spluttered, and was going to answer when the squealing crunch of a car coming too fast off the road into Paley's gravel court made both women glance through the window. Fenny's fingers hardly paused, but she frowned, caught her needle on the thumb that held the binding taut and had to put it to her mouth. Damn Paul. She wasn't up to the hassle he represented, especially with this work to be finished.

"I'll go down and hold him off," Anna said.

"He's not easy to hold off. He'd only be rude. Let him up."

Anna sighed and went. Fenny heard the door-knocker and Anna's voice. She went on sewing as Paul's voice brusquely answered and his feet came up the polished wood of the stairs. She was stitching-in the end and snipping it off when she heard the confident tap and Paul pushed the door open and stood there. He expected her to look up and she didn't, threading up with the gold thread once more.

"Come in, then," she said. "You'll have to talk while I work."

Paul had a neat, well-constructed face with a short,

belligerently tilted nose, small clear blue eyes fringed with thick lashes, and the habit of carrying his chin at a jut. The well-cut brown suit was his concession to the country, with a green and brown check shirt and mud-colored silk tie. Drop Paul in the shit, thought Fenny, returning to her work after the short glance, and he might not come up smelling of roses but at least he'd look the same.

"Well, Fenny," he said, and began wandering about the room examining the design on the corkboard, fidgeting with the skeins hanging on the wall, spinning the colored spools on their nails, and picking up and putting down her chalk, the marking wheel, her scissors, her thimble, the gold silk; running his hand up and down the letters, bills and receipts on the spikes by her writing space, peering through the geraniums out of the window; and coming back to rattle the pencils and crayons in their pots and pick up and stare at the bottle of rubbing spirit.

"What's this for? The odd booze-up?" He put it down on one of her sketches and she moved it. "It's such a mess in here. I don't know how you manage."

"I do. As you see."

"You'd be far better off in a properly organized place."

"This place suits me perfectly. And it's very highly organized. Everything is where I need it to be."

Paul's grimace gave him the look of a discontented small boy. "With a proper office you'd soon know the difference. You could hire someone to do all this admin stuff for you—" he flipped the pile of pierced letters "—and you've said you hate the correspondence side."

What I really hate, she thought, is people bothering me while I work. "It would be absurd to hire anyone for the tiny amount we deal with."

"But it could be a really good business, Fenny. It has such potential. Make us both a pot of money." Paul parked himself sideways on the window sill and, picking up Fenny's long scissors, began to open and shut them, with a faint metallic sound like a bat's echo-sounder. Fenny overcame a desire to snatch them from his hand, and concentrated on her sewing. The needle's movement usually soothed her, but the scissors' noise, out of synch with her pace, put her off.

"Did you come here to ask me anything?" She took the scissors out of his hand calmly, used them to cut the thread and put them down out of his reach. That he chose to look out of the window with great attention at this point showed that he had at last decided to say what he wanted to say, and he spoke in an abstracted tone.

"Well . . . there's an opportunity come up. A first-class opportunity."

She threaded up and rapidly carried on setting invisible stitches along the next stretch of binding. She was not going to ask what the opportunity was because for one thing he wanted her to ask, and for another she guessed what sort of thing it was and did not want it.

"You know the big barn by Dollond's Corner? Near Hawkhurst?"

"I've driven past it. I think I know the one. It had a sort of tractor graveyard."

"They've cleared all that. It's for sale. With forecourt and outbuildings."

Fenny sewed on, conscious of Paul waiting for questions she wasn't interested enough to ask. He was now trying her spare thimble on his little finger, without success. His hands were well shaped and well kept, but a little fleshy.

"It'd make the perfect place for all this." His expansive gesture shed the thimble in a glinting arc to the floor, and he bent his head under a chair. "The business. We could expand." He emerged and put the thimble down as though she had dropped it. Fenny removed it to her other side.

"You know I don't want to expand. You know I'm quite happy with things as they are. Why do you keep on when I'm not going to do it?"

He settled on the sill again, sleeking back his hair. "You *know* it's sense to expand. This is the perfect chance. The things you make are just being taken up, and they'll be in fashion for a while. It won't last long, so we must seize the market for the work you and others can produce. I've told you that Rusty Kate wants as much as you can do. More than you're doing now. I have gone into it with the bank and they're ready. Now we've got the premises—"

"What are you planning to do with this barn? Put *me* in it?"

"You and Mrs. Deal and Mrs. Price, Julia Whatsername, the others. Rationalize it. You're forever saying that you're always interrupted here. If you work there, no one can bother you."

"Have you got planning permission?"

"It's in the bag. A rural home industry—people doing what they were doing at home anyway."

"They won't want to, Paul."

"Not want a proper workroom, time to get on with things? Mrs. Deal's got no room at all, clearing away all her work every mealtime."

"She has to be at home every mealtime, too. She can't get to Dollond's Corner and back twice a day. There's no bus. She hasn't the time either. None of them has the time."

"It's not going to take much adaptation. People find time when they can see money in it," he said impatiently. "You can only see difficulties. It's going to be a real chance for them."

"I'll tell you what it's going to be," Fenny said. She laid the jacket on the table and turned toward him. "It's going to wreck the whole set-up as we have it, all our comfortable arrangements here with the shop and our timetables, doing just what suits us and our families, all to do what suits *you* with your expansion and business ideas."

"I've talked to Julia and her sister and they're in favor." There was sly triumph on his face.

"And the others? You've not talked to Lady Mary, she's away. I can't see her fitting in with this. Mrs. Deal can't and won't. *I* can't."

"Nobody's thought it out as I have. Don't condemn it without giving it time and talking it through. Think of advantages instead of complaints. You're so negative, Fenny. Think of working as long as you like, nobody walking in, nobody to mess your things up—nobody can borrow your scissors." He smiled, looking sidelong. "And don't think Mrs. Deal and Julia don't *need* more money, just because you don't. Julia jumped at the idea."

"All right, set up Julia and Susan in your barn and get a lot of girls with machines to run things up for Rusty Kate."

"They don't want that sort of thing; the market's asking for your kind of stuff." He plucked at the jacket, dislodging her needle.

"Thank you so much, Paul. Now look. I knew something like this was coming; you've been trying to push us toward it. But I'm like the others. I've all my things here, in order and in the right place. I couldn't work in the same room with Susan or Julia, and Lady Mary wouldn't move and Mrs. Deal can't. If we did expand there'd be more organizing and paperwork, that nobody wants to do. I know you're wanting to get more out of us for what you put in—and your finance has been a help—but it won't work."

"All you can do is find fault. You've no vision, Fenny." He leaned forward, the small boy ingenuous, pleading. "We can shift all your bits and bobs from here easily enough and set them up in the barn; and we can get a bigger shop than that poky affair over the road. We needn't depend on Rusty Kate either, not for ever . . ."

"The shop's been fine—"

"And on bank holidays, when the village is full of people, it's shut; and it's often shut because none of you can spare—"

"Anyone who's interested can come across and ask—"

"It's a one-horse, inefficient amateurish affair, and my money is being wasted."

"I've told you that Jake will buy—"

"If only any of you relied on the business for a living I'd get more sense out of you. I'm not getting myself thwarted by—"

"No, Paul. I won't."

"You sit there on your fat little fanny—" Paul ignored the evidence of his eyes as to Fenny's build in favor of rhetoric—

"and you say 'I won't.' But I believe in what I can see. You all make these terrific clothes and quilts and things. There's a mint in it. I can't take no. We'll talk. And look, I meant to say, has Ysobel told you about the weekend?"

"No. What?"

"I've got a chance to have my roof fixed, they're coming this weekend, and when I rang up here I got Ysobel; who said of course I could stay here. That's all right, isn't it?"

"It has to be," said Fenny.

"I told her about my plans. She was very interested."

"Really? Well, Paul: see you at lunch, then."

As he went, another car tooled in on the gravel, an upright and ancient Lanchester. Fenny had not seen it for some time, but she knew it. Christopher Thorn had arrived. Fenny had looked after the house for his sister Kingsley during Jake's first marriage, and she had felt that he still thought of her as a housekeeper, but later she realized he looked at everyone like that. She heard Ysobel, her voice clear in the front hall, welcoming him.

". . . Don't expect to meet Jake or Fenny until luncheon. They're both working."

Fenny bent over the rich velvet armful and sewed on. She glanced up only once, hearing her son's treble. On the back of the door hung his costume for the fête, dazzling scraps of flame, yellow and orange material making the feathers of a small Firebird.

Jake's voice momentarily surprised her, but then he wasn't writing. For him, writing might entail striding about the room, or furiously roaming the garden, or sitting in stunned trance in the small terrace beyond his workroom, or lying supine on the decrepit chaise longue, or scribbling with frenetic speed. It didn't entail staring out of the window and humming.

A white coupé edged between the gateposts and turned neatly in next to Christopher's, in a space only just sufficient. A warm husky voice called. Morgan Carradine swung her long beautiful legs out and came toward the front door and out of sight, but Jake answered her. She wasn't due till after lunch, surely? Fenny thought, I bet Jake asked her to lunch and just somehow forgot to tell me. Is that why he was in the hall? When his book turned into a money-spinning TV series he had copped the unexpected bonus of Morgan as *The Late Lady*.

Her famous husky croak, gin floating over gravel, echoed in the hall, and the company moved off to the drawing room for drinks. Fenny liked Morgan very much, although she would have been happier had Jake liked her rather less.

Anyway Morgan would keep Jake in a cheerful mood and stop Paul talking business at table. Dom would be pleased. He thought Morgan was the cat's pajamas. Morgan as a cat would be, perhaps, an Abyssinian with topaz eyes and oval paws, a cat with a touch of the exotic. Fenny pushed her fingers through her hair. A comfort not to be in competition: dogs must know their place. It would all be more simple if she could dislike Morgan.

Better go down now. Anna might be thrown by the advent of another person, and it was no good to tell her that, as Fenny had observed, Morgan hardly bothered to eat at all.

Shutting her door, she paused for a moment, then put a hand in her dungarees pocket and brought out a key. So Jake thought she was paranoid. His mother didn't pop into *his* study to borrow his typewriter, a writer's room was sacred, and anyway he was a *man,* doing important work. Ysobel did warmly acknowledge that Fenny's "hobby" had kept the wolf from the door, one terrible year before Jake's success when Ysobel's accountant had made a gruel of her tax affairs. Fenny's income meant nothing now that Morgan had made a runaway success of *The Late Lady;* her work was quite unimportant; it was "fun," and with this had come a habit of treating the workroom as a family source for needles and thread, or for scissors or paste. Fenny locked the door with superfluous vigor. She heard the voices in the sitting room, glasses clinked, Jake was genial. Another noise, trundling hideously on the parquet, sounded below and Dom crossed the hall kneeling on the old brown skateboard, oaring himself with a cricket stump.

"Hallo, darling," she said over the landing balustrade, and he tilted his head up.

"Hallo, Mummy. Morgan's here. I'm going to show her my canoe." He disappeared below.

Fenny saw herself in the long glass halfway down the stairs. Pink dungarees, violet shirt, fine; and then appeared the pleasant, plain face. No, let's go and look at Morgan. It cheered Fenny up to look at something nice. Her feet tapped down the honey-brown wood of the stairs.

2

Bone had both front windows of the car down, and he rejoiced in the flow of cooler air over his skin as he drove; pleasant to feel it on bare arms, not to be in his usual constriction of shirt and even jacket, to be off duty even to the extent of wearing teeshirt and jeans, the uniform of the younger man. His daughter had approved. "Mr. Grant wears *shorts* and his legs are really jungly." She was going to be collected by Mr. Grant, together with his daughter Prue when—was it Janine's?—birthday party was over, so Bone might get a glance at the gorilla legs himself when Charlotte was delivered home. He could imagine the covert grins at the station if he came in wearing shorts.

He was still smiling when he swung off the roundabout onto the bypass. He saw the big truck in the lay-by, its brake lights glowing, and saw the girl being dumped by one arm from the high cab. Her legs kicked and her mouth was shouting. A black cloth holdall was dumped after her; she tried to catch it but was too busy shouting to attend to it. Bone saw the lorry's signal just in time before it swung out into his path. The driver must be in a fury to pull away as wildly as that. As the girl gazed after it, all the fight seemed to leave her and her shoulders slumped. She looked no more than Cha's age, though she was dressed like an exaggeration of Prue Grant. Bone, having been forced to slow, swung into the lay-by and stopped. The girl turned swiftly and was lugging her holdall toward his car as he leaned across. She wore a clinging black teeshirt, and black harem trousers caught at the ankle into little black cotton boots.

"Trouble?" he asked.

As she bent to talk to him, her hand on the car door, he realized the question to be superfluous. The teeshirt was scoop-necked, she was made up matt pale with a brown lipstick outlined in black. The hair swinging forward in two points at her cheeks was so lusterless and jet black it must be dyed. She might be Cha's age but she *was* trouble.

"Trouble?" she echoed. The eyes gave him and the inside of the car a once-over. "Nothing I can't handle. Not going anywhere near Benenden, are you?"

For a moment he connected this request with the classy girls' school there. Her accent, though slightly disguised by the demotic now fashionable among the top layers, was suitable. However, in holiday time?

"I can go through there," he said, opening the door. Benenden had for him the welcome association of being on his way to Adlingsden where Grizel Shaw lived, though to his present frustration, Grizel's brother and his family had taken their usual summer advantage of her living in a pretty Kent village to ask themselves there for a fortnight. The undecided terms on which Bone and Grizel stood could be disturbed by family opinion.

The girl slung her holdall in, rocking the car, slid in, shut the door, and reached for her seat belt, eyeing Bone speculatively. He got out into the traffic with ease. He had meant to go home, but it seemed to him a good idea to get this young woman where she was going. Her handling of trouble so far had earned her bruised arms.

He was silent. Acquaintance with Cha's increasing circle of friends had shown him that questions were regarded as interfering, condescending, uncool. One method of the interrogations his job entailed was a receptive silence, and he was very good at it.

The girl tucked up her feet, sat sideways, and stared at him. Bone, amused, idled down the A21 at a regulation sixty. Finally she said, "Married?"

"No." Bone no longer hesitated over this question.

"Divorced?"

"No."

"Gay?" Either self-consciousness or incredulity made her voice alter on this question.

"No."

"Playing the field, then."

He let that alone. At least she hadn't placed him as past such activities.

"What's your name?"

"Bone."

"Bone?"

He had heard all the jokes, and then an extended repertoire of them through having a daughter named Charlotte. Charred Bone was her official school name, though like himself she had been called Skeleton at school; Prue Grant's fierce and combative friendship had ensured a brief life for any name Cha objected to.

"God, it's as bad as mine." The girl was pleased.

"Is it?"

"No. Nothing could be. Marsh. Get called Bog."

Bone, whose job also involved correlation of facts, knew that the writer Jake Marsh lived on the outskirts of Adlingsden. This dramatic object might belong to him.

"I forgot it was sodding bank holiday when I came. The train was Hell. Should have waited another day, only that shit-awful place—" she shrugged. "You been to Belgium?"

"Yes," said Bone, who had very much liked it.

She began to laugh. "It was a rotten con. This family lived just outside Bruges, and I thought, well, I could go in and see what life there was. And I never got to go anywhere alone! Moomi and Papa escorted us to museums and canal boats

. . . But to be not just bored shitless but groped by Papa as well . . ."

Bone grinned. If her present dress was habitual, Papa could not be blamed for getting the signal; only for not knowing it wasn't aimed at him. "Poor old Papa," he said.

"Do you grope?" she asked.

"With no aspersion on present company, I go for the mature woman myself."

"Fumbles at forty."

She was reasonably accurate about his age, and though the reduction to pathetic passes was somewhat wounding, he was not fool enough to show it.

"Where were you going—Bone?"

"Going?"

"Go-ing. Today. If Benenden isn't far out of your way, where were you going?" She spaced it out with ostentatious patience, as for a crumbly.

"I'm just a kind Boy Scout."

"Dib dib dib," said the girl. "Do you have a first name?"

"I do. And a second. And you—were your parents extravagant? One name? Two, or three?"

"Don't know about extravagant. They were wet. Named me after the place I was conceived in. Don't know how they knew."

"If that caught on," Bone said, "it could be very interesting. A girl called Wigan. A boy called Adelaide."

She snorted a half-laugh. "So it could have been worse." She was still resentful. "They went to Gibraltar that year too, and Morocco. But they had it off successfully in Ravenna, and Dad won't say how they knew that was it."

Dad won't say; therefore Mum is not around, Bone noted. "You were lucky. But I dare say if it had been San Gimignano or Poggibonsi they'd have skipped the idea."

"My mother's an explorer," the girl said. "She couldn't stand village life in Kent. My uncle Chris thinks she's probably up the Amazon somewhere, gone bush."

The story was vague in Bone's mind. Jake Marsh's wife,

given to quietly sloping off on expeditions, had not come back. It was twelve or fourteen years ago. "You can stand village life in Kent?"

"Some of it's all right. Some of anywhere's all right. Even school." This depressed her, though. She hunched herself up and fell silent as Bone drove through the summer lanes. The day had clouded over and he put the window up on his side against a suddenly chillier breeze. She glowered through the windscreen.

He took the road for Adlingsden without any remark from her, and she only roused herself to say abruptly, "Here will do." They were opposite a side lane, little more than a cart track although it had once been asphalted; a finger-post said Public Footpath, and on the wall a half-obliterated wooden board: Footpath only to Station. Part of the footpath's wall was the mellow brick of a large house, with a side door.

He could hear canned music over a public-address system somewhere, and diagnosed a bank holiday fair. A peacock shrieked in competition. He leaned to give a heave at her luggage as she hauled it out. She slammed the door, ducked to say "Dib dib dib" again and waited for him to drive on. He wondered if scouts still did say dib dib dib, and if not, whether they'd ever live it down. He started slowly on into the village, seeing her cross behind him to the lane. Police cones lined the village street, which was certainly narrow enough for visitors to the fair to block with parked cars otherwise. His eye was caught by a bright array of colors in a shop to his left, and he pulled up and looked. The window held a tumble of scarves; quilts, coats and sashes had been deployed, embroideries and metal and patchwork. Cha would like that waistcoat. The shop of course was closed; he could bring her along at the weekend to look. Probably Grizel knew this shop—she must do. Bone had been putting from his mind that she lived here, that she might be at the village fair; perhaps he might not have stopped the car to look in a shop window in a village where he felt less at home. Perhaps, such were the mazes of the human mind, he had stopped on purpose to think of her, before he realized it. He was sure now that he had seen her in a jersey of olive and indigo once, that might have come from here.

He was twisting his head to try and see a price tag on the most brilliant of the three waistcoats, a confection of violet, pink and emerald scraps seemingly held together with gold thread, when he heard the scream. It rose high above the pop music but it did not come from the direction of the fair and there was no confusing it with the cry of the peacocks. It came from the house across the road, the house into which Ravenna had gone, and Bone had never heard a cry of such anguish and horror.

Bone was out of the car and across the road. His feet scattered gravel in his race for the open front door. He paused for a second on the threshold to take in the scene before him. His pulse sounded in his ears.

Two women lay on the polished wood floor, like bodies on a battlefield. One lay on her side, hands pressed to her chest, gasping. The other sprawled inert near the stair-foot, her head too far toward her left shoulder, like a dropped puppet, dark hair spread around. Facing him in a doorway under the stairs gallery, Ravenna stood with her hands to her mouth, staring.

Priorities. Bone strode to the gasping woman, knelt, took in the pallor, the sweat, the struggle and clawing hands, and got his arm under her shoulders and raised her up. Ravenna, released from paralysis by his movement, ran into a room on the left and could be heard rummaging. The woman on Bone's arm, eased by being raised up, relaxed a little. Her lips were bluish, her eyes shut tight. The hands gripping the fronts of the indigo housecoat were slender, veined, and loaded with rings that glittered as she breathed.

The other woman lay as he had seen many lie, too still. One foot was bare, the other in a wood-soled sandal. She must have tripped somehow on the stairs and that scream, which still rang in his ears, must have been her last cry.

He raised his eyes to calculate the pitch of the stairs and all but stopped breathing himself. A woman stood at the top, in the shadows, looking down, her fingers pressed to her mouth.

"Dear God," her voice came faint and hoarse. "What happened? Anna?"

Ravenna had come back, was prising the lid off a small plastic container with her bitten, black-painted nails, shaking out a small white tablet, presenting it to the bluish lips, her hand trembling.

"Granny. Come on, Granny. It's your tablet. *Please.*"

Her grandmother made an effort, the lips parted, the mouth opened wider. Ravenna peered and got the pill under her tongue.

"You'll soon be all right." Ravenna sat back, nearly colliding with the woman who had come down the stairs and stood looking at the still figure there.

Bone said to Ravenna, "Where's the phone? Your grandmother needs an ambulance."

"Not a doctor?"

"Hold her, will you? Where's the phone?"

"She's got one in her room. In there." She pointed as she moved to take over from him. "Fenny! Gran's having an attack! *Help* her. *Fenny.*"

"Anna's dead." She had not touched the woman at her feet. *"Anna's dead."* Bone checked for a pulse, but could not find one. He had thought as much from the start.

"Don't move her." He stepped over the grandmother's feet and went into the room on the left; it was a room of luxury and taste, a décor in pink and gray, in which it took him a moment to spot the gray telephone. He called out. "Ravenna. What's this house called?"

"Paleys."

He tapped the emergency code and, while he spoke, giving his name and rank to speed things if possible, he saw the woman called Fenny now crouched by Anna's body, touching her softly, murmuring to her. "Anna. No. No. Anna, do wake up . . ." Bone found a doctor's number as soon as he opened the gray spring-pad by the phone: DOCTOR, and the local code. He dialed.

The woman called Fenny stood up, tall and slender in bright pink dungarees. Her face, broad-mouthed, pug-nosed, could have been attractive in its plainness but was distorted by shock. She sat down on the stairs, leaning forward to touch Anna's shoulder, and began to cry.

Ravenna was looking at him over her grandmother's head. The elderly woman was more at ease now, though still a bad color.

The hair disordered by her collapse was streaked with silver, so elegantly it might even have been by design, her nails and lips pink-tinted. Cuban-heeled blue kid slippers clad her small feet.

"You're police," said Ravenna.

He agreed, and glanced around the hall as he stood waiting. Ravenna bent solicitously, her hand on the ringed ones. Twenty minutes ago in the car he wouldn't have taken odds on this girl showing tender loving care to anyone, let alone a granny. It was undeniably curious that while the girl did not seem to care about the fate of Anna, or Fenny's tears, beyond an occasional glance at her, neither did Fenny appear sharply concerned for the fate of Ravenna's grandmother.

Anna's other sandal lay against the wall by the front door, together with a skateboard. The house was silent, with a feeling of space, of a good many rooms. This hall was two stories high, with a big window over the door, and a good deal of waxed wood. A very fine quilt in shades of rose and crimson hung on the staircase wall.

The doctor arrived quicker than Bone would have thought possible. The crunch of tires on the gravel was swiftly followed by the entrance of a dour-looking man in a brown linen jacket and tan trousers, carrying a case. Bone recognized the grim features of Dr. Monro Walsh whom he'd met on a recent case.

"I've called an ambulance."

Walsh nodded. He glanced at the grandmother, gave a moment of attention to Anna and shook his head. Fenny now sat with her head on her crossed arms on her knees, silent. Walsh went back to the older woman and reassured her. Then, straightening up, he looked at Bone.

"Is this a police matter? What's been happening?"

"You tell me." Bone regretted the flippancy as soon as he'd said it. Walsh gave him a dark glare.

"It takes no expert. Miss Dudley has broken her neck, apparently from falling downstairs. Mrs. Marsh is having a heart attack." How like Dr. Walsh to pull no punches. Bone wondered yet again how it was that Walsh was a very popular and even beloved doctor. It could not be for his tact and it was unlikely to be for his expression. Could it be that his patients were frightened to die on him?

He was now watching the woman on the stairs; and as if she were conscious of this she raised her head.

"Can't you do anything for Anna?"

Walsh's expression did not change, but his voice did. "No. I couldn't. Superintendent, is there a bedspread in Mrs. Marsh's room . . . ?"

Bone had been leaning on the doorjamb. He peeled himself off it and went back into the pretty bed-sitting room. The bedspread was of heavy gray ribbed silk, but a silver and brown Madras shawl lay folded on the chaise longue and he brought that and put it over Anna. Walsh was asking where Mr. Marsh and the little boy were.

Fenny said in a monotone, "They're at the fête."

"Ah, yes."

A strong voice outside called, "Anyone here own the blue Vauxhall over the road?" and Bone saw a large young uniformed constable coming over the gravel toward the door. He circled the recumbent Mrs. Marsh and strode out.

"It's mine. There's an emergency here. I don't think I've identification with me but I'm Detective-Superintendent Bone, Tunbridge Wells."

He was apologetic—authority left his voice and face with comic speed. "Could you get your car off the road, sir? We've—"

"I will. And can you go along to the fairground and have Mr. Marsh called on the Tannoy? He's needed here. There's been an accident."

"Sir."

Bone backed his car into the lane, despite the cones there, which he removed and replaced after him. Dr. Walsh's car had the last space on Paleys' forecourt. He was putting the last cone back when the ambulance came nosing down the street and he hurried to the gate of Paleys and beckoned.

The ambulance took Mrs. Marsh, and Ravenna in attendance, to the hospital. Fenny had offered to go, but a brusque "She's *my* grandmother and nothing to do with you" was reinforced by Dr. Walsh's "Certainly not. You're in shock." The ambulance men had carried Anna's body to her room to await the services of the district nurse and the undertaker. Fenny stood in the hall, which looked strangely uninhabited to Bone's eyes with nobody lying there; a phenomenon he had noticed before when accidents and deaths had taken place. Walsh had gone into the kitchen.

"It's not that I'm unfeeling about Ysobel. It must have been an awful shock for her. But she'll be all right and Anna—Anna's my friend. I've relied on her dreadfully, we all have. I simply can't understand—I don't believe it can have happened. She shouldn't even have been here. I didn't know she was in the house. She was at the fête."

"You don't know why she came back?"

"I didn't know she had! I was working—machining, which is probably why I didn't hear. Didn't hear Anna, I mean. I *thought* I heard Ysobel call; but, well, I thought: I'll finish this seam and then go and see if she did call."

Dr. Walsh emerged from the kitchen with a small glass, which he presented to Fenny. "Here, Mrs. Marsh. Drink this and come and sit down."

When she was gone, shepherded away by her dour sheepdog, Bone picked up the skateboard and climbed the stairs. The board's wheels were precisely as far apart, front and back, as the skidding scratches on a tread just below the turn of the stairs. He had descended, when a car roared in at the

gate and right up to the door. Feet hit the gravel and a man
came hurtling into the hall, followed closely by what looked
like an outsize cockerel of scarlet and orange. The man, tall,
thin and haggardly handsome, stared at Bone with the same
very light blue eyes as those of Ysobel Marsh.

"Who are you? What's happened?" He strode to the door
of Mrs. Marsh's room and looked in. "Where's my mother?
What is this accident?"

Bone noticed that he didn't ask where his wife was, but
any explanation was precluded by her running from the
kitchen; at the sight of her face, Marsh strode to her and
wrapped her in his arms.

"What's happened, love? I'm here."

"Anna—Anna's dead. She fell on the stairs, I can't
believe it—" She stopped, having caught sight of the
skateboard in Bone's hands. Her eyes widened and she drew
breath. "Oh no! Not that *bloody* skateboard!"

The small boy in the bird costume shook his head
vehemently. "I didn't. I put it away."

Someone had been standing just outside the front door,
and now she stepped in, a darkly glowing woman in green
trousers and shirt. Bone knew her face but could not place it.

"Dom, you can't have put it away. You left it on the
stairs."

"I *didn't.*"

He stood with his arms full of little souvenirs from the
fair, a blue bear, a picture book, a toy engine. The bird
headdress framed an incomprehending frightened face, pale
in the shadow of the yellow beak. A silver balloon bobbed
on a string tied to his wrist. Above the blue bear, a red
rosette showed, pinned to his chest. The tall woman said,
"I'll take Dom upstairs with his prizes," and she guided him
away with a hand on the back of his head. Jake and Fenny
watched them go with dazed faces; Jake said, "Fen, where's
Mother?"

She looked guilty and bewildered, as if his mother's
condition had until now almost escaped her memory. Dr.
Walsh spoke from behind her, coming forward. "She is

recovering from a heart attack. She'll be at the hospital by now. Detective-Superintendent Bone here had already sent for an ambulance by the time I came, and Ravenna went with her to the hospital."

"Ravenna?"

"Yes, she was here, Jake. I don't know how. And I don't know why Anna was here. She was at the fair, I thought."

"She came back for a jersey," Jake said. He kissed Fenny's head.

"I gave Ravenna a lift from Tunbridge Wells," Bone said. "I gather there was an awkwardness with the family she stayed with in Bruges; the father . . ." He let it go.

"I'll get to the hospital," Jake Marsh said abruptly, turning. "I'll sort out Ravenna on the way back, when I've made sure Mother is comfortable." He turned back to Fenny and took hold of her once more; he dropped his voice and spoke about Anna.

"I shall be all right," she said. "It's just hard to believe. Just like that."

"Did Mother see it?"

"She was here in the hall. She must have come out and found . . . Oh Jake."

"I'll be back as soon as I'm sure Mother's all right. Where did they—what about Anna?"

"In her room." Fenny choked. "I said I'd rather. Until . . . It's locked. Dom can't walk in and see. Jake, would you burn that horrible skateboard?"

"I'll take it away if you like," Bone said. He made for the door. "Have you a friend in the village, Mrs. Marsh? Someone who can come and be with you?"

"Morgan's here," Jake Marsh said. "You'll be all right with Morgan, won't you, love?"

"Oh yes," Fenny said. "We'll manage." She gave him a push. "You go and see to Ysobel, darling."

Morgan. Morgan Carradine. Of course. Star of Jake Marsh's book-turned-series *The Late Lady*.

As Marsh left, Dom could be heard crying upstairs. He

had come back with his prize, and his trophies, to a tragedy he could not understand, and for which somehow he was to blame.

As Bone got into his car he heard once again the skirl of the peacock, and thought he would never again believe it resembled a human scream.

3

Bone drove back toward Tunbridge Wells, going by way of Benenden and taking his time. Just out of Benenden past the girls' school, he saw a man clipping a hedge, someone so familiar that he pulled up without thinking. The man looked over his shoulder, and then turned, regarded Bone for a moment and said, "Well. It's a long time. Bone, isn't it? You'll be my excuse for stopping for a cup of tea."

Bone moved the car onto the asphalt driveway's entrance and got out. "I'd no idea you lived in this neighborhood, Mr. Whitmore."

"Bought the place some years ago to retire to." They fell into step up the drive. "What have you done with yourself? Must be all of ten years since we met. At the school jubilee, was it?"

"Oh, it must be." They were much of a height, the schoolmaster more loose-limbed, with a shock of thick silver hair, and black eyebrows imparting a fierceness to his direct regard. "I'm in the police," Bone said.

"Ah. Yes. I remember." The garage was open, and Whitmore stopped there to wipe the shears with a J-cloth and hang them up. "I remember reading the news about your wife and the little boy. I'm sorry."

"Thank you . . ." It was all but four years ago now. He thought: Even a year ago I might not have stopped when I saw Whitters; am I becoming less thin-skinned or more gregarious? He followed Whitmore into the house and leaned on the dresser in the big kitchen while the kettle was filled and switched on. There were blue check curtains and red Le Creuset pans.

Whitmore pointed a spoon at him. "I remember your Regency project. I wanted you to get the History prize for it, but some oaf without imagination was going to Oxford to read History, and I was told you had a couple of years to try again; but in the nature of things you had no chance to produce anything of that kind afterward. You traveled all over the place on that, didn't you? Polesden Lacy, Osterley?"

Remembering those schoolboy journeys, Bone smiled. "Really enjoyed myself. I'm glad I didn't know about the prize. It was a bit of disinterested research. Great fun."

"Research. You like being a policeman?"

"Some of it. It brings one up against the unattractive sides of life somewhat. I was thinking just now that it changes one's nature . . . There was a fatal accident just now at Adlingsden; a young woman, a housekeeper and mother's help, fell on the stairs. I heard her scream . . . and I thought how often I've heard neighbors and passersby say: 'Well, I heard a scream' or 'We used to hear them crying.' But *I* was in that house before I knew. It gets built into you."

"You were rather a self-contained fellow," Mr. Whitmore said, putting out cups and reaching down a battered cake tin whose muffled rattle portended biscuits. "Minding other people's business would be a change. Can't have been easy. Yet I recall you were an efficient prefect, so perhaps it was latent even then." He put sandwich biscuits with jam-tart tops onto the plate and made the tea.

"Have you been living here long?" Bone asked. He hoped

the change of subject was not too obvious, but he did not wish to be discussed further. The plate of biscuits would not fit on the tray, so he picked it up and stood aside for Mr. Whitmore. He did wonder why he had come out with that reflection about himself and his job in the first place. It might be Grizel's influence, as he had begun to open up to her about his thoughts. It might be the distance between Mr. Whitmore, whom he'd always liked, and himself. He followed, into a sunny front room overlooking the garden.

"I retired two years ago. We'd lived here quite a while by then; and Meg died just before I retired . . ." Whitmore poured tea, and stood with the pot in his hand looking out over the garden. "Didn't want to uproot again, so I stayed although the place is too big. I can look after it, luckily."

Bone wouldn't have known there was no woman's hand here. The place looked cared for and comfortable.

"It's a damn good thing, Bone, to have something you've got to do when you retire. I'm still teaching evening classes and coaching a bit. D'you remember Bookham?"

"I'll say I do. He dragged and coaxed and coerced me through Maths. When I was a third-year he scared the living daylights out of me, but I suppose by fifth year one's growing up a bit—" fifth year: Charlotte's age!—"and I cottoned on to his methods."

"He was here last week. Heartily disapproved of my *modus vivendi*. Piddling about housekeeping. Should shift to a labor-saving flat and do something Worth While. Such as a book on my subject. D'you know, all I could think was: Why? Why should I? I've done a lifetime's work. So I nodded away, and totally rejected all he was saying. He's running a sports center."

"He'll be good at that." They exchanged an amused smile over the teacups.

"I'm sure he is. Have a biscuit."

Bone had not a sweet tooth, but he took one as part of the ceremony of being entertained to tea. Whitmore, eyeing his own biscuit, said, "Don't know why I still buy these. Well, I do, yes. Meg liked them. One does things like that."

"Yes," Bone said. He still remembered, and even read, poems because of Petra; still noticed flowers, still kept a window box going that he didn't particularly want.

"You've a daughter, haven't you, Bone?"

"Cha's fifteen. All but sixteen. We look after each other."

Perhaps too much, he thought. When she was climbing back after the crash, starting to move, to walk; through the various infernal operations, the therapy, the clinics, she had all his attention and his spare time. He had used to the limit his leave, his colleagues' good nature, all the resources he could wangle. Cha's social life had dwindled to Prue Grant, luckily a host in herself, a lively subversive girl tireless in visiting, talking, supporting, crying with Charlotte at the pain, giggling with her over whatever it was girls giggled about so inexplicably. Bone's social life, always at the mercy of his job, had only recently begun to emerge from this hibernation. Their friends had mostly been Petra's; Bone had not grown up in the Wells and old school friends weren't around; and he hadn't missed them. Colleagues, and few others, made his world.

He had been musing. During this time the telephone had called Mr. Whitmore away, and now a sudden snore made Bone turn sharply and see an elderly Jack Russell asleep on a beanbag bed in the sun behind his chair. He was smiling when Mr. Whitmore returned.

"That was *my* daughter, very apposite. A piece of irony there too, you know. We stayed in this area because Vicky and her brood lived in Cranbrook; her husband managed the chain-store grocer's there and we know the area because we lived in Adlingsden. Now her husband has been moved to Wimbledon! I'm not moving to Wimbledon where they'd be the only people I knew. I've made a life for myself here."

That's what I've done so far, thought Bone. Before so very long, Cha will be acquiring boyfriends, shy though she is. Eventually she will probably marry. And I . . . will Grizel risk marriage again? And could I ask her, when every policeman's wife is a secondary one?

The Jack Russell now snorted itself awake, and came to

investigate Bone, grumbling in its chest about strangers. Bone's trouser leg must, to a canine nose, reek of Cha's cat who marked him religiously with scent-glands every morning during breakfast, and had been very thorough that morning because he was in clean jeans. Having in the course of duty been faced with a good many strange dogs, Bone made no overtures to this one, and it moved on, hoovered up a jetsam piece of biscuit, sat down on one of Whitmore's feet and regarded Bone peaceably.

It was a pleasant meeting. Whitmore talked a little of old times but plainly they did not much interest him. He was living in his present day. Bone unwound a bit from his tension after the shock at Paleys. His profession, always taking him into other people's lives, made this contact the more attractive because it was no forced intrusion.

"Didn't have many friends at school, did you? Solitary chap. There was Derrisford you used to go around with."

"He's in Devon." Bone grinned. "Five children, three dogs, two ponies and a parrot."

"Heaven protect us! I've been very lucky," Whitmore said.

Bone set off for home with a cordial invitation to dinner the following Thursday. The Jack Russell trundled into the road after him and could be seen in the rear-view mirror barking as he receded. It was a great improvement on peacocks.

Traffic going into Tunbridge Wells was not too bad for the evening of a bank holiday. He had known worse. Cars moved sluggishly toward the Frant roundabout but in nothing like the metal porridge of the old days before the bypass.

His thoughts occupied themselves with supper. Mrs. Ames had cooked a chicken to eat cold over the weekend— "It'll last you till Monday, Mr. Bone, with salady things, though not if your daughter brings her friends home; but the freezer's stocked up." The salady things, lettuce, beetroot, endive, cucumber, tomatoes, potato salad and red peppers, had disappeared quite early on. It would have to be macaroni with a fry-up of the less appealing bits of chicken still left, together with onion, sultanas . . . Bone was good at making fry-ups out of not much, and he was always touched by how good Cha was at eating them. She had been known to reject a perfectly good casserole left by Mrs. Ames for them, to demand one of her father's fry-ups. Of course this evening she might not be home. After Janine, or Janice, and her barbecue lunch, Cha had prophesied things might get dead boring. Still, Cha's return would depend on when Prue Grant had instructed her father, he of the hairy legs, to collect them.

Finding a place near his flat to park the car was a minor triumph these days. Bone remembered the luck Kojak always seemed to have in the matter; this time he achieved a Kojak, gliding to the curb outside his door. He and his daughter occupied the two large floors above the insurance office on street level. He let himself into the building in a good mood, not dampened by the rock music pervading the staircase from above. Cha was back. He ran upstairs to the beat of an insistent drum and walked, smiling in anticipation, into the sitting room.

Facing him, sprawled on the sofa, and drinking beer from a can, was a total stranger.

The uniform was there, skinny bare chest under the denim jacket, faded grayish jeans that had obviously been victim of a mad axe-man, jagged gashes showing the skin beneath strangely whole. The hair, which was bleached white, seemed to Bone to be in a confusion of styles, in frail ringlets on the back of the neck, cropped very close above the ears and standing in a longer brush on top. The left ear had three silver studs along its rim, from the right ear a diamanté object, perhaps a cross, hung nearly to his shoulder. Traces of black eyeliner made Bone think of Ravenna, which he had no wish to do. The face was smooth; the boy had very likely no need to shave yet. Skin of an almost pearly pallor was drawn tight over cheekbones, the lips seemed hardly able to close over the teeth. It was a young skull that stared back at him, with a not unamiable expression.

"Ah," said Bone, lacking inspiration. It could only be that Cha had brought this home. Bone indulged in a fleeting thought of it as a burglar, who had shinned up a drainpipe and was now making free with the beer before vandalizing the flat and departing with Petra's silver bonbon dishes, but he dismissed this fantasy, and along with it a distinct desire to yank the young skeleton to its feet and boot it down the stairs.

"Oh. Daddy, this is Justin."

Cha had been delving behind the sofa collecting Ziggy, who now burst from her arms, jinked around Bone and disappeared upstairs. Bone thought: You and me both, Zig; but he nodded at Justin, who was certainly not going to get to his feet or do anything conventional like handshaking. Cha looked on anxiously as Justin returned the nod and waved his beer can in what seemed a friendly enough way. Bone, deeply conscious above all of not wanting to upset Cha, pitched his voice to carry through the rock beat to inquire hospitably, "More beer? Plenty in the fridge."

Something in Cha's face as he said this prompted the thought that there might now be rather less than he imagined, so he addressed himself to her. "Party all right?"

She stood behind Justin, not looking up but picking bits of cat hair from the sofa back. "Oh, bit boring. After the barbie people just sat talking and playing dreary old records so Justin and I split." She was using the rate of speech for strangers, slow and careful, to obviate the impediments that lingered still in her talk; and loud to be heard.

"Paul Grant didn't collect you, then?" Even as he spoke, Bone knew he wasn't going to like the answer.

"Oh, he wasn't coming for Grue till six. She's much more Janine's friend than I am. Justin brought me back."

She moved to go and turn down the sound on the player. Bone sat on the arm of the chair opposite (never sit lower than the person under interrogation) and asked, suddenly loud in the ensuing near-quiet, "You've a car, then?"

The boy might be seventeen, might even own a car, could borrow his father's (and what did his father think of him?). The skeleton stirred, and put the beer can down on Bone's cherished copy of *Great Houses and Gardens* so that Bone had to force himself not to lean over and snatch it up. What was a dust jacket, anyway? and the can was, perhaps, dry underneath.

"No. I gotta bike."

Only this last week Locker had been lamenting the stupidity of a young neighbor thrown off her boyfriend's bike, wearing no helmet, and now in intensive care.

"It's all right, Daddy. I wore the spare helmet and we didn't even go fast."

Bone was sorry that his face had betrayed anxiety, but he wondered if she was any judge of how fast they had gone. Slow bank holiday traffic could tempt a motorbike driver to weave and speed.

"You're police, aren't you?" Justin's tone made it sound as respectable as peddling dope, and perhaps by his standards the police were the more obscene. He wondered what, when Cha told him what her father's profession was, the boy had commented. He could not see Cha taking kindly to having her father referred to as a pig.

"Yes. Detective-Superintendent," he said.

"Wow." The boy sat up straight, light glinting on his earring. "Supers are up top, right?"

Bone felt a sign over his head should flash *Big Pig* at this point. The boy's pretense at being impressed was not overdone. Bone hoped, first that Cha would not take it in, because it could upset her, and then that she would, so that she might be put off the boy. He produced a genial smile.

"Long way to go before Chief Constable, and I dare say I shan't make it."

This amused Justin. The teeth his smile revealed were fanglike but very white. "Get nicked yourself for something on the side? Get found out? The Bone Bust?" He got to his feet and Bone, following suit, was annoyed to find the boy was the taller. Gray, rainwater eyes looked down at him. "Must be a bind having to keep your nose clean."

It was one of those remarks to which there is no answer. Nothing was likely to convince this boy that not everyone's natural instinct was to be on the make or bend the rules. Although Bone was used to such an attitude to his profession, and knew pretty well how far it was justified, he did not care to hear it from this youth in front of his daughter. He said nothing, always one of his stronger cards.

The boy turned to Cha.

"I'm going, then. Seeya."

Cha, not looking at her father, escorted Justin from the room. They descended to the front door, the boy's boots clumping on every stair. There was a murmur at the door. Bone found himself hoping furiously that there was no more than that.

Ziggy came cautiously downstairs and began sniffing around as though the place needed disinfecting. Bone addressed him in a whisper, hearing the stuttering roar of a bike start in the street.

"That was *Disgusting, of Tunbridge Wells.* You were well out of it, chum."

Needled, nettled, what was the word? He listened to Cha coming up, and took the beer can to the kitchen bin. Unluckily the bin already contained small plastic bags of wrapped rubbish, so there was no satisfying clunk as it went in. He heard the irritation in his tone as he said to Charlotte, "Where did Janine dig that one up?"

"He's not Janine's friend," she said, muted. "He's living with the Grants."

"Good God." That meant Cha would see the oaf all the time. "For how long?"

"Don't know. He hasn't anywhere to live. Mrs. Grant being a counselor she took him in. There's room, with Martin away."

"A deserving case, is he?"

"Yes." Cha flared up, startling him. "He damn well is. His father beat him up for years, nearly killed him. He was in care but he got badly treated there."

Bone crammed back *I'm not surprised.*

"And when he was sixteen he had to leave the home anyway and he'd nowhere to go and had to live rough, and he got put into a detention center for stripping pipes out of empty houses. And the houses were derelict anyway, so somebody might as well have got some good out of them—"

"Cha, even derelict houses belong to someone. It sounds very reasonable, but it's theft."

"Well, what could he do? He couldn't get a job. He tried laboring but he's not exactly Schwarzenegger and they gave him the sack."

"He seems to be able to afford a hairdresser."

"A girl at the squat did it for him; and Grue trimmed it. You're being horrible, Daddy."

"But take a look at him, Cha." He reined in his voice to calm. "These boys complain they can't get work, and they get themselves up so no one would take them. Most of the men with work to give out are square, set-in-their-ways types. Who's going to employ a chap with hair like that? Rebellion is all very well, but if you rebel then you have to expect that the world you're rebelling against isn't going to accept you. Look, he's saying to the rest of society, 'This is what I am, take it or leave it,' and it's no good his being surprised if they'd rather leave it."

"Well, but you're terribly conforming. You have to, in your job; only *you* mostly seem to understand people."

"I try. But I don't want to see you getting into that."

"I'm not *getting into that.* He gave me a lift home from a boring party and I gave him a drink. I'm not *getting into* anything. I like him. He's had a hard time and he's really brave. But you're judging him all from the outside."

Bone looked hard at the table top. He was silent a moment. Cha had struggled to be coherent when her speed, her vehemence of feeling, blurred the sounds. It went to his heart.

"I'll try, pet." He picked up the pencil from the kitchen notepad, and drew an oblong. Beneath it he added four little strokes, at one end a snout and floppy-cornered ears, at the other end a corkscrew tail. Cha came to look.

"Hn'h?"

"Square pig," he said.

Charlotte, her arms around Justin's body, felt its thinness even through the leathers he wore. They were second hand and didn't fit, and their bulk shifted on him.

When he called, and stood on the doorstep saying in a spoof accent "Care to come for a spin, what?" she had been hugely flattered. She also felt guilty at accepting because her father had made his opinion of Justin rather clear last night, and she hurried to get ready before Mrs. Ames should arrive and see her escort. Justin, standing in the doorway of her bedroom—he had refused to stay downstairs, refused a beer—was a masculine, exciting presence. He looked at her posters, not at herself getting leggings and boots, and when she was ready he turned and led the way without a word.

She had hoped he wouldn't talk about her father, and so far he hadn't. When they stopped at traffic lights and he turned his head, it was only to comment on a pair of stout women crossing, laden with grocery bags. "What they want to shop for? They could live for a month off their hips alone."

She giggled. She wondered if anyone who knew her was around, and she hoped not, but the helmet was disguising. Once they were clear of the town, she plucked up spirit.

Justin didn't seem inclined to speed, but she felt once more the vulnerability of bike riders. Cars seemed so heavy, so fast and oblivious. They came out of side roads as if an approaching bike didn't exist. She swayed with Justin as they swerved and avoided, and could hear that he swore, casually and without heat. He pulled up at Cross in Hand, and asked if she was doing all right. The machine vibrated quietly under her.

"I'm fine." She looked at his profile in the jaws of the

helmet. Today he had no eyeliner, it must have been only for the party. Then she saw he had mascara. He twisted further around, putting a hand on her thigh, a thin hand, larger than one expected because it was a boy's, smeared with oil and grazed on the knuckles. She asked, "Are we going to Brighton?" since that was the road ahead.

He considered. "Unless you want to. Thought I'd cut around east. Come lunch time we'll get a sarnie and a beer somewhere. Brighton's not much cop if you've got a cash flow problem." He twisted yet further around and made an amused sound like *kih!* "Lemonade for you, kiddo. No one'll take you for eighteen."

Cha put on a droop and a mournful face.

"But that's all part of your charm." He gave her a pat and turned back. Tendrils of white hair lay on his collar. She put her arms around him, got her foot on the stirrup and they were off. *Your charm!* She had charm for him! He was amused by her not being even sixteen yet. She remembered how when you're little you count your age in halves and quarters. A copper's daughter, fifteen and three-quarters. And the copper didn't like him; last night at the door he'd grinned and said, "Daddy hasn't taken a shine to me."

She liked the way he maneuvered the machine, swinging it through the lanes. For a little she was anxious about where they were, until a signpost told her. He slowed a little, put his visor down and gestured; she put hers down and took hold. The landscape, a bit obscured by the visor's grime, began to flow faster, the vibration under her strengthened. Around his shoulder she saw the road straight ahead, almost empty, switchback. They crested a hill and swooped. She gripped hard. It couldn't be that dangerous, whatever it felt like; and the fear gave her a kick. Air battered at her, streamed through her clothes to her skin, the hedgerows blurred. She caught her breath, exhilarated. This is terrific!

They were slowing, to her regret, running now past houses, and now they tooled into a small town. She could feel the small movements as he drove, not just the sway of his balance but the small reflections in his midriff of the moves of arms and legs. She hadn't noticed it so much before; perhaps she wasn't gripping so tightly. It was good to be confident on a road. She still felt nervous in a car, though the desperate tension of her fears during the year or so after the crash had lessened. She wondered what Mother would have thought of Justin. Her leg was beginning to ache. It was cold, and not quite comfortable at the angle she had to sit.

Justin was slowing at a crossroads, and stopped. "Any way you want?"

Cha read the signpost, saw ADLINGSDEN, and pointed. "There's a shop there with clothes Daddy thought were good. We could look."

"If Daddy thought they were good," Justin said sardonically, and shrugged. He very likely thought her father would approve of little-girl dresses. He turned left, though, and drove quietly along the summer lanes, down a slope in a tunnel of green, and came to houses.

"Where is it, then?"

"It's at one end of the village. I don't know which end." Justin had never, after his first surprise, shown any difficulty in understanding Charlotte's speech, so that she did not have to think about choosing words she could say clearly. "That house is where my form-mistress lives. She's a biology teacher." She didn't say anything about her father and Mrs. Shaw; she wasn't sure where they stood, she wasn't sure how she felt. Besides, Justin might make fun.

She saw, as they came near the far end of the village, a shop window with a flame of color in the sunlight.

"Hey!" She shook his coat. "That—there."

He stopped outside the garden wall of a big house; not a garden really, as it was mostly gravel for cars, and a Suzuki was parked there. She crossed the road, finding she was unsteady on her feet, and looked into the shop. The side wall of the window was hung with a quilt in beautifully shaded block shapes. There was a denim-patch sling bag and a matching big beret hat. Right in the center on a stand was a brilliant kimono robe in silk patches of kingfisher blue, violet, indigo, lilac, purple, turquoise . . .

Justin had come up behind her.

"Is this what Daddy saw?" he demanded.

"Oh yes. He said patchwork. But it was a waistcoat he saw."

"Then it's grown a bit."

Charlotte spluttered a laugh.

"They got waistcoats hung up inside." He could look over the board to the back of the window. He took off his helmet and moved to the shop door. "Shit. It's closed," and bending to see a handwritten notice under the CLOSED sign, he read out, "Sorry we're having staffing problems. If you want to see the shop please apply to Fenny Marsh at Paleys opposite."

He straightened up. "Okay. Paleys opposite."

"No, don't let's. I can't buy anything." Cha pressed her face to the door and peered. "Oh look, that rainbow jacket. And that waistcoat."

"Not bad."

"It's all my best colors. Bet that's the one he saw."

They turned to look at Paleys. A black-haired girl in a poison-green teeshirt and black mini above black leggings stood in the doorway watching them. She called out something and made the shoulder-hefting, hand-spread gesture of inability to do anything about it.

"Oh well," Charlotte said. "Have to wait till Friday. I expect Daddy'll be better pleased—" but Justin had set out across the road, not toward his machine but toward the gateway to Paleys. Damn damn damn, thought Charlotte. She's older, she's his age. She's allowed to wear a skirt like that one. And dye her hair.

She waited for a slow van and three frustrated cars to go by, and trailed after Justin. By the time she arrived they were talking. Justin said to Charlotte, "Ravenna's stepmum will be back, but guess what, she's at the undertakers." He rounded his eyes.

"The shop key's locked in her workroom," Ravenna said, to Justin. "She has to get lunch, so she *better* be back."

"I'll come again on Friday," Cha said.

"They'll have sold it come Friday." Justin looked at Ravenna, who was made up like white porcelain. "Get them to put it by for you."

"Or if it doesn't fit, at least you'd know," Ravenna said, glancing at Charlotte for a moment with raised eyebrows. "I think it's all a load of bloody expensive tat, but some people still go for it."

Justin said, "Who's got green eyes, then? That stuff's brilliant."

Cha, who had been feeling dashed, perked up. Ravenna, putting on a theatrical mocking smile, said, *"Don't* tastes differ."

Justin swung to survey the house front. "You live *here?*"

His incredulity seemed to provoke Ravenna. "Come on in, see around the estate."

Cha hoped Justin would refuse, but he was disposed to go along with Ravenna, who walked slightly ahead, swinging her hips. Cha at the best of times could not walk with that easy movement, and said to herself: Who's got green eyes now?

The hall was high-ceilinged, wood-floored. Ravenna said, airily waving a hand, "Someone was killed yesterday falling down those stairs."

Cha's exclamation was drowned out by Justin's "Anyone you knew?" and she saw Ravenna appreciate that. It's a whole language, Cha thought, that I'll never learn. I'd never in my life think of saying that. Justin had returned an unplayable ball. She felt proud on his behalf.

"Housekeeper," Ravenna said offhandedly. "My little brother left a skateboard on the stairs and—POW." She led the way past the stairs down a passage and into the garden. It was landscaped and showed a gardener's hand. The brick path went under a pergola covered in small creamy roses. The bricks were not level, and gave Charlotte a little trouble, but Ravenna had hooked a hand on Justin's shoulder and they could not see her as they strolled ahead. A thud and a patter of feet could be heard.

"This is my part of the garden, where my little brother is playing. Oh no, go on, Dom; who cares?"

"I didn't *know* it was yours," the small boy said, coming around the end of the pergola and looking up with puckered brows. "I thought it was all Daddy's." He held a multicolored rubber ball to his chest.

"But *this* part is mine because it belonged to my mother. Gran gave it to her."

The strip of garden between the pergola and the high retaining wall didn't look like much, being only mown grass. The wall, which was stone, had ferns and various flowers growing on it. It leaned slightly backward and was dry-stone laid, bulging here and there.

"Here, give it over." Ravenna held out her hand imperiously, Dom gave the ball with doubtful slowness. She skimmed it at the wall. It came back at an angle and Dom ran, missed it and chased it into the roots of the pergola roses. Ravenna, about to walk on, saw that Justin had squared up to the wall and was looking at Dom, having shed his jacket under the roses.

"Your throw, kiddo."

"No, it's Ravenna's. I didn't catch."

"For heaven's sake, Dom. Just throw," Ravenna said. Thus discouraged, Dom hurled the ball, which went almost straight up in the air off a spur of stone, and Justin ran in and caught it. He seemed completely inconsequent: he entered this game with apparent absorption. Perhaps Ravenna saw this. She leaped for the ball when a face of the stones sent it her way, and sent it hard at the surface again. Justin had to jump to reach it. Cha did not try, save once when it came straight at her. Dom, wholly outclassed, stayed watching for a bit, then backed off and ducked under the roses. Cha wished she could go with him, but she had to stay smiling, a good sport, while Ravenna and Justin thudded the ball at the wall, breaking ferns and flowers, running for missed catches with howls of fury, shrieking at clever catches, agile as cats.

Ravenna was playing at Justin, showing off for him. He looked to be playing the game for itself, using his height to reach for the ball as it soared overhead, sure-footed in his laced boots, his grin showing the white crooked teeth; yelping as he pounced for the ball. His teeshirt had come loose from his jeans and was falling off one shoulder all the time. However thin he was, and the shoulder seemed nothing but bone, he had strength. The ball came back at Ravenna with more force than she liked, and she yelled at him.

Into the middle of this erupted a tall man in a blue shirt, with a shock of gray hair. His eyes were bright light blue and wide open and furious.

"What the hell are you doing? What in the name of all the gods at once is this infernal bloody racket when I'm working? Didn't you know I was working?" This to Ravenna. He wasn't young, the skin of his face had seen better days, but he was good-looking. As her mouth opened he went on, "Get the *hell* out of this garden. Somewhere else. *Anywhere* else."

"Like Mother?" said Ravenna. His mouth stayed open, like a sick cat's. He fixed his eyes on her and said in a completely different soft voice, "Get the hell out of here, my darling, before I wring your bloody little neck."

"You're lovely, too, Dad," she said, and stalked off down the garden, her head up. Ravenna's father paid no apparent attention to Justin and Charlotte, but returned the way he had come, across the tended lawn to french windows on a small pavilion annex.

Justin retrieved his jacket and, still playing with the ball, tossing and catching, he jerked his head at Charlotte and said, "Let's go."

Cha, already nervous and upset, felt very uncomfortable at walking through someone else's house, particularly when the someone had just given them the push. She drew back behind Justin's shoulder when they met a woman in turquoise dungarees in the hall. She had a sad, rather long face and glanced at them vaguely, then stopped and summoned up an inquiring half smile.

"Friends of Ravenna's," Justin said.

"Oh yes. Are you here for lunch? I need to know because of the macaroni."

Justin hesitated. For a moment Cha thought he would accept. Then he said, "No, thanks," and walked on. Cha gave the woman a placatory smile and trailed after him. It wasn't until they were at the bike that she remembered the shop key. It would have to wait until Friday, and she was just as glad. That woman had been crying. Justin said as he climbed across the bike, "A free lunch is a free lunch, right? But there was a bit of atmosphere." He oared the machine into the roadway with his feet. Cha settled herself, putting on the helmet. "Ravenna and me got something in common," he added. "Our mums took off. I sh'think hers was the same as mine: couldn't stand her dad."

4

The lights dimmed, leaving the chat-show host and Morgan in silhouette, pretending to maintain their animated talk while the credits swam slowly up.

Fenny abruptly thumbed the *off* button on the remote control. She expected a routine protest from Ravenna, deep in the stage of taking everyone's actions as an infringement on her liberty, but no one spoke. Jake stayed gloomily slumped at her side, long legs crossed, chin sunk on chest where his hand kept propped a nearly empty whiskey glass. He really was drinking too much again. At the moment he seemed to have passed the bolshie stage which had prompted him to snort and chiack whenever the presenter mentioned either Jake's name or *The Late Lady*. She hoped he had entered the somnolent, reasonable and peaceful stage; if he didn't drink more there would perhaps not be a scene with Chris.

Jake's ex-brother-in-law was exactly the guest she could have done without just now, but to put him off had been impossible. The most practical reason for this was his unpredictability; in Spring when Chris was last in England, Jake had overcome his dislike of Chris and, for Ravenna's sake, issued an invitation to him to come and stay when he got back from the Peru expedition. Jake had achieved his aim, for Ravenna had come out of character—losing Stroppy Teenager for a joyful greeting. Typically, Chris had not let Fenny know until Monday morning that he was coming, although he had been at home, at Beeches with his father and aunt, not ten miles away, for a day or so. Jake had suggested that Chris must be long accustomed to turning up in the middle of nowhere and making the best of it; Fenny maintained that Paleys did not in the least resemble a native village and that Chris's hosts were the ones who would have to make the best of it; she did not say this aloud, as it was after all for poor Kingsley's sake that Chris was asked. Fenny also suspected that Ravenna had bunked off from the Belgian visit because she knew her uncle was likely to be there. She sat now at her uncle's feet, picking up and leafing through copies of the *National Geographic* he had been looking at, as though she wanted to share his experiences. Fenny wished, briefly but vigorously, that he would take Ravenna with him one day, not just back to Beeches as he was quite likely to do, but abroad somewhere she couldn't bunk back from.

Ravenna stared at her stepmother now, under her eyelids, head tilted back. "I thought that jacket looked really dated. All that patchwork. Very yesterday. Wasn't it, Chris?"

He had just her intense regard. Fenny thought it was self-regard, an inward look that never saw other people. He had exactly the same air of not caring if he offended so long as he asserted his own opinions. Why the natives he had encountered on his expeditions had not long ago clubbed him to death was a wonder to Fenny; perhaps that look made them believe he would get working with his club first.

"I can't say that I noticed the jacket. *She* looked all right."

Oh, well, yes. Ask any man what Morgan Carradine was wearing and unless it was nothing at all they wouldn't have seen it. Clothes were only ingredients in that aphrodisiac recipe making Morgan. Chris was grinning to himself over the magazine.

Fenny threw the control pad on the sofa beside Jake, making him start and clutch his glass. She got up and walked to the door.

"Uh—supper?" Jake asked.

"Why, yes. If anyone wants supper they know where the fridge is. Goodnight." She shut the door and stood for a moment, gathering up courage. When she was a child, their house had had no two-way switch on the stairs. You had to go up in the dark, not knowing what lurked above. Now the nightmare had altered—she had to go up those stairs thinking of Anna. She would not surrender and use the back stairs. She wondered if any of the others had thought all day of Anna as she had done. Since it happened, she had gone over the accident ceaselessly: what she had heard, what she had seen, blaming Ysobel for having a heart attack—weren't the tablets supposed to control it? Why not take a tablet instead of coming out and calling? But poor Ysobel, in distress, only wanted help. Then Dom, leaving his wretched skateboard in such a place; herself for not having seen it before they left for the fair. You could end up blaming yourself for having been born.

She couldn't turn to Jake for comfort as she usually could. He was absorbed in worry for his mother. Anna had meant very little to him, only a pleasant, useful person about the house.

As she crossed the hall, Fenny could not help thinking how nice it was not to see Ysobel's door open; and whether her light was on or off, the quiet voice would ask, "Who is that?" or "Which of you is that?" It was always friendly, and Ysobel loved to feel included in the goings-on of the family from which her condition kept her a little apart. Ysobel was no demon mother-in-law. She adored her son and his children, and if her kindness to Fenny was ever so slightly gracious, it was because Fenny had first come to the house as Kingsley's aide and friend, referred to by Ysobel innocently as "the housekeeper."

Such thoughts do not go into words. They fly through the mind in images. Fenny wished she had known what Ysobel's faintly-heard call had meant, she wished she had gone to answer instead of finishing the seam. She might or might not have seen the skateboard, she might herself have been dead at the foot of the stairs, but she would not have heard Anna's terrible cry. But Dom, poor little Dom then!

When she crept into his room he lay fast asleep, and she hoped for no repetition of the nightmares he'd had last night. He'd been fond of Anna too, relied on her. He wasn't old enough to admit he'd left the skateboard on the stairs. It was far too much for him to face. She hoped he never would realize what he'd done. As Jake said, it was necessary for Dom to manage to believe that indeed he hadn't left it . . .

Jake was not long in coming to bed. He stood by the window in his dark green pajamas, looking out and listening to the rain. The steady drumming on the roof, hundreds of little feet marching, soothed Fenny, but Jake hated rain.

He twitched the curtains shut. "There'll be a flood in the lane by morning."

"Jeremiah."

"We need sodding doves, not peacocks. To send out for a sign of life."

He was cold, so she cuddled him. He spoke into her shoulder plaintively: "Chris is a bastard."

"Yes; but he has to be here for Ravenna."

"She hates me."

"No, darling. She's at the awkward age."

"I'm forty-three. *That's* the awkward age."

"The age men look around for the new wife?" She thought of Morgan. He moved his head against her breast.

"I *like* the one I've got."

Before he slept, he muttered, "You know I'm sorry about Anna. You do know? I use words so much that when it's serious they come out as if I'm writing them."

She lay awake a long time listening to the rain. Because of Chris's presence in the house she thought of Kingsley. She'd been been Kingsley's friend, had kept house for her so that she could be free to go as she pleased; and so it had seemed natural, when she herself wanted to spend time on an absorbing hobby that became a small business, she should ask Anna to come. She liked Kingsley very much: a difficult, restless woman. Jake had never got over her ditching him like that. Certainly Ravenna still expected her mother to walk through the door one day. Lawyers could rule that she might be presumed dead, her estate parceled among legatees, her husband marry again, but Ravenna hadn't stopped hoping. So had Fenny, even after her marriage. Ravenna had been such a loving child, and Fenny longed for her to grow up and be affectionate once more . . .

The rain increased in violence, the little feet on the roof stamping lemming-like toward unforeseen disaster.

She had dropped off when the crash came. Jake woke too and sat up. She flailed for the light switch.

"What the hell? Like an earthquake. No, avalanche. Has the roof fallen in?"

"I think it was outside." She picked up her watch, and after a moment her bleared eyes made sense of the figures. Two fifteen. "It sounded to me to be in the garden."

"Bloody hell. I know what it is. It's those spectacularly infernal children. It's the wall."

He was out of bed, nearly smothering her with the thrown-back duvet. Rain slashed at the windows as he peered out, shielding his eyes with cupped hands. His hair was all on end, and Fenny was so busy with how endearing this was that he had to say twice, "Turn the light out." As she obeyed, he said, "It's the wall all right. I can see half of it's in the garden. I could *skelp* that tall lad. He did it."

"The rain did it, Jake." She thought about going to look, and then thought it would still be there in the morning and was not worth getting up for, when she had arranged the duvet and was comfortable. "It must have been on the point of collapse for years. Come back to bed. You can't go out and build it up now, and it's the council's job anyway. It's their wall."

He grumbled his way back to sleep, as he sometimes did, in the middle of saying something. She was surprised no one seemed to have woken at the noise. She listened for Dom, but he did not call. He may have thought he dreamed it. The house was quiet. On the roof the little feet lost their urgency, began to falter.

Outside, the ferns lodged in what remained of the wall ceased to be dashed against the stones as the rain lessened. They ceased even to flutter, except as a drop slid from a frond, releasing it. They dripped in the dark as the eyeless face behind them looked down into the garden.

5

Bone, coming out of the house into the garden, had the familiar sense of being a vulture: we arrive when there's death. He emerged into the bright sunshine of still quite early morning, and walked straight into a swathe of wet roses.

Locker and his team were treading carefully about in the taped-off area of grass. Halfway down the pergola's arcade, Jake Marsh stood with a glass in his hand. He was in jeans and a cream cotton sweater, and he eyed Bone's shirt and tie in what seemed like silent comment, but turned his attention back to the wall.

They could see through gaps among the twined stems of roses. Bone had once thought himself unaffected by the sight of a skull, but that was when he had only handled a demonstration piece, scrubbed and sanitized. It had not suggested much connection with the person who once had used it. Now he was envious of Marsh's whiskey. The thing in the wall looked almost genial, but in that threatening fashion always recognized by mankind: to this shall you come at last. Bone was aware all of a sudden that his own skull waited inside his skin. The other, in its niche half visible behind the ferns, brown and with perhaps a trace of hair, regarded its discoverers.

Bone moved to have a word with Locker, and the canvas screen which had dropped from place was hurriedly put back, cutting off Jake Marsh from his view. Locker's men were picking up stones, putting them aside, and combing the rubble and the ground. That had all to be done before they could come at the wall. Bone went back to the roses as the fewer feet on that patch, the safer. Marsh had not moved.

"Why should one be sorry for an archaeologist?" he demanded rhetorically, waving his glass. "Because his career is in ruins."

He finished the glass.

"I'm told you made the discovery, Mr. Marsh."

"Yes. But I know you, don't I? You were the bloke on Monday. Yes, I came out first thing. There was all that rain in the night and an almighty row in the middle of it. We've a security spotlight at the back door around there. Enough light for me to see the wall was half down. So first thing, I trotted out . . ." He pointed at the wall with his empty glass. "It's not fun. Those sodding children did it, playing here yesterday. My daughter and a couple of friends. Shook it loose ready for the rain." He looked twitchy, and perhaps he had been drinking since first thing. Bone asked the important question, part of his attention on the pathologist, Ferdy Foster, who had arrived and was leaning this way and that to see the find, illuminated suddenly by a powerful lamp. Cameras whirred and clicked.

"Oh, it would be . . . thirteen, fourteen years ago. They wanted to raise the lane level with the road, and that meant a retaining wall. The council built it. Can they have reverted to the ancient heathen practice of walling someone in to give it strength? I remember Kingsley telling—"

He whirled to stare at the screen that hid the wall, and seized hold of an upright rustic pole of the pergola, shaking rainwater down on them both from the roses. He plunged his arm through and pulled down the top of the screen, gestured and opened his mouth as if to speak. After a moment he managed, "Oh Christ. No." At this moment Ferdy's gravelly drawl could be heard, in a detached tone.

"It may be a female."

Bone said, "Come into the house, Mr. Marsh."

"No. No, hell if that is Kingsley. It can't be. My wife, my first—" The canvas slipped from his hand and sprang back into position. He clawed at it and then set off for the end of the pergola with the evident intention of walking around it to see. Bone circumvented him and stood in his way, putting up a hand.

"No, sir. You mayn't go in there."

"But that was when she went away. The wall was being done. The lane . . . she walked off, she always did. These expeditions, I mean. Oh God. I've got to be sure. You must see I've got to look." His eyes didn't see Bone, they were still occupied with what he had seen in the wall and his face was contorted like a tragic mask.

"Come into the house, sir." Bone applied the simple tactic of invasion of body-space to make Marsh retreat, but he stood his ground and even pushed with the glass at Bone's chest.

"She liked to walk off with her pack, no fuss, no goodbyes. And come back the same way, just walk in. They were building up the wall, they had lanterns up and the footpath barred off. But she'd set off from the side door, you see, into the lane. My mother said she heard her leave during the night. She could have fallen behind that new wall. God knows how." His wide stare suddenly relaxed. He stepped back. "No. I'd forgotten the card. She sent Ravenna a birthday card. There was the card. Thank God, that's not Kingsley. She sent the card."

His color had come back. He said, "That was a very nasty moment."

"Very nasty," Bone agreed. "I'm sorry, sir. Can we go into the house now? We need to know more about the building of that wall."

There was a subdued breakfast going on in one of the

rooms as they came through the hall. Ravenna, not part of it, was visible in her grandmother's room, sitting on the floor watching television. Marsh opened another door, into a pleasant sitting room that overlooked the garden. It had comfortably sagging sofas in glazed-chintz loose covers, and several small tables handy for ornaments and books, and an impression of flowers—two large vases, and pot plants, begonias and geranium, and a collage wall-hanging. Marsh had gone to the sideboard and was refilling his glass. Down the garden a peacock gave an admonishing screech. The door Bone had just shut opened and a woman said, "Oh do get something to eat instead."

It was Fenny Marsh, in pale blue dungarees this morning, and a pale green shirt. She saw Bone and was confused, but reverted to her husband. "What about some toast, love? You could—"

"I bloody *need* a drink," he said, putting half of it back. "Just now I thought that—" and he waved the bottle in the general direction of the wall—"was Kingsley."

"Oh Jake. Oh no." She went to him and clasped his arm.

"No. It's all right. Ravenna's card, remember?"

"It's too horrible."

"Don't tell Chris what I thought." Jake's voice had the slight carefulness of the drunk by now.

"Of course I wouldn't. Thank goodness it's all right. Listen, I'm going to bring you some toast and coffee in a minute. The coffee's perking."

Jake bent his head to kiss her nose. He came toward one of the sofas, Fenny still on his arm, and let her lower him into it. He had a cautious eye on his drink, keeping it level. He said to Bone, "Chris Thorn is Kingsley's brother. He's convinced she's living somewhere with a tribe she took to. She told him she'd always wanted to go back to them, and that's what he thinks she's done. And I hope so. I've always hoped so."

"Ravenna had a card from her mother," Bone said, one of his statements that was a question.

"When she was four," Fenny explained, sitting on the sofa

arm by her husband. "The card came for her birthday, a few months after Kingsley left. Ravenna still has it, of course. The stamp on the envelope was from Ecuador."

Bone thought it very possible that a woman who planned to be away from civilization for some time might engage with a friend to post a birthday card to a little daughter. It was as possible that a woman leaving her house on a dark night to set off for the station might lose her footing in the earthworks of the new wall, and slide down into the gap behind it, perhaps stunned or with her neck broken, beyond calling for help. That it should be an unknown, never reported, female stranger who had fallen was too unlikely. He said, "You knew more or less where she was off to."

"Within a few thousand square miles," Jake agreed. He took his wife's hand. "We made enough inquiries. I married Fenny, after they couldn't trace Kingsley and there was no sign of her. We took it that she didn't mean to come back." His voice betrayed that this had been painful to come to terms with. "Fenny and I married seven years ago. We still miss Kingsley."

There were more helpful ways of deciding against marriage than walking out on your husband and a three-year-old daughter, and Bone did not think that Kingsley had made that decision.

The phone rang, the sound coming from two directions. Fenny freed herself from Jake and went to the phone near the window.

"Yes . . . Oh, I forgot, and I meant to ring you . . . but you see we've got this disturbance, they've . . . Paul, I . . . It's Anna's *funeral* on Friday . . . I suppose you could, but . . . yes . . . oh very well . . ." She rang off and said to Jake, "I tried to explain to Paul, but he simply doesn't hear anything that's not what he's decided."

"You really ought to be tougher with him," Jake said, downing his whiskey. Fenny looked anxious; it was an expression constantly incipient with her, and Jake did not seem to have any great idea of protecting her. Bone had noticed that many people's idea of help is to give advice that the one concerned cannot, by nature, take.

"What can you do when he's got dry rot?" Fenny said.

Bone banished his instant picture of an unknown Paul crumbling from fungus, to hear Jake saying, "When is your friend arriving? Patty? Will she be here?"

"Tomorrow, I think. She said she'd *try* to get here today, and she can stay for at least two weeks, and we may be able to get someone before then."

"Don't *worry,*" Jake said furiously. "And if you're going to the hospital today, just keep all this quiet from Mother."

"Oh yes," said Fenny, now looking harassed. She went out, meeting Locker in the doorway. Locker was the size and shape of a door, if slightly less tall. He stood back, but Bone had met his eye and came out after Fenny into the hall.

Locker had plastic gloves on. He was holding a small booklet covered in white mold, and he opened it with great care. Inside, though buckled and foxed, the pages were legible, with stamps, dates and visas. He opened the front, as the passport's spine gave way, and showed Bone the first page:

MRS. MARY KINGSLEY MARSH

Bone nodded, and Locker said with slight awe, "Did you think it was?"

"Seemed likely." He heard Jake Marsh help himself to more liquid breakfast. There was certainly what an American journal had called "undue use of alcohol" in there. He had better talk to the man before he was too drunk. The news might sober him, of course, somewhat. Was he drinking because he knew all along about the wife in the wall?

"Come with me. Did you meet Marsh?"

"Only when we arrived."

They went back into the drawing room. Marsh had gone to the windows and was unbolting the french door. Bone said, "Mr. Marsh."

He turned. "God, you look like doom," and he crossed toward them, very slightly weaving, a faint smile on his wide mouth as if he would entice them to smile too.

"I'm sorry, Mr. Marsh." Bone embarked on the copper's least liked task. "You were right in your fears, it seems. I'm sorry to have to tell you that the body appears to be that of Mrs. Mary Kingsley Marsh."

Jake Marsh stood still, with the smile gradually changing on his face until he became recognizably a rictus of pain. He lowered his full glass onto the pembroke table nearby. Perhaps contrary to the evidence so far he's not a lush, Bone thought, for wouldn't a lush have to take a swig here? Nice if he isn't, because *The Late Lady* has wit and pace and invention.

"I'm not sure that I'd got myself convinced," Marsh said slowly, as if his voice had become fragile. "You said 'appears to be.' Does that mean you're not sure or is it police talk for 'is'?"

"There was a backpack, sir," Locker said. "We've been examining its contents. It has a waterproof pocket that preserved the papers inside—"

"Yes. I see." He did not look at them, or at the passport Locker was waiting to show. "I thought, if she was dead, it'd be in the Amazon somewhere. I thought she must be dead. She would have been in touch. She used to send messages when she could. D'you know she once got some bandits to mail a postcard from her: she would have told us if she had decided to stay. There's Ravenna, you see. I thought, I hope she died among her villagers. I was hurt that she didn't say goodbye somehow. Then I thought that very likely she could have sent it and it didn't get through. And all the time—" now his voice rose "—all the bloody time she was here."

His face was wet and he rubbed at it with both hands. He turned, looked for his glass, picked it up and put it down again.

"I'd like to talk to Fenny," he said. "Can I—do you need me for anything else?"

"We'll have to ask you sooner or later exactly what happened at that time: but it can wait, Mr. Marsh."

He looked from Bone to Locker and back. "But nobody killed her? She fell into their bloody roadworks."

"We've no reason to think otherwise," said Bone.

Marsh said, angry but with an effort at reason, "You've got your red tape. Fill in the forms, account for the details, wrap it up and file it. And then you can forget it."

Bone held to a not unsympathetic silence.

"Yes, all right. I'll try. Now rather than later."

He paused and sat down again, folding himself into the sofa, and said irritably, "Do sit down."

"I'll get on with things, sir," Locker murmured. "I'll send Shay?"

"Right." Bone took the wing chair. "Can we start, Mr. Marsh, with who was here at that time?"

"Well, of course *I* was. My mother. Fenny. Ravenna. No one else that I can remember. And I would remember because I've been over and over it since. I knew she was going. We all knew she was going. She'd got a hatred of ceremonial send-offs and goodbyes. She said," and he stopped and turned to see out of the window, "she'd read somewhere about the road beginning at her door. She liked to walk to the station across the fields, so that she was at once on her way. She was so bloody independent. My mother once said to her, 'Why did you marry?' and she said, 'For Ravenna.' Mother was disarmed. She's partisan, my mother." He might sound smug about it, a favored son, but his voice sank again to the flat tones of shock. "I still can't think of that—that thing out there—as being Kingsley. It's too horrible. Grotesque."

"Can you tell me about the day she left?"

"The night she left. It was at night. My mother said she thought it was early morning. She wasn't in my room because we'd had an argument. We often did. Nothing to it, no rift in the lute; I thought next day that she chose to sleep on her own so she could leave without waking me up. In the morning she—she'd gone. I always sleep like a log. I didn't hear her go." He sighed. "I wish to Heaven I didn't know about this. If it hadn't been for the bloody children the wall might have stood for ever and she'd be no worse and we wouldn't know. Do you think she suffered?" He lurched forward, trying to struggle to his feet. "Do you think she was conscious, in that lousy hole? And we were so near. Oh damn that boy."

"Boy?" Did he mean his son, the child Dom? Hadn't he been blamed for the accident on Monday?

"Long stringy bleach-job, playing fives with Ravenna against the wall. I don't know where she picked him up. I'd like to give him a boot up the backside to connect with the cross in his ear."

Conceding that there might be, within the area of Kent, more than one long stringy bleach-job with a cross in one ear, this particular example did seem likely to be Justin, if only because of the common reaction he produced in disparate men of roughly the same age.

"Little blonde with him inflicted no damage. She just limped off after him when I chucked them out. What the hell inspired them to play anything so stupid? Destructive morons."

Bone, distracted by this first intimation that Cha had been here, had been out with Justin again, barely took in that Shay had silently joined the company. Jake Marsh, who had appeared concerned with the destruction of the wall, and the consequent revelation of what had happened, more than the actual death of his wife, said suddenly, "D'you think she suffered?"

Shay shifted and, in response to a minimal nod from Bone, spoke: "Dr. Foster said he thought not. There was no sign of struggle, she was in a quite relaxed position."

Marsh gave Shay a moment of the wild blue stare, then a hoarse "Thank you." The gaze fixed on Bone. "Telling people bloody awful news must be run of the mill for you. Always in at the death. God, that's not fair. Sorry." Now he did get to his feet. "It's my turn. I have to tell Ravenna about her mother and it isn't going to be fun. I wish you could do it. I'd like to get it over with if you don't want me any more."

Fenny showed strain. Her face with make-up would have looked *jolie laide;* as it was you could say it was a face of character. She said, "We're trying to keep Dom from finding out what's been discovered. We've said the police come when there's an accident. There's been a very nice police-man who showed him the inside of a police car, and he seems all right. You want to know about the time when Kingsley left, I suppose."

"Please."

"The trouble is, I can't tell you anything. Fourteen years ago! I think I was probably tired out and slept all night. Ravenna was a very active little baby—well, child. She was three. And I was decorating the studio then. It's my work-room now, but it was where Jake worked until we built the pavilion. I can remember the day *after,* and how quiet Jake was, and Ravenna cried. She'd been saying 'I don't want my mummy to go away' for a week or so, and it was driving Jake mad. Ysobel was wonderful, though. She took Ravenna off my hands, and she talked to Jake about Kingsley needing her freedom, and that he'd known and agreed and so on. And we all tried to think of Kingsley speeding away to where she wanted to go."

She began to cry, walking over to the window, her head down. "And she wasn't." She searched her pockets, found a pink tissue, and blew her nose and turned. The strong, plain face settled itself courageously; Bone thought he saw why Jake Marsh, a man with fame and charm and money enough to attract any number of beautiful women, seemed to cherish his wife. "Don't think I'm always dissolving," she said. "I don't much. It's Anna, and now."

Bone was about to produce some banality when the door was flung open and a man strode in. Shay moved at once to block him off, but the man stopped short, ignoring him and addressing Bone.

"Are you telling me you believe it is my sister out there?"

The tone was an instant hackle-raiser, the stare that came along in the package was no mitigation. The eyes were intense under the straight brows, the nose hawk-like; the mouth had a theatrical curl of scorn. Even more theatrical was the single, pirate's earring in the man's left ear. While it might be an improvement on Justin's jumbo cross, there was something challenging, a deliberate affront, in a man his age wearing it at all.

This difficult customer had elected Bone as the unsatisfactory assistant in this particular shop.

"Just what grounds have you for this absurd idea?"

"Her passport."

This blow to the wind actually shut the man's mouth, Bone was satisfied to see. His stare, though, seemed to judge whether Bone were a liar or merely an idiot.

"And you, sir, are Mr. . . . ?"

"Chris Thorn." His tone said, How could you be so ignorant?

Bone turned to Shay and said, "I'll see Mr. Thorn in due course, when Mrs. Marsh and I have finished talking."

Thorn wheeled and strode from the room. Bone began to wonder if there was something in the air here that made the men larger than life.

Fenny sat sideways on the arm of the blue and green armchair. "What else can I tell you? Goodness, I don't think I've ever seen Chris put down before . . . Oh dear, this is going to shatter Jake all over again and it's going to be awful for Ravenna. When she heard we were going to be married, she must have been ten, she said, 'What will you do about being married to Dad when my mother comes back?' I said we'd probably get divorced, but it shows how she's always been thinking. I am so fond of her and it's a horrible age to be, hating everything and everybody."

With a brief fervent wish that this symptom might never attack Cha, Bone stood up and went with Fenny to the door.

"I hope the little boy will be all right."

She glanced up with anxious eyes. "They're very resilient."

Locker and Ferdy Foster were coming into the hall, and Bone knew that look, that expectant, contained expression in Ferdy's deep-lined face. Locker said, "Mrs. Marsh, do you know if Mrs. Kingsley Marsh was wearing any jewelry when she left?"

"Jewelry? I didn't see her go, you know. At home she did. You see, she enjoyed the change. She wore skirts and dresses at home. She said wearing jewelry on expeditions was only a method of getting robbed."

"A formula for robbery," Chris Thorn said, "and possibly murder." He was descending the stairs, hands in pockets and, to Bone's eyes, tiresomely trenchant. It was a pity, he felt in a surge of irritation, that no one had removed Thorn's ear for the ring.

He said, "Ferdy," and motioned Dr. Foster into the sitting room. Locker came as well, and Bone shut the door on Fenny and Thorn.

"What have you got, Ferdy?"

The pathologist held out on his palm a small sealed and labeled plastic bag. It contained a couple of brown pieces like broken stone, one very small indeed.

"Hyoid bone," he said. "Horn broken off. Cause of death, strangulation."

6

Strangled," Bone said. "That's why you asked about jewelry."

"We'll have to inquire more closely whether she could have been wearing a neck scarf," Locker remarked, "but there's no trace of one. Knotted material might survive. Could've caught on something; or it could have been a necklace though we've not found one yet."

"Conditions were rather good, considering," Ferdy conceded, his gravelly drawl cheerful. "Drainage and air, and protected by the backpack overhead." He made it sound salubrious, something any corpse would vote for. "But that broken hyoid means thumbs."

Locker showed Polaroids, dealing them out on the table. As they moved to look, a car started up at the front of the house. There was a shout, the roar of an exhaust and the scutter of gravel coming across the hall floor; more shouting, and a car taking the turn out of the gateway with a shriek of brakes. Feet pounded gravel, there was more shouting, and by this time Locker had shot from the room and a fume of car exhaust seeped in.

"I'm sorry, sir," came Shay's voice from the gravel court. "Couldn't stop him, sir."

"Who was it, man?"

"Mr. Thorn. Do I put it on radio?"

Bone called, "Come in here. What happened?"

Shay came striding, flushed. "I ran out, sir, but he all but ran me down reversing. He said he wasn't going to hang about."

"Just that?"

"Something about country cops, sir."

"Which nobody can deny," Bone observed. "Got his address, Steve? Good. We'll trot down there when we're through here. I'm not proud. All right, Shay. You'll have to take up sprinting." Shay, who was serious about fitness, became reproachful, a wounded bull terrier.

Bone went back to the Polaroids, in which the mortal remains of Kingsley Marsh grinned out with manic benevolence in successively fuller detail as the focus changed. Steve Locker and Ferdy spoke in turns.

"The backpack was here, sir, tilted above the head. Still the frame left and the waterproof lining and some of the contents."

"One arm may have been above and behind the head. Part of the metacarpel process and some finger joints were resting on the skull and one on the left clavicle. The rest had subsided to the ledge just under the pelvis here."

"Another detail, sir: the pack lying across like that, it could've been wrenched off by her falling down a narrow slit inside the wall, but the way it's lying, across over the head from side to side, looks like it was dropped in on top of her."

"Jake Marsh was talking about the building of the wall. Let's hear what the process seems to have been."

"It seems, from what Mrs. Fenny told me, that the old lane had deep ditches either side and a sharp rise to the road level. The council decided this was a hazard and after some time they moved men in to fill the ditches and surface the lane right across, and raise the whole level of the lane for about a hundred yards, she said, to make it a more gradual slope to the road. This meant building a retaining wall either side instead of the lap fence this side and a hedge the other; so they built up this garden wall first, and they were infilling all along the lane with aggregate. Just here there was still a long slit and a pile of filling marked off with trestles and poles and lanterns. The whole lane was shut off the same way from the road and marked Closed, with a diversion sign telling how to go around to the station by road; but it seems a lot of folk still used it by bike or on foot because it was a short cut to the station in those days. Mrs. Fenny says Mrs. Kingsley must've left the house by the side door and slipped."

"Did she fall," said Ferdy Foster, and held out his palm with its tiny burden, "or was she pushed?"

"We'll need to try and trace the workmen. How did they manage not to notice this macabre bit of infill?"

"I expect you'll find, Robert, that the contractors responsible either never recorded who was on what job, or have, a month ago, happened to destroy the records."

"Don't encourage me so, Ferdy. You'll make me too optimistic."

"I don't know if I'm reading too much into the angle of the backpack. It may have altered anyway with having aggregate piled in on top, and with subsidence and decay." Ferdy sighed. *"Yet*, it does seem to have been chucked in on top of the body."

"Unless that arm over her head had been through a strap."

"The skeletal structure of the torso has maintained a degree of coherence, apart from a settling of the head; there is complete disarticulation of the shoulders and ankles." He spoke with a certain satisfaction.

"Not a great deal of help, Ferdy."

"On the face of it—if such an expression is suitable in the circumstances—*not* a great deal."

"What amazes me is that you found that hyoid in all the rubble."

Ferdy's treacle-brown eyes narrowed in a smile. "Part of the service, Robert. It's losable so I always look for it at the start. I'm so pleased to have provided a puzzle." He pushed his spectacles up his nose once more and, nodding, left them, swinging his bag.

After a word with the scene-of-crime sergeant, Bone prepared to follow Chris Thorn to his home, Beeches, some ten miles off. Locker was talking of a house-to-house inquiry, to start with the question "Were you living here fourteen years ago?" and Bone looked in at the Paleys' kitchen to say he was leaving. To his surprise he found Morgan Carradine there with the little boy Dom. They were at the table with a Dulac picture book. She raised her head and smiled across the table. She was pale, though not as pale as the ghost who always started the episodes of *The Late Lady*. Her face was wide across the eyes, generous as to the mouth, and her hair, dark nut-brown and gleaming, was untidy in its waves, pushed back from her face. She now wore a white silk shirt and blue trousers and sandals; on her lightly tanned hands and feet the nails were silvered. There was something about her presence that made one think of the way the white silk was lying on her skin.

"They're all in Jake's study, I think. Can I fetch any of them for you?"

"Thank you, but I'm off. I expect we shall be around for some little time yet."

Dom said, "They've taken the wall away, you know."

"Yes. They'll see it's safe before they go."

"That boy and that girl broke it."

Bone nodded. He was going to have a few words with that girl this evening, and wished he could be as equable with her as he could manage to be at work.

Both Morgan and Dom suddenly smiled at him warmly, and he realized that he had smiled at them.

"Here we are, sir. This must be Beeches."

The great wrought-iron gates were discouragingly shut. Bone and Shay got out of the car and looked through them.

This courtyard was very different from Paleys' car park. A stretch of gravel led the eye down to the house, thin gravel green at the edges with a fur of moss. In the center a fountain, not working, rose in a small basin, all dappled with lichen. High hedges stood on either side, imprisoning the space between their dark ranks. There was silence in which the loudest sound was the tick of cooling metal from the car.

"Wonder why it's Beeches when the hedges are yew?"

"What I wonder is if this is the right entrance. It doesn't look used." The whole house didn't look used; the facade was a stage set, dark, regular, two stories and a long roof with dormer windows. The gates were locked. "There doesn't seem to be a bell," Bone added, looking at the brick pillars that flanked the gate.

"Bell here, sir," Shay said. "Shouldn't think it works, though." He was experimenting with a contraption of wires wrapped around one of the gate bars, shedding flakes of rust like autumn leaves.

"You're wrong there. Watch the birdie."

The door in the center of the stage set had opened. A woman stood there for a moment before advancing with slow dignity. They had plenty of time to take in every detail as they watched, the long brown pleated linen skirt, brown shirt and paisley scarf, the sensible shoes that made the gravel squeak, and the face of a calm horse under the loosely piled gray hair. She reached the gates and examined Bone's warrant card with detachment. Then she asked gruffly, "What d'you want?"

Bone caught something of Chris Thorn's challenging look in her dark glance. Could this be his mother?

"We would like to speak to Mr. Thorn."

She was turning away. "You can't. He sees no one."

"Mr. Christopher Thorn."

She paused, and turned back without, however, coming any closer to the gates. "Why should you want to see him? He's been abroad until a day or so ago."

"I'm sorry, but it's necessary, Mrs.—?"

"Miss Thorn." She must, then, be Chris's aunt. Fingers, a little swollen at the knuckles yet long and elegant, inserted a heavy key in the lock. The police were evidently to be allowed in. Bone speculated on the Mr. Thorn whom nobody saw; the father, most likely, of Chris, and therefore of Kingsley who also didn't see people any more.

They stood waiting while she locked up again, and matched their pace to hers on the advance to the house down the gravel. On either side, the great hedges stood darkly. As the tree reached the door, Bone regarded with pleasure the proportions of pediment, engaged pillars and well-kept oak of the doorway.

"Who was it, Antonia?"

They had stepped into a hall that was a large room, with a fireplace at either end and sofas ranged before each. Doors to sunlit rooms stood open along the far side and from one of these came a wheelchair gliding at startling speed along the polished wood floor. He was against the light, but the intonation of the voice was Chris Thorn's despite some constriction of speech. "Who the devil are these people?"

"Police, Lewis."

"Police!" The chair whisked to face Miss Thorn. "What are they doing here?"

"They want to talk to Chris."

The chair spun violently around to face Bone again. Lewis Thorn stared at him in silence and then backed a little and turned his head as if to look at his sister once more. His eyes, however, remained fixed on Bone.

Bone was grateful for a long schooling in impassivity. Lewis Thorn had put himself into a dim light from one of the windows, and Bone could see that the right side of his face was not all there and what was there had the rippled pink scars of burns across it. He hoped Shay did not give away the shock that he felt himself.

A door slammed at the back of the house, a door that needed an extra pull at the handle to shut it. A key clicked, feet padded across the wood, and Chris Thorn came into the hall and stopped dead. Then he strode forward.

"What the hell do you mean by following me here?"

Bone, whose thought was: What the hell did you mean by bombing off before talking to us? said, "You made it necessary."

"What have you been saying to my father?"

"Chris, stop sounding off; and remember that your aunt dislikes swearing. As you have been hardly three days in the country and have got across the law already, it might be in your interest to be civil."

Antonia said dryly, "I don't like his earring either but he continues to wear it. I'm sorry to say he's a grown man and has been legally of age these twenty years. I am going to see to the soup. Would you like some coffee?"

Bone declined. He wanted no social cups in the way.

"I want my coffee," Lewis Thorn said. "Bring a pot, Antonia. These gentlemen may reconsider."

A faint snort from Chris greeted the appellation.

"Come and sit." A wheel snarled on the wood as he turned and headed for the left-hand fireplace. Christopher stalked after him, hands in pockets and shoulders a little hunched. The earring would have looked less conspicuous with shaggy hair. Perhaps that was why its owner wore short back and sides.

Lewis brought his chair to a stop in the gap next to the fireplace, Chris leaned on the back of a wing chair at his side. The Force deployed itself on the two sofas that enclosed the square before the hearth. Bone was pleased at the absence of a coffee table, an object that was always near enough to prevent stretching the legs, too far to put a cup or glass on without bending double, and kept the fire off one's feet in winter. He was unlikely to be here in winter or to visit Beeches again; which all went through his head in a second, while they were sitting down; the reason for their call was foremost in his mind and he looked at Chris, a steady and significant stare. Chris, suddenly and in a loud fast tone, spoke.

"Lewis, before this crew shoot off their mouths, there's bad news I'd rather tell you myself."

"I've been waiting, since you got back from Paleys, for you to tell me what it is."

"It's Kingsley."

That was all he said, and Shay's eyes waited on Bone, expecting him to explain more. Lewis Thorn stared ahead for a moment. Then the chair shot backward, swerved, and moved to face the window. Chris didn't stir. He seemed to be intent on his own crossed arms on the chair-back.

"How?"

"At Paleys. She was murdered."

Shay's head turned sharply but no one else moved. Bone said, "How did you know?"

"Hell, Kingsley had been all over the world. She'd crossed rope bridges eighty feet above flood rivers. She was not going to fall into a pothole outside her own back door."

"Nothing more likely." Lewis voiced Bone's answer.

"In that house? With Jake hating her independence and that creeping-Jesus Fenny waiting for Kingsley's sheets?"

"Chris. Go and tell your aunt. She'd prefer to hear it in private."

Chris peeled himself off the chair and strode away. Perhaps Lewis had intended a reproof for the way he himself had heard the news, but he now, after a moment, came slowly back. He said to Bone, "Is 'murder' true, or a drama of Chris's?"

"It's more than possible."

The eyes' forceful stare was the family characteristic, which Bone had first met from Ravenna. "How was it discovered? What pothole just outside the back door?"

Bone explained about the raising of the lane, the wall, and the hole behind it. "It seems she went out of the house by the kitchen door into the lane. Her body was found early this morning when part of the wall collapsed."

The stare had been held, unblinking, during this time. Now Chris returned, carrying a tray and followed by his aunt. She came to Lewis and stood behind him with her hands on his shoulders. He raised his right hand stiffly and put it on hers. She had been crying, and still wept in silence as the heave of her chest showed, but her face showed nothing of her distress.

Chris brought his father a large mug, practically a stein, of coffee, and took up his post behind the wing chair. Antonia retired to the table, and brought coffee and biscuits to the police without regard to Bone's earlier refusal. She brought a sturdy Jacobean stool for a table between them. She offered nothing to her nephew, but came and took the wing chair.

"Are they going to get away with it?" Chris demanded.

"We shall be looking at all possible evidence."

"Looking at—what sort of shit is that?"

His aunt stirred at this, and a spasm of impatience twisted his mouth. "Look at Fenny, won't you?"

"Please, dear—"

"You will have some consideration," Lewis said with authority.

Chris leaned over the chair-back and murmured what might have been an apology. Antonia nodded slowly. She said, "Superintendent: how did my niece die?"

"Are you sure you want to know?" Lewis asked.

"Of course I'm sure. How was she killed, Superintendent?"

"By strangulation, we think."

"Then she *was* murdered?"

"Not necessarily. A scarf could have caught on some object as she fell; or a necklace, if it was a strong one, but I understand that she never wore jewelry on an expedition." Bone avoided the brutal truth.

"There was one thing she always wore, though." Miss Thorn put up a hand to her own throat. "Not a necklace. She showed me once when she was here. You remember, Lewis. It was the day before we heard that she'd left for New Guinea."

"I remember. Kingsley never said goodbye, Superintendent. She did not say she was going anywhere. I thought afterward that she might have considered that expedition riskier than usual, since she had come here before leaving."

"If it wasn't a necklace, Miss Thorn, what was it?"

"It was an amulet." Chris had moved to lean an arm along the mantelshelf.

"A funny little figure, a man, very primitive, with his hands like this." She lifted her hands, palms forward, in front of her shoulders close to her body. "It was made of some green stone or other. She wore it on a cord that went through a hole in the little creature's back."

Chris said, "She never went anywhere without it. A shaman had given it to her years ago. He told her it'd protect her against all evil."

Lewis grunted, and passed his mug to his sister for a refill. "Didn't work, then. Thought you believed in that sorcery stuff."

"I do." Chris drove his hands into his pockets and leaned on the wall, looking down at his father. "It didn't work because she wasn't wearing it on the night she was supposed to have left home."

Lewis twisted to see his son and asked, simultaneously with Bone, "How do you know?"

"Because I saw it around Ravenna's neck on Monday. I knew then that Kingsley wasn't alive."

7

There was a silence while they looked at him. Then he spoke to Bone.

"I asked Ravenna where she got it and she told me Fenny gave it to her. It's Fenny you should be grilling, not coming here with your plodding questions. Fenny was there then, Fenny took it off Kingsley when she killed her; perhaps it fell off in the struggle, perhaps she pulled it off. Christ, it's so obvious! The second Mrs. Marsh."

"Did you speak to her yourself?"

"I thought on Monday that Kingsley might be dead in the Amazon or knifed in Bahia. I thought she'd forgotten to take it. She was used to protecting herself; she used to bluff; she was good at defusing situations or ducking out of them. She'd learned it. I didn't realize Kingsley's enemies were at home."

Bone got to his feet. "Thank you for being so helpful. Thank you for your time, Mr. Thorn. I don't think we need to bother you further."

Shay almost showed his surprise at this abrupt departure. Chris stayed where he was but Lewis Thorn came to the door and Miss Thorn accompanied them, of course, to the gate. This time she was not silent as they walked.

"When I was a girl we left even the front door open. But times have changed. Your work must be the harder for it . . . My brother very rarely talks to people, Superintendent. He was a pilot during the war and was wounded in the spine and badly burned, as you can see. The children's mother was a nurse at the MacIndoe hospital, a dear girl I still miss very much . . . I've been sure for many years that Kingsley was dead, you know; neither Lewis nor I had any objection to Jake's having a legal declaration, for he asked us at the time. I was at college with Ysobel, and Jake met Kingsley because of that friendship. Things turn out so differently from what one expects! Ysobel was to become a doctor, and we all thought she would be splendid. She met Jake's father and that was that. I'd always thought she was so ambitious she would never give it up, but for love one does these things. Nothing turns out as one would think—Lewis, for instance; but we were none of us brought up to whine, and he's made a philosophy for himself."

They had reached the gates. The tall hedges, the gray stone of the house, the silent fountain, were going back to their solitude. Miss Thorn had a little difficulty in turning the key, and cried, "Oh, bother getting old! Not being able to do what once you did so easily . . . Kingsley is spared that. She loved to be free, to do just what she wanted." She held the gate without opening it, as though now she was talking, it comforted her to go on. Bone reflected that being shut up with a man who never saw people might well be a lonely life. Neither her brother nor her nephew struck him as easy listeners. "Do you think you'll find who did it?" The dark gaze was the more intense for the graying hair above.

"We'll do our best; but after fourteen years . . ."

She sighed, and swung the gate wide. "Chris has missed her so much, all that time. You know, although we were sure she must be dead, there was always a hope, an irrational— we've talked of her, one of the things Lewis talks of when the pain is bad and he can't sleep. And Chris, you know, was always vying with Kingsley, which would be first in finding something, going somewhere out of the way. They were so fierce about it, Lewis and I would laugh . . . I hope you're successful, Superintendent."

Inside the bars of the gate, she watched them go.

Bone sat beside Shay as he drove back through the lanes toward Adlingsden. Used to associating this drive with the prospect of visiting Grizel Shaw, Bone felt sour, morose and critical. He had been thinking of Grizel while he was at Beeches, and traced the particular reasons, Lewis being the name of her ex-husband. No doubt his mood was partly hunger, but partly it was reaction to Lewis and Chris Thorn. Lewis had shown his face, when they arrived, in deliberate aggression. Well named Thorn; had Kingsley been as belligerent? It made her murder more likely.

A motorbike burst past in the other direction. Suppose Cha was spending today riding around on Justin's pillion instead of busying herself on course work with Prue?

She hadn't told him last night that she'd been out with Justin that day, let alone demolishing the garden walls of complete strangers. Then Bone was switched from resentment to thankfulness that the wall hadn't come down while she was there.

He wished there was a chance of calling in on Grizel, but as they passed her house he saw a strange woman sunning herself on the seat in the front garden, a brief glimpse of a heavy body in a flowered dress totally unlike Grizel's feline slenderness. Was that her sister-in-law, and did she envy Grizel's figure? He had never seen Grizel slumped, inert. When she slept she might sprawl, she might curl into the very spirit of repose, but her body when she abandoned it to his wakeful eyes was always informed with life.

Shay had announced their advent by radio and Locker was at the mouth of the side lane. As Shay pulled in, a dark bronze Mercedes turned in at Paleys, right up to the door. Pressmen, herded back by police across the street, were clattering cameras, but could have had little luck as Jake helped his mother out and ducked in at the front door, which firmly shut.

"She's back early," Bone remarked.

Some of the press crossed to question him, and Bone gave stock answers with all the curtness of hunger, and turned his back.

"Let's rustle up some lunch, Steve, talk while we eat."

"Oh—Mrs. Fenny gave me a bite."

"Trust you. Ian?"

"I've got mine in the car," Shay said.

"Peanut butter sarnies," Locker said. "Our resident vegetarian."

"Bring 'em along with you. We'll try at the Pig and Biscuit." Bone got back into the car. "We'll give Ysobel Marsh time to settle in and have a rest before we talk to her."

"The hospital rang soon after you'd gone to say she could be fetched home, sir. I reckon she had it like my mother-in-law. They kept *her* in a couple of days, gave her an ECG and kept her under observation, no further signs or symptoms so they sent her home." Locker was clambering into the back and the car swayed.

Bone exerted a bit of conscious charm on the landlady of the Pig and Biscuit, a cheerful Tudor pub at the center of Adlingsden which was shut after lunch. She directed them through a black beery passage into the garden, where sunlight fell through the branches of apple trees, and long wooden tables with fixed benches stood on the short dried-out grass. A little girl clearing away rubbish said severely, "You're too late for lunch," and Bone said that he knew.

Shay had got it across to Mrs. Burnett that he had his own lunch, but Locker had said nothing, and she brought a tray with two plates of microwave-hot steak pie and two beers and a pint of cider. She said to Shay as she put a bare plate before him, "You keep them sandwiches quiet, now. I don't want the trees hearing I let anyone eat their own here."

Bone had started on the fragrant pie before she spoke, and

dry sweet flakes of pastry crumbled in his mouth with spicy gravy and a slightly resilient chunk of beef. She left them, and for a moment there was silence in the orchard except for birdsong, a clatter and hum from the kitchen, and a car or two on the road.

"All right, Steve. You had the edge off your appetite already. What did Mrs. Marsh give you?"

"Ah—bit of soup, and spaghetti on toast," Locker said deprecatingly. Bone grinned.

"Then you can talk. I'm famished but I can listen." Bone thought, as he ate, that even as short a spell of hunger as his job often imposed on him made it very easy to understand how all over the earth people could kill one another for food.

"I talked to Jake Marsh before he left for the hospital, and to Mrs. Fenny after that. Dr. Foster's still enjoying himself sorting bones from the debris out the back."

"Isn't there anyone on his staff to do that for him?"

Locker gave his Super an almost pitying look. "Dr. Foster says he knows what bones look like better than anyone else; the stuff they've got is stained by earth, it's hard to differentiate."

Shay said comfortably, "Dr. Foster's one of those as can't stand to let anyone else do what interests him," and then shifted as Locker's foot connected with his leg under the table.

Bone said, "Some people are like that."

Locker, boot-faced except that his eyes were smiling, admitted he'd heard of such people. Then, without further prompting, he started an account of his morning's work, and Bone drank cider, sharp and dry, and listened, and watched leaf shadows on the wood beside his plate.

"I got onto the District Council, sir. Jim Hobden there isn't too sanguine about tracing the workmen who did that lane and wall, after so long. Casuals, very likely, he thought. It might even be Saxhurst Rural, that far back, before they centralized. I'd like to know what those men found when

they came to work that morning. How they didn't spot their
hole had been part filled."

"If they did, I reckon they'd not kick up about being given
a hand," Shay put in.

"They think the wall builder could be easier to trace. He
would have to be a professional and might still be working
for the council. Any road, that's to be seen. Now Mr. Marsh,
he's an odd one. Apart from having been drinking fairly
extensively, so that he was solemn—a bit deliberate—he
was swinging from being joky, and then to being sad. Like he
caught himself joking and realized it wasn't the thing. And
superior with it."

"We had a bit of that from Chris Thorn," Bone said.

"Mr. Marsh told me he found it hard to keep down to my
speed of working. I said perhaps he better change gear."

"Nice. What did he say to that?"

"He laughed, so we got on better. But he's a smooth
operator, sir. Perhaps comes of being a writer. He could lie
that black was white, *and* you'd come near to believing it."

"Facts, Steve?"

"Facts as before, sir. He was in bed, slept well, heard
nothing. He knew he heard nothing because he was so
surprised his wife'd gone. It made him think back and
wonder at how quiet she'd been. He'd known she *meant* to
go, but thought it'd be not yet."

"It can't be that easy, Steve, to choke the life out of a
healthy woman, one who knows how to protect herself,
without at least some noise. It's clearly not a stranger or
she'd have been on her guard. Someone she knew could get
close enough."

"Could there be anyone else we haven't heard of, like a
lover? I know a rendezvous in your own kitchen sounds
weird, but could someone else have come in to see her?"

"And are we ruling out a random attack in the lane?"

They paused. Locker said, "Mrs. Fenny—she's got something on her mind. She's not easy about that night. She says
she slept and heard nothing, but her room was right over the

77

kitchen where, she says herself, Kingsley must have been packing a few stores. There were a couple of tins in the backpack, and so on."

"How did she do for money on these trips?"

"She'd see to that in London, apparently. She traveled cheap, she'd have booked her passage they thought, but when the inquiry was on, they couldn't trace a cargo or small ship that could have taken her. They did trace all such ships sailing from English ports for South America, but as for passenger lists . . . and Mr. Marsh said she needn't have sailed from here; she could have crossed to France, sailed from Spain, Italy—if she'd gone on the ferry there's no record anyway. Jake Marsh said he reckoned she'd sent him some goodbye letter that didn't arrive. But someone in that house has got to know what did happen; and on present judgment it could be either of them."

"Fenny's motive, to make sure Kingsley didn't return and she could eventually 'step into her sheets' as Chris is certain of." Bone went on to tell Locker about the amulet.

"Mrs. Fenny's the one that cleared all Kingsley's belongings into the loft when she was finally presumed dead," Locker said. "Mrs. Marsh senior told her that Jake wanted it done but that he would not say so. Mrs. Fenny and Mr. Marsh got married three weeks after the presumption of death came through."

"But that took seven years. Hardly a rush job. Whether Fenny took the amulet off Kingsley's neck, or out of her room later, it proves nothing at all except to the heated mind of Chris Thorn."

"Why'd it take so long?" Shay said. "Seven years, I mean. I thought presumption of death could be done sooner."

"Presumably because they went to all that trouble trying to trace her. And that could be a very good cover-up for someone who knew where she was all the time."

8

To Bone, the door of Paleys was already familiar. He grasped the knocker, a brass ring in the mouth of a disagreeable animal with a snarl. The snarl was matched on the face of the man who flung open the door while Bone's hand was still descending from the knocker, almost as though he had been lurking behind it. It was Jake Marsh, and he was still drunk.

"Well? Here to scoop up some more vertebrae?" He thrust his face at Bone, who stood firm to sustain the blast of whiskey. "When will you be through with buggering us about? Kingsley's dead. It's fourteen *years* ago. For God's sake, what are you expecting to find at this date?" Bone wondered if there was anything he did not want them to find at this date. In shifting his feet, Marsh stumbled slightly and hung onto the latch to steady himself. Beyond him, a door on the left opened and Jake, following Bone's glance, turned to see his mother standing there. She wore a loose jacket and trousers in lilac and cream, with a cream silk shirt. Her silver hair was tied back with a little lilac scarf. Her face, pale and strained, inquired of them.

"Go back, darling, lie down, it's all right—the bloody

police again. I'll get rid of them." He let go of the door and crossed to take his mother's arm to usher her back into her room. The resemblance between them was remarkable, two tall, thin and handsome people with brilliant pale eyes and ravaged faces as though living had literally worn them out. Yet Ysobel, who must be at the least twenty years older than her son, had at least as much of the violent spirit that had hollowed both faces. She was resisting Jake's efforts now.

"No. I am perfectly all right, Jake. They would not have allowed me to come home if I were not."

"But you need rest. They said you had to rest—didn't they?" He added the appeal in a ludicrous change of tone. Bone could not imagine him the victor in any clash with his mother's will, and this gave him a new impression of them both.

"They said I was to lead a normal life." Ysobel's kind smile directed at Bone included the police in this definition.

"I'm glad to know that, Mrs. Marsh, because it would be helpful if we could have a word or two with you. Is that possible?"

"No it is *not* possible." Jake lurched forward and Bone, who had advanced into the hall, wondered if he were going to have to deal with a punch. Locker edged forward. Jake's mother, with the same idea, came forward and took her son's arm, and turned him.

"Darling, you look after me very well." She smiled at him. She was almost his height. "Still, I'm quite well able to look after myself and I don't in the least mind a talk with the police."

Jake, dubious, was more overruled than persuaded. "Bloody persecutors . . ." The tone was now protest. Any command of the situation he may have thought he had, was out of his grasp. "Hardly back from hospital and they're hounding you. What can you tell them?"

"I shan't know until they ask me. And the sooner I see them the sooner it will be over. Why don't you go and listen to some music in your study! This has been a terrible day for you."

Bone was amused at Jake's automatic response to this motherly coaxing and sympathy: he allowed himself to be led down the hall, and he disappeared around the corner under the gallery. A door opened and shut. Ysobel came back toward them, and her walk showed that she was still frail. Before she reached her door, a burst of furious music came from beyond the corner, music evocative of a large number of people thundering about on horses. Then it was muted to a muddled buffeting of strings and bass.

"The poor boy," said Ysobel. "Come in," and she led them into her room.

It shared her elegance. The walls were papered with a silver-gray Regency stripe. The curtains, and an Osborne chair, were of yellow velvet, the carpet a gray so pale that Bone feared he must be marking it with gravel from the drive. Locker looked about for any chair up to his weight, and Ysobel pointed out a two-seater sofa covered in a chintz of yellow honeysuckle, gray tendrils and green ivy. A maidenhair fern fountaining from a porcelain pot on an adjacent table trembled as he sat down. Bone took the yellow velvet chair as Ysobel herself sat on the bed and put her feet up. It was a small French bed like a boat, both ends curving up in gleaming mahogany, and its cover of ribbed gray silk was protected where her feet were with a *Radio Times*. Overhead, a brass coronet fixed to the wall allowed swags of coarse ecru lace to form a canopy, spreading out over the bed-ends. Ysobel had evidently been sitting there before they came; she leaned back on the pile of lace-edged pillows. She was wearing a little rouge, and had placed it well, but the skin lay flatly under it instead of glowing through it. It was like a flag of courage. She was not prepared to look ill.

Bone read the statement the room made: the quiet luxury, the taste. There were small china pieces, Meissen perhaps, and Chelsea figures. The air held a soft musky scent of potpourri, although the french windows opposite the door were open on a small paved courtyard where a white table and chairs stood, and a tub of pink and purple fuchsia.

81

"So. How can I help you? It's Superintendent Bone, isn't it? I believe I owe you thanks."

"No. I happened to be there when you were ill. I'm very glad, Mrs. Marsh, that you feel able to talk to us; though you must tell us if at any time you feel tired and would like to postpone further talk until you're more rested."

"Certainly. I'm stronger than I look, you know." Certainly she looked better than on her last appearance. "I was lucky that Ravenna was so quick with my pills on that dreadful day. It seems so much longer ago than Monday. I'd got up, I think, in rather a hurry, and went out into the hall; I believe I meant to fetch something from the drawing room, but I can't think what. I felt ill, and called out. It was—I felt if someone could fetch my pills . . . It's no good wishing now that I'd been stronger or more sensible, but I shall remember that dreadful moment, I think, all my life. Poor, poor Anna . . ." Her long fingers with their heavy antique rings of pearl and amethyst pressed the silk over her heart and she looked, for a moment, older than before. Bone suppressed a pitying thought that often the people who could afford beautiful rings were no longer in possession of hands that could show them off well. Ysobel's hands, long and slender, were also brown-spotted and wrinkled.

"It's not good to dwell on the past—though I believe that's what you've come here to do, isn't it? Well, first I can offer you some tea."

Bone demurred, but she had risen and crossed to a cupboard whose panels were covered in striped wallpaper. Opened, the cupboard was a miniature kitchen. She poured water from a filter jug into a tall electric kettle, switched it on, and arranged cups on a tray. It all seemed very much like her life, everything where she wanted it and under control. She had arranged matters so that she could cater for herself, keep a sort of independence, with the minimum exertion. There was a little chintz-seated chair nearby and she sat there waiting for the kettle to boil. "I expect you want to hear about Kingsley. She was very like her brother—you've met her brother? Yes, well then. Very forthright and single-minded. She knew, as the phrase goes, what she wanted in life. She was lucky, too, in that fortune placed her where she could live as she liked. I admired her, even though she had little time for the things that I believe make life worthwhile. She was never scornful or critical; I don't mean that. She was not immature enough to believe one way of living was more worthwhile than any other, only that she must live in the way that her nature drove her to live."

She stood up and turned to a wall phone, lifted it with a small clack of rings, pressed a button and said, "An—Patty —are there any buns?"

Bone almost protested that it was too soon after lunch for them to want such a thing, but in the tail of his eye he saw Locker spread his hands on his knees and take breath in happy anticipation. Besides, perhaps the buns were for Ysobel herself.

She made tea, and Locker forestalled her in carrying the tray to the low rosewood table. The door opened after a brief tap, admitting a short roly-poly woman with a cheerful face. She was carrying a plate of buns.

"Oh, Mrs. Marsh, I'd've made tea if you'd said! You shouldn't—"

"I'm quite capable of making tea, Patty. I am supposed to take a little exercise fairly continually, thank you." Ysobel's quiet, controlled, gentlewoman's voice overrode Patty's. "That will be all until four o'clock."

"Oh yes, Mrs. Marsh. I hadn't forgotten." Patty took herself off. Bone expected Ysobel to make some comment on her, but he was wrong. He saw that it was not in Ysobel's code to disparage or to make excuses; he had read her thoughts from her expression. She poured tea.

Bone had in the course of business drunk tea you could trot a mouse on, from a thick pottery mug; and mint tea, and Earl Grey, and teabag tea in a chipped mug. Ysobel made good tea, hot and clear. A luster rose in the bottom of the cup shone through it, and he declined milk.

"Kingsley was not domestic. Not interested in housework and babies. She was very conscientious about herself when she was carrying Ravenna, and I admit I expected a change in her once her own baby was born. But no! she was consistent in that as well. Off she went—" Ysobel gave an expressive flick of her fingers—"as soon as she was sure Ravenna would be looked after. Yet she seemed fond of her. Little presents would arrive, and when she was here she would talk to the child as if she were an adult . . . the marriage—the wedding I should say, had been very sudden. Jake telephoned from Milan to announce it, and brought her home. She was a surprise to me in more ways than one. She wasn't pretty." Ysobel looked at Bone as though to invite his surprise too. "I'd always thought that Jake would marry some exquisite girl . . . sometimes I wondered why Kingsley had married at all, she was so independent. Yet they seemed very much in love, and she and Jake got on beautifully together. She installed Fenny here to housekeep and to nanny Ravenna. It may be that she later thought that had been a mistake."

Ysobel drank tea, and looked out at the fuchsia bush with eyes that saw something different.

"I suppose even an independent woman can resent someone taking her place; or making for herself a place that Kingsley had not seen was there. Kingsley had her own room, you know. She kept her collection of bits and pieces there, from her expeditions. They are all in the loft now, I believe . . . Jake had the room above this one, and I sleep very lightly . . . one becomes aware of comings and goings. For some time during Kingsley's absences . . . though I still think of this last absence of all as one of her journeys because for so long we believed it *was* . . . well then, Jake used to go to Fenny's room. I found it inexplicable, I have to say. One can perfectly well understand his being attracted to Morgan Carradine, for she is lovely—" Ysobel seemed a little proud of Jake's philandering—"but it seemed as if Jake perversely went for plain women. I'm giving you a picture, however, of how things were at that time."

Bone wondered if the plainness were less a factor than was

the strong-mindedness; it might be that Ysobel had herself to blame if he sought women who might dominate him—run things and make decisions for him. Was Fenny strong-minded?

"Did you observe any scene between them, Mrs. Marsh? Did Mrs. Kingsley Marsh show any resentment?"

She hesitated. "I thought there was a situation between them. I heard and saw nothing direct. On Kingsley's last stay at home . . . but you want to know particularly about that final night, and I think, now, that things were—" She bit her lip, and this symptom of indecision seemed oddly uncharacteristic of her, as if hesitation and doubt did not come often into her life. She raised her eyes to stare again at the brilliant shrub in her garden. Then, as if she had made up her mind, she went on. "We all knew Kingsley was about to set off again. She liked to leave without any ceremony, but all sorts of things had to be seen to before such an expedition. All we did not know was when she planned to go. I heard her in the kitchen. She used to eat only when she was hungry, which was not a very sociable thing to do, as it didn't by any means always coincide with family mealtimes. I knew it was Kingsley because she used to hum to herself. I like to keep my door open because I feel cut off down here, in a way. I supposed Kingsley was getting herself something to eat. Then I heard voices. Women's voices. They didn't talk for very long. It sounded . . . it sounded like an argument in which they were both having to keep their voices down. They would boil up and then hush. Then there was a noise . . . I can't describe it quite. As if someone had stamped, or put something down awkwardly. Then there was quiet, and then the outside door, I think, shut. I listened, but that was all. I must have fallen asleep, I suppose. I don't think anyone came up the front stairs, but the back stairs are far more used, for some reason."

The reason might well be someone who kept their door open onto the front hall, Bone thought. Ysobel still gazed at the bright plant, and Bone did not interrupt with any questions. In the silence there came a distant desolate cry from a peacock.

"All these years I've had, like her brother, a hope that we'd not seen the last of her."

And we hadn't, thought Bone. Who was it who hoped they had?

9

Patty heard your sergeant say poor Kingsley was strangled." Ysobel put her head back and shut her eyes. "It means everything has a different aspect. Is it possible to be sure after all these years? Is there no possibility it was an accident?"

Bone remembered that Ysobel had begun medical training. He said, "We found nothing that might have fractured the hyoid bone as she fell." He did not add Ferdy's opinion that "fall" was not the word he would have applied. A sprawling fall would not in likelihood have resulted in the tidily placed bones that were found. "She's been tipped into there," Ferdy had said, with a two-handed hooshing gesture, "lay you a monkey." A man could have carried her the few yards down the lane, but a wheelbarrow in the garden shed outside the kitchen door was a handy method for a woman to transport her.

Ysobel sighed. "I see. Jake did his best to break it to me gently, but he's very much distressed. His own feelings made it . . ." She sat up. For the first time, her voice was betraying emotion. "Poor Jake. All this all over again.

87

Whatever I thought before, I really dread for him now. It all looks very different now." She got to her feet, with graceful slowness, waving away Locker's offer of help. "No no. Sit down, please." She walked to the window and stood there with her hands clasped at her mouth, pressing her thumbs against her lips. Finally she spoke, and now her voice was constricted with pain. "Fenny is a dear girl. She's been a good mother to Ravenna; and Ravenna does know it although she's going through a rebellious phase and finding life so difficult. Fenny's managed marvelously to run the house and her own hobby. Those lovely designs." Turning, she said with sudden strength, "I don't want to think what I'm thinking—" and coming back to the bed—"I shan't even contemplate it." She sat down. "What else do you want to ask?"

"Had Kingsley any local enemies? Or distant ones?"

"No, I'm sure she had not. Of course, some of the articles she wrote seemed to provoke the most vituperative answers from other people in her field, professional ethnologists and so on, but *enemies,* I don't think you could call them that."

Locker said, "Mr. Marsh thought you would have a photograph of Mrs. Kingsley. You have all the family photographs, he said."

"If you look at the shelf just behind you, you will see a row of albums. Kingsley's pictures should be in the one marked Four." She sat forward, and held out her hand for the book. She was smiling. "I've kept these all Jake's life." Bone and Locker exchanged a glance as she took the album and opened it. "This is *my* hobby, Superintendent!"

He could not avoid the thought that, compared with Fenny's work which she also designated as a hobby, Ysobel's was not precisely creative. It depended on Jake's creativeness, apparently, for she went on to say that later volumes had press cuttings about his works. "This, though, is still a family one. Yes, here's a clear one. I've called it a wedding photograph, although they were married abroad—I took this when they came home."

She turned the book, and Bone took it from her to look.

Kingsley might not be *pretty* according to Ysobel's require-
ments, which where her son was concerned would obviously
be stringent, but it was a handsome face, with strength and
charm, a thin humorous face, the straight dark hair framing
it in a bell-shaped long bob. Jake, behind her, twenty years
younger than now, smiled joyfully. Kingsley looked at the
camera with a reserved amusement. Certainly she resembled Chris too much to be called merely pretty. Bone
thought of the face in the wall. Given that all life is sacred,
then the good-looking, the humorous, the ones who contributed to the extent of human knowledge, were not more
sacred than others, but it was human to regret them more;
the picture fueled in him a sudden flare of the professional
anger that, with curiosity, drove him.

He gave the album back, and she turned a few pages and
extracted another, single photograph, which she gave to
Locker.

"You may have this one."

He saw, as he went to the door, that Locker had managed
three of the little buns.

Out in the hall, they could hear the music from Jake's
room still conveying fitful struggle, *ignorant armies clash by
night.* Locker had shut Ysobel's door as if it were made of
china. Bone, remembering, turned back to open it a little.
Her voice saying "Thank you" followed him across the hall.

They were approaching the garden door, along the kitch-
en passage, when Fenny came softly down the back stairs,
making "stop" gestures. She joined them by the door, and
said in a low voice, "Let's go through the garden. I don't
want to disturb Ysobel." For which read: "I don't want
Ysobel to know," thought Bone, as he followed her out and
around to the sitting room french windows. He reflected
that the number of exits at Paleys would be ideal for a
French farce. The side window of Jake's study was curtained
at the moment. He would hardly want to look across at the
pergola, the screen, and what they hid.

Fenny, in her pastel dungarees and shirt, pulled the door
shut and turned quickly.

"I have to speak to you. About that night when Kingsley must have been killed. I went into Jake's room."

She stopped and put her hands together. She had flushed. Bone remained quietly attentive, noting that Fenny's communication came at twice the speed of Ysobel's; and that the style of the sitting room, with its bright colors and battered sofas, the wall-hanging and a big scarlet and gold modern painting, was her room just as the haven of feminine elegance was Ysobel's.

"I didn't tell you before. It didn't seem necessary. And I didn't want to—to admit it. But now if it's true she was killed, it's different. He'd been drinking a little because he was upset about Kingsley needing to go, and he fell asleep, and I watched him a bit, and then I went to check that Ravenna was all right, and went to my room. I could hear voices downstairs. They were sort of night-time voices, kept low I mean, but then they'd burst out a bit, and then drop. But then after a bit there was quite a long quiet. I'd gone to bed, and I was almost asleep when a door woke me, a door shutting. There wasn't any other sound." She was pressing her hands together. "I think Ysobel was having another try at persuading Kingsley not to go. Kingsley told me, it must have been a few days before that, that Ysobel had suddenly come into her room and pleaded with her not to go, to 'stay and save her marriage' she said. Kingsley told *me* the really dangerous thing in her marriage was having to live in Ysobel's house. It was Ysobel's then, she hadn't given it to Jake. But she said to Ysobel, she told me, 'I keep Jake by setting him free; I don't cling around his neck'; and that made Ysobel stalk out and leave her."

"There are difficulties about living with a mother-in-law. You've experienced some yourself?"

Fenny drew a deep breath and did a little mime of tension and endurance. "Kingsley said that the Japanese ideograph for discord was two women under one roof. Really Ysobel's rather a nice kind of mother-in-law. She *is* wrapped up in Jake, but then"—Fenny grinned apologetically—"so am I."

The music next door reached a zenith of conflict and she said, looking toward the study, "He's playing Beethoven very loud and Ravenna's stunning herself with a Walkman and rock music; and I've got to help Patty who doesn't know her way around yet. Ysobel has only got her thoughts."

And her scrapbooks, Bone thought.

Suddenly, as if the music next door had been an incantation to conjured violence, there came a ringing crash and a heavy thud against the party wall. Fenny started—indeed they all did—and Bone and Locker were out of the door, Fenny at their heels, heading around to the study. The door jarred to an impact and Bone had to shoulder it open. Locker's greater bulk thrust the door back with a force that propelled Jake and Chris Thorn away down the room. Jake, on uncontrolled trajectory, had hold of Thorn's arm and swung him, letting go only when his long feet caught up a Kashmiri rug and he fell, stumbling, one outflung hand tipping a thesaurus from the top of a book pile onto a badly balanced wire tray that hurled papers far and wide as Jake cannoned off the desk, his other hand now hitting the keys of the word processor which obligingly responded with a line of green digits. Thorn fetched against the bookshelves, jarring them into ejecting a few volumes onto the floor. Whiskey dripped from the edge of the desk where a glass rolled to and fro. In his progress Thorn had dragged the curtains open. He now sat on the floor at the foot of the bookcase looking stunned, his ear bleeding down his shirt. Fenny ran to Jake. Along the hall floor in the momentary comparative quiet came a curious trundling sound. Bone, watching Thorn who was getting his feet under him, wondered if the child Dom had got his skateboard back, when the noise stopped outside the study, the door opened, and Ysobel appeared in the doorway with a trolley. Somewhere a clock struck four. A faint screech like a choked peacock came from Ysobel. A vase on the mantel with some deliberation toppled over and crashed into smithereens on the hearth.

Bone, observer to the scene, felt it was not appropriate that all the men were in possession of their trousers and that no soubrette was trying to cram herself out of sight in a cupboard. He wondered why Chris Thorn, whom he had left at Beeches, had been dancing a tango with Jake Marsh, here at Paleys. Time would show.

Ysobel advanced down the room to where Jake leaned on Fenny. His shirt had a red smear down the front; Chris Thorn was clasping a tissue to his ear and it had reddened between his fingers. He now raised both hands and tilted his head to remove the earring delicately. His ear bled generously down his chest.

Jake's blue stare focused on Bone. He seemed to be almost dangling between the two supporting women, as his feet pranced, but in fact the arm around Ysobel was supporting *her*.

"You're—damn *late*. Get tha' madman *outa* here. Walked in and went for me."

"The shit was *dancing.*" Thorn spat out explanation. "My sister was murdered and he was *dancing.*" His nostrils were flared in distaste. His free hand described a pirouette in the air as if he illustrated the outrage.

"I was bloody not dancing," Jake roared, erupting from his women toward Thorn and finding himself up against Locker's solidity.

Bone pulled a chair around from the desk and offered it to Ysobel, who with a slight inclination of the head, sat down, visibly making herself relax. Bone said with emphasis, "You are upsetting your mother, Mr. Marsh."

"Jake, Ysobel's brought your tea," Fenny said. "Chris, did you come to see Ravenna? I think she's in her room."

Chris had moved to the desk, and mopping the spilled spirit with his tissue he applied it to his ear, hissing as it touched the torn lobe. He swung to look under his brows at Fenny. It was a brooding and forceful look. He did not answer, but turned and strode into the hall with the abrupt energy that characterized his movements. They heard him run up the stairs.

"There, dear," Ysobel said, in her clear, husky voice, "he's gone. Sit down and have your tea."

The trolley bore a promising blue brocade tea cozy, a plate of nice little sandwiches and a plate crowded with slices of two kinds of cake, more of the buns, and some petits fours.

Jake made a slight hash of sitting down on the little settee. His mother brought the trolley to him and sat at his side, pouring tea, and arranged the tray for him. Fenny watched this with an expression Bone diagnosed as sardonic, and turning to Bone was about to speak when Chris Thorn appeared in the doorway and said harshly: "If you weren't dancing, what the hell were you doing?"

Jake raised his head, looked blearily at his ex-brother-in-law and in a distant soft tone said, "Piss. Off."

Locker headed for the door to implement this; saying, "Not the time," he crowded Thorn out and pulled the door to.

Fenny said, "I'll come and clear up in here in a minute, darling. Have your tea and forget about Chris."

Ysobel glanced at her with eyelids lowered, as if at her recommendation that Jake should have his tea. He was drinking from a very large Rockingham breakfast cup, and Ysobel put a sandwich on his plate. Fenny after a pause said, "Yes, well then," and went out.

"Mr. Marsh."

Jake was patently surprised to find Bone still there.

"Mr. Marsh, what were you doing to give Mr. Thorn the impression you were dancing?"

He thought Ysobel was about to intervene, but her son spoke. In the same precise soft tone he said, "I was— mourning. I think that's the way to describe it. Not Chris's bloody business and not yours either; but you are a poseel— policeman. Duty to ask questions." He waited, his eyes giving Bone the same message he had spoken to Chris.

"Thank you, Mr. Marsh." As Bone closed the door he saw mother and son both engaged in the little ritual of tea, like some nursery vignette, in the midst of the room's chaos.

There were sounds of the winding up of activity in the garden. Bone went to watch from the doorway by the pergola. The screen had been removed.

He wondered what Jake's mourning rite had been, that Thorn took for dancing. Perhaps it was dancing such as the "primitive" people Kingsley loved might use at a wake, and Bone liked this idea. It might have been some catharsis of grief. It might have been, perhaps, celebrating. Further down the garden in their enclosure were the peacocks—the male dragging a molting train and screeching that agonized empty cry. Bone wondered what Locker had done with Chris Thorn. They seemed both to have evaporated. He emerged from the garden door, and entered the rose-laden tunnel of the pergola.

Ravenna and Justin stood at the far end of the arches, regarding the police, who in overalls and plastic gloves were packing the soil samples. Shay examined the shoring-up of the wall. Bone, aware of relief that Justin was not with Cha, strolled along under the creamy roses. Ravenna and Justin were in the jeans of their age's uniform, and she was barefoot, her toenails bearing chipped signs of having been painted in black. She wore a loose black teeshirt with some indecipherable logo on it, and the thong of her mother's amulet showed around her neck. Justin's denim bomber jacket was open on a milky chest bare even of hair; his ribs stood out so emphatically that the team might have been tempted to pack him in among their findings. He had dyed his hair rose, which imparted a touch of the flamingo, and he greeted Bone with a friendly "Hi."

Ravenna's eyebrows showed surprise at this cordiality to one of Bone's profession. She said, in a tone that would have suited her grandmother, "Are *you* in charge of this case?"

Bone had been condescended to by the young often enough to be undisturbed. He said, "Yes, ultimately. It's Inspector Locker's case."

She turned back to watch. Her face showed nothing, not even interest. Her hands were in her jeans' front pockets. Bone wondered at her presence here: was it a teenager's normal fascination with the morbid, or was she here in attendance at her mother's grave? Her lack of expression might be shock, or it might be that refusal to display emotion, which he often met. Dealing with shock was so endemic to his trade that some of his colleagues thought to ignore it was the best method. He had developed his own ways of dealing with it in himself, but he thought: She ought not to be here.

"Just another job for you," she said.

"Yes."

"Something like this happens and right off the place is crawling with the shit."

"The doctor was all right," Justin offered in mitigation.

"Yeah, but he's not police," Ravenna countered.

"He let Ravenna touch one of the wrist bones."

"Scaphoid," she said shortly.

Typical Ferdy. "Did he offer, or did you ask?"

"I asked. I suppose he'll be in trouble for it, now you know."

"He's Home Office. I'm not his boss."

They were rolling up the plastic sheeting. Dave Roberts raked the flattened grass, sneezing intermittently. Bone said, "There's no reason Dr. Foster shouldn't have done that, if it's what you wanted. I wouldn't have stopped him."

"She was *my mother*." Ravenna seemed to agree, but so angrily that it was more like a protest.

"Exactly."

Ravenna looked up at him under her brows. "I suppose you think you understand because your wife was killed."

Bone could rely on his face of granite, and he kept still so that no body language might betray him. Part of his mind observed that he would like to hit the girl; another part traced her probable source of information through Justin to Charlotte. Subliminally he lived the car crash again, the customary nanosecond's horror. "Perhaps," he said. "I hadn't thought of it."

She tossed the dark hair. "The official line of thought, according to all the women within reach, is that my mother lived her life as she wanted to and that I ought to think about that. It's supposed to help."

Bone turned the corners of his mouth down in comment, but he said nothing. Roberts, sneezing, took the rake to the shed by the garden door.

"I can understand Fenny telling me that," Ravenna said scornfully. "She has to think that, doesn't she? But I didn't think Ysobel would. She's not a cliché type. Except that she lives for Daddy—" she stuck out her chin to emphasize the phrase—"which is a cliché all right. Fenny's got her own life that she wants to live. Dom and the Arty Crafts, that's her life. It used to be she would have done anything for Daddy."

Including the removal of his first wife? Bone thought. Just because it was Chris Thorn's idea it wasn't being ignored. The person who had killed Kingsley Marsh would have had plenty of time to bury a sense of guilt, wrap it away, almost be able to convince themselves it had not happened as it had. Jake had gone to the hospital first thing to break it to his mother about the discovery in the wall; so that all three of the people in the house the night Kingsley died had time to be ready, of course, he thought as he went back into the house. A noise on the landing was Shay and Roberts maneuvering the loft ladder down to set its feet on the gallery carpet. There was not likely to be any clue among Kingsley's belongings up there, but they must look.

As Bone left the house, he met the tall somber figure of Dr. Monro Walsh coming in.

"Hallo, Mr. Bone. I hope all this police palaver isn't preventing the invalid from getting her rest?"

"She's having tea with her son at the moment," said Bone, going his way, "but you'll find she's had a little exercise."

10

He was still in the forecourt of Paleys, contriving not to give a statement to the pressmen who had swarmed across the road at the sight of him, when he saw Grizel. She was walking past Fenny's shop, on the far side of the road, listening to the woman with her. It was her sister-in-law, walking with the slight backward tilt of the pregnant. Grizel saw him, and gave no sign—perhaps she too became fleetingly rigid of face as she looked away, as he did. That he was successful in showing nothing, he knew because no reporter turned to glance her way.

As he got into his car, he experienced disturbingly an isolation he had not known before. He drove off without attention until he passed Grizel and her companion further along in the village. He might have scattered the press or taken off in the path of a coming car for all he knew. Now, as he left Grizel walking and drove past her house and on up the road, he was alone. Conventions, the social opinion Grizel must observe on account of her job and where she lived, prevented him from seeing her freely, kept her from acknowledging him before others. She did not want her family to consider her committed to him, to question, to

97

expect; here we are, he thought, in the liberated late twentieth century, bound and kept apart. He needed her company, her quick mind and sympathy, her electric presence. He needed her closeness, her voice in the dark.

They both hesitated about an engagement. He was diffident. Her wretched marriage had smashed her confidence. She feared, only too reasonably in his view, a future so unpromising as to include a stepdaughter and a policeman husband; anyone might doubt their power to deal with such a life. Bone silently agreed that he could offer only too little in mitigation. How could he say: "But look, you'd be marrying *me?*"—a man who would have to ring up or, worse, detail another to ring up, to say: "I can't be there for your birthday/the dinner party/the holiday—someone's been killed."

It had been dangerous, he thought, to have had someone to talk to. He had taken his exhaustion to her, had begun even to let go and talk to her of the emotional shocks and the involvement of feelings which were the industrial diseases of his trade and to which no one admitted. He had always felt solitary. Now he felt alone.

On the A21 back to Tunbridge Wells, Bone was overtaken by a trio of motorcyclists, on the stretch after the eucalyptus nursery. They zapped past like wasps, anonymous and menacing in helmets with dark visors. He remembered the messengers of Death in some Cocteau film on television. He wondered if Justin were one of them. His reluctance to talk to Cha about her little wall-breaking jaunt with that youth yesterday was making itself felt, physically, like something undigested lying on the stomach.

The late afternoon sun shone hard on his back as he locked the car—once again in a space outside the house—and glanced up at the windows. There was no Charlotte fluttering a hand in welcome, as sometimes there was. As he slid the key in the door, he speculated on the chances of finding Justin, fresh from Paleys, drinking his beer on the sofa again, and as he climbed the stairs he attempted to face the possibility and determined to behave in a civilized manner. Whatever that was.

No music greeted him this time. He could hear the singing of the kettle and the clink of china, so Cha was certainly in. He prepared a smile that must stay even if Justin were with her, but the kitchen contained only his daughter, in violet teeshirt and pale blue jeans, making coffee, her head at a rather dejected droop. The kettle's noise prevented her from hearing his step, and when it cut off and he spoke at the same time she gave a start and splashed steaming water on the Formica worktop around her mug.

"Daddy! You scared me."

"Wish I had that effect on villains. You'd be confessing everything by now." You might even, he thought, be telling me about yesterday's little outing. "Don't mop that yet, it'll be too hot."

Cha was looking at him anxiously. He noticed there were dark circles under her eyes, something he had been very familiar with in the long months when her hip and leg had been so bad after the crash. Has that young beast ditched her? he thought, and went taut with rage. Nothing could be better, in fact, than that they should part, but the initiative ought to come from Cha, not from the wretched Justin.

"Like some coffee, Daddy? Had a bad day?"

Her anxiety seemed to be for him and he was touched. Perhaps his smile hadn't looked genuine after all. He unhooked his mug, a large black one with his Crab star sign in gold on the side, and plonked it down beside her green Scorpio. She put a spoonful of Gold Blend into it and poured, frowning, while he ripped a couple of sheets off the kitchen roll and mopped the spilled water.

"Not a good day, I suppose. I was at Paleys."

"Paleys?" she asked. The name was new to her?

"Where you were yesterday with Justin."

Cha's spoon shot its load of sugar into her coffee and slid after it with a splash and a clatter. She looked at him. He did what he usually did when he wanted people to talk. He did nothing.

She took hold of the spoon again and did what he was doing, stirring coffee. She pushed a strand of blonde hair off her face. She was wearing a new style, one he disliked in other girls, combed across the top of the head and tied, the ends teased into an aggressive clump of crimped ringlets arranged so as to half mask one eye. The sort of style, he couldn't help thinking, that a boy like Justin would appreciate. Was it got up for him?

Cha spoke with muted indignation. "There was nothing wrong about what I did. You don't have to go on about it."

Bone repressed a sharp objection to the unfairness of this. To disclaim nagging would make it worse. She was picking up the criticism that had been silent. Wasn't it mothers who were traditionally accused of nagging? How would Petra have managed?

"I thought you weren't going on that bike again."

"I never said that. And you never said I wasn't to."

"You knew well enough I didn't want you to." The coffee steamed untouched, as impossible to drink as molten lead.

"It isn't dangerous. Justin doesn't speed." There was something in her eyes that suddenly remembered otherwise. Bone had not expected to be using his private organic lie detector on his own daughter. Now a thought occurred to her. "Who told you? About us being there? Did that man complain?"

"Do you mean Jake Marsh?"

"Whoever. The beast. We were only playing a game, and *she,* that girl, she said she *lived* there. So why shouldn't we be playing there? And he came out and shouted at us." The echoes of that shouting were in Charlotte's look. Jake Marsh, choleric even if not drunk, would be a redoubtable apparition. "All we were doing—well *they* were—was chucking a ball against a wall. It's not as if we broke a window or anything." She paused, with her coffee at her lips, and said, "Why did he get the police, though?"

"The wall fell down. In the rain last night."

Cha put the mug down. "How awful. But it must have been in a rotten state. It must have been crumbling." Then she almost grinned. "I bet he shouted all right when he saw it."

"He did, I should think. He called the police because of what showed up when the wall fell down."

"Showed up?"

"There was a body. At least, there had been. It turns out it was someone who was missing for fourteen years."

He didn't normally talk about his work to Cha, and goodness knows why he did now; except that it would be in the papers anyway, and because he was angry. He had all her attention.

"Who?"

He was already ashamed of having thrown it at her like this. "I shouldn't have told you. It was his wife—Jake Marsh's first wife. Look, I'm sorry. Forget about it, pet. My work isn't nice and I shouldn't bring it home with me."

Charlotte picked up her coffee and drank. Her face, always quickly expressive, was thoughtful and sad.

"That girl. Ravenna."

"Ravenna. It was her mother, yes."

"How did she get there? In the wall? Is there something fishy about it? There must be. But how lousy for her. I didn't like her, she's bossy and stuck-up. All the same. And it was her mother's garden, that part. All the rest belonged to her horrible father, but she said that bit was her mother's. It's rotten for her."

"Yes. She's not a likable girl, but all the same . . . Your friend Justin was with her today, so I suppose that's a help. She doesn't seem to have much time for anyone in the house."

Had he been disingenuous in "your friend Justin"? She had glanced at him, and then away.

"Justin's got tickets for the charity concert at Hammersmith," she said, too offhandedly.

"Has he? I thought he was short of cash."

"Someone gave them to him. I mean this person put them up for a draw and Justin won."

Bone knew that delicately treading tone.

"That's nice for him." He knew what was coming and he didn't want it. "Lot of big names appearing, are there?"

"Everybody. I mean UB40 and the Craze and Sweetly and the Eurythmics and they think even more. Some people haven't said yet. They think Archangel."

Bone finally drank his coffee. He said nothing. Cha was driven to go on.

"Justin asked me to go with him."

Bone took breath. He'd had time to find an answer but not to find the detachment that could make it the right one. "What a damn shame. I wish you could have gone."

Cha didn't at once reply and he felt irrational hope. He had meant, by his answer, to avoid confronting her—an adult's cunning sidestep of seeming to take her part. The businesslike tone of her reply was marred by tremor.

"I could, Daddy. It's not like the Wembley stadium or Milton Keynes. There's seats. It's a cinema. I wouldn't be standing all the time."

"Cha, everybody stands all the time at these things. They stand on the seats. I wasn't born yesterday, pet, I know about pop concerts."

"But I mean I could sit down when I felt tired; or when it was a group I'm not interested in. And Justin says you can sit in the bar. He'd thought of it."

"Not good enough, Cha. You'd still be standing far too long." He said nothing of his vision of her getting off balance while waving her arms and dancing on a cinema seat, and crashing down between the rows; or in the crush for the exits at the end.

"I'll be sensible, Daddy. I'm not stupid and I know when I'm tired." She was offering him, with an effort at firm reason, an argument and not a wild plea. He did not like "I will be," her assumption that she could go.

"And transport?"

"Well, it'd be the bike of course, but Justin—"

"The answer's no. I wouldn't let you ride that distance on a bike, and back in the dark around midnight, even with the best police motorcyclist there is. It's not on."

"If Justin looked like one of my stinking cousins, all short back and sides and clean and polite and WET you'd let me go. You would. It's all because he looks like that and because he's got enough imagination and nerve to be different. You think he's not to be trusted because of the way he looks, but it's all prejudice. I didn't think you were like that—"

"Cha, for God's sake, I'm not being unreasonable, and no, I wouldn't let you go with the cousins either. They're an insensitive pair and I hold no brief for them. I've told you I won't let you go that distance on a motorbike pillion. They told you at the clinic that riding horseback could strain your hip, and—"

"A bike isn't *half* as wide as a horse, and it doesn't jounce."

"The answer's no, Cha. No. I'm sorry, I don't like disappointing you, but that's it."

She looked at him, her mouth shut tight, and then turned and pounded up the stairs. She stumbled once, fetching Bone in anxiety to the door, but she recovered, stamped into her room and flung the door shut with a reverberant crash.

After a moment, Bone picked up the coffee mugs and swilled the brown liquid down the sink. He washed them, hung them up, dried his hands, and went into the sitting room, picking up his briefcase on the way. He spread out his work, and looked at the forms to be completed: the reports on his staff; a request for his version of a procedure on which a complaint had been made; a confidential letter asking for a nudging of the rules; authorizations for his signature. He had expected to get on with this at home. His colleagues stayed at the station to work, away from the distractions of home. He thought of Charlotte upstairs, furious, perhaps crying. Why the hell had she set her heart on something so manifestly impossible? When did an excited child ever sit down because it felt tired? After sixty miles' pillion on a roaring, vibrating machine poor Cha would be tired already, even in pain. When the concert started she might be carried out of that by the battering sound, the show and the shared, whipped-up euphoria. Then afterward, with the unknown factor of a teenage biker perhaps drunk but certainly on a high from the noise and the frenzy . . . If I could have taken her there it would have been just possible.

Why the hell did the first boy to engage her attention have to be this specimen? Unfairly equipped with a battered childhood and the emaciation of a waif, offering her a viewpoint on life rivetingly adverse to her own, evidently also "kind," the wretched boy was also "kind" enough to offer her this unlikely treat. Was Justin sorry for Charlotte? On the face of it, she was not a girlfriend who could confer kudos: too young, unsophisticated, conservatively dressed. Bone did not want Cha to be pitied. Damn it, she was pretty, acutely intelligent, courageous—Bone remembered Justin with Ravenna at Paleys. Why could he not have invited a girl so much more his type? That girl knew her way around. Bone knew too much to judge by the blatant sex appeal of modern girls' clothes. Most girls dressed for fashion and had little awareness of the message they were giving out. They intended to say, "I'm up to date, I'm cool," while any male would hear "I know the score." They were saying, "I'd like to be admired, I'd like a boyfriend"; the boys were quick to read "Get it here, I want it too."

Ravenna's appearance was not a fake. Her first sizing up of Bone had told him that. She was choosy, but she knew the score. Why, with a girl like Ravenna in reach, did Justin have to invite Cha to this infernal concert?

Bone went to the foot of the stairs and listened. No sobbing. No music either. Silence.

Bone said to the shut door: I am not going to apologize for protecting you. I can only say I'm sorry I couldn't do it any other way.

He went back to his work. He needed, badly, to consult someone, to talk to Grizel about this, to have her opinion on whether he was being too protective.

He thought of the exhausted Charlotte climbing onto the back of that bike at midnight, and shook his head. It was no consolation at all to be sure he was right.

11

Ravenna!"

It was as if a peacock had acquired speech. Jake, coming
to his study window, saw Fenny in the pergola through the
roses. He heard his daughter's defiant tone in reply, and
strolled across the rugged stones of the patio. He knew
Ravenna was far more distressed by the discovery of her
mother's body than she was able to show.

Fenny, near tears, stood on the path under the arching
roses. The pergola had an odd appearance which, after a
dazed moment, Jake traced to a complete dearth of flowers
on the side nearest the wall. Creamy roses clustered on the
one side, and hung thickly overhead. He could see through
the leaves on the denuded side of the broken wall, the niche
where Kingsley's body had dwindled through the years. The
niche was paved with flowers. Ravenna, a jar of the roses
between her hands, stood inside the police tape that still
barred the site, and glowered at Fenny. He was surprised to
see that Fenny was in tears. She was wearing jeans and a
washed-out old blue shirt that had never suited her, and she
hadn't done her hair yet.

"—spoiled the roses—"

"They're my roses. All this side is mine."

"But we could have bought any amount of flowers—"

"They're my flowers and it's my mother and I don't want bought flowers. All you bloody care for is—"

"Shut up. Shut up. BOTH of you."

Fenny turned to him, pointing. "Jake, look. She's—"

"Fen, it's her garden too. Look what she wanted them for. Surely she can take them for Kingsley."

Ravenna's hair looked very odd, a great tuft sticking out over her left temple.

"But why didn't she take them from all over instead of stripping one side? They look so—"

"All you care for is the look of it," Ravenna shouted. "You don't care about my mother. You never did."

"Hey, no, that won't do. No." As both sides began again Jake raised his voice, the hoarse note of fury silencing them. *"Shut up.* I don't know how the two of you have the heart to wrangle. Fen, it's Kingsley we're talking about. Damn the pergola, what's it matter?"

"I know. I know. We're all having a horrible time. Only I don't think anyone minds about Anna the way I do and I thought of some roses for, for the funeral. And Ravenna has no right to say I didn't care about Kingsley."

She was mopping her nose and eyes with a cotton offcut from some patchwork effort, and he said, "Oh God, Fen, don't be so pathetic," and held out a tissue from his own pocket, and cupped her head for a moment.

"Ravenna, you do know how close Kingsley and I were—"

"So close you shared Daddy." Ravenna jutted her head forward with viperish speed. "You were sleeping together all that time."

"Pack it in," Jake said. "Do stop this. Both of you."

Fenny gave a final mop to her nose, took a breath, and drew herself upright, straightened her shirt, sniffed, blinked, making the small motions known as pulling oneself together, and then, avoiding Jake, went into the house. They heard

Dom's voice: "Mummy, what's the matter? What's the matter, Mummy? What's the matter?" until a door shut.

Jake looked at Ravenna. Angry, she unpleasantly resembled Chris. There was the flare of nostril, the fastidious lip, the bitter stare.

"Well, Princess Charming," he said. "Men aren't monogamous, you know."

"Tell Morgan," she suggested.

They stood there a moment like two cats, waiting for the next move. Jake made it in a neutral tone. "What's up with your hair?"

"I cut it for Mother."

He took this in, then said, "Your customary suits of solemn black don't give much scope for expressing mourning, I agree. Only I don't think anyone but an anthropologist like Chris will get the point. It's not in the modern European canon."

"So?"

"All right, pussycat. I'm on your side, don't shoot an own-goal. Christ, you can shave it all off if you feel that way."

He thought for a moment that she might cry, and since the sight of his daughter crying would make him cry too, he turned sharply away and went back to his study.

Paul moved in during the morning. Patty showed him his room, "—and the bathroom next door, Mr. Lackland. You share it with Mr. and Mrs. Marsh, but the other bathroom is right at the other end. Mrs. Marsh thought you'd rather—"

"Oh yes. It doesn't matter," Paul said, with an instant geniality that vanished as he asked, "Where's Mrs. Marsh now?"

"You mean Fenny? She's working."

The term had a definite meaning for her, but one quite other for Paul. He strode along the landing and turned the handle of the workroom door. It did not open so, knocking, and hearing a movement within, he said, "It's Paul," and stood back, smiling in readiness for the door to open. When nothing happened, he knocked again, harder, and repeated in a raised voice, "It's Paul!"

His tone suggested that this information must be so pleasing as to act as an *Open Sesame!* After a moment Fenny, preoccupied, said, "I'm working, Paul. Not now."

Disconcerted, he stood there frowning, more puzzled than annoyed. "We must talk, Fenny. And no time like the present."

"Which is why I'm using it," she called tartly. "Hop it, Paul."

"This is exactly what I was talking about on Monday," he said triumphantly. "If you were away from home no one could interrupt."

"You would," Fenny said. "Now do go away and leave me alone."

"I want a word with you before the others come. I've called a meeting this afternoon."

"You've *what?"*

At least in one thing he had succeeded. The door was flung open and she stood facing him. He was surprised to see that her eyes were red. "You've called a meeting? Where and when?"

"Here and this afternoon. We need to discuss the expansion among the whole group, everybody concerned. It's got to be soon because the chance of the barn won't wait. I've got to finalize by Monday."

"Then forget it. It won't work." She was flushed, and he thought it didn't become her. Skinny women with straggly hair and no style couldn't afford to look upset.

"Let's discuss that this afternoon, shall we? I did want to give you a chance to hear the whole scheme before the others do."

"Oh, did you? Well, you'd better treat us all alike. And don't interrupt me again. You are not privileged any more than anyone else in the house, and if a child of six can learn not to come bothering me when I'm working then so can you. When you said you wanted to stay here I thought: I bet he comes waltzing along like God's gift to busy women, in spite of all I've said and all he's said that he understood. And you did. And now you've found that I really am working and I don't expect to stop for you. So cancel your meeting; *now.*"

She shut the door. Paul stood for a minute staring at the panel, his mouth tight and his head forward. Then he turned and went down the stairs.

"Hallo." Ysobel was leaning forward on her sofa, smiling at him through the half-open door. "Is that Paul? Come in and have a chat. Everyone's making me rest too much."

12

Bone drove to Whitmore's in a gloomy frame of mind. He and Charlotte had been polite and stilted in converse. Neither of them had mentioned Justin, or talked indeed on any subject. There was an air about her that made him wonder if she meant to defy him and go to this infuriating concert. He hated to be on such terms with her, and was not looking forward to an evening of reminiscence with Mr. Whitmore. He could not think why he had let himself in for it, except for an offchance, pretty unlikely, of hearing more about the family at Paleys fourteen years ago. The Chief did not seem to put much urgency on the matter of Kingsley Marsh's death; perhaps, Bone hazarded in one of his flights of fancy, because if Jake Marsh should be the culprit his arrest would be unpopular with the three or four million people who habitually watched *The Late Lady*.

What a gift that title had been to news editors. Hardly one of the headlines, last night, this morning, had not bellowed "His Late Lady," alongside pictures of Jake and, from the file, Kingsley, the resolute aristocratic face, with that hint of the chancy in it, Chris Thorn's eyebrows but in neat circumflexes, Ravenna's mouth but more controlled. Two papers had managed to include a picture of Morgan Carradine, *"The Late Lady* of Marsh's TV series," completely irrelevant but for the sake of popularity. One paper emphasized that Jake had not met Morgan until well after Kingsley's disappearance, almost seeming to suggest that had they met before, Kingsley's death would be wholly explicable. After all, Morgan as the ghost of the series was the enchanting phantom for whom the men showed understandable willingness to commit any number of crimes.

Mr. Whitmore had always been a dandy dressed in a profession more famous for shabbiness. He wore a dark blue poplin shirt, a gray and blue striped tie, dark blue trousers and cardigan. He ushered Bone in with a wide gesture and said, "This is very nice," and Bone hoped it was.

At first, not. They sat with a weak g-and-t talking of past events. Bone wondered if Whitmore were regretting the invitation. They started dinner with pink grapefruit. All the segments had been neatly cut free, and Bone, who had once shot a hard-wrestled piece of grapefruit into his prospective father-in-law's breast pocket, pictured Whitmore conscientiously dealing with the fruit, and felt gratitude. He told the anecdote, Whitmore roared with laughter, and they both relaxed. The dog, which had been roaming under the table, sat down by the small wood fire that glowed on its heap of ash in the chimney, and regarded them with attentive complacency.

"I'm doing steak, Bone. Come into the kitchen and we'll drink wine as I cook."

The kitchen was large, untidy, and comfortable. Bone was put at the table with his wine, Whitmore cooked and the Jack Russell sat in the doorway. Whitmore removed his cardigan and put on a butcher's striped apron, and as he cooked, he drank and refilled the glasses. He was a little affronted at the slowness of Bone's drinking.

"I can't afford to be caught," Bone said. "Some of our fellows'd grin and let me off, and they'd chat about it; others might let me off hoping for a return favor later. Some would be delighted to nail me. Yet I'd be very likely to get home without meeting a soul and without being stopped . . . but to be tedious, I suppose it's on principle; and because I've met drunken drivers."

"It must make a good many differences to your life, being a policeman." Whitmore perched on the table, tongs in hand.

"I can't tell. It's a while since I was anything else."

"Are you one of the people concerned with this somewhat grisly find at Paleys?"

"Yes."

"Wretched thing for the family. My daughter was sad when I told her. Talked to her on the phone this afternoon. She used to go there in her teens—rather often, in fact, and we feared she was making an utter nuisance of herself to the family although they were easygoing about it. I suppose one's apt to be anxious about one's own children. God knows I've dealt with enough anxious parents in my day, and some of them hopelessly critical, ready to undermine their poor offspring at every turn. Vicky's not academic and she was self-conscious—a big girl is at a disadvantage. We worried about her a great deal. But the Marshes said she was no trouble. We lived in Adlingsden itself then, near the green."

Bone's concentration on Vicky Whitmore's friendship with the Marshes was disturbed by a vision of Grizel Shaw's little house below the church green, secluded behind its hedge and front garden, and that was therefore the house he saw the Whitmores in, with their big unacademic daughter making her way to Paleys.

"What attracted her about the Marsh family in particular?"

"I suppose they were less time-bound and less at the mercy of routine than we could be. Marsh being a writer was probably part of it, and Mrs. Marsh would take off for five or six months at a time, a year once, I believe . . . Mind you, they had their routines. Vicky was full of talk about them, and I rather let it flow over me, you know. Mrs. Marsh senior would give her son tea at four o'clock, and the housekeeper wasn't allowed to do it. Vicky thought that was so nice. If I'd been Jake Marsh it would have driven me mad, I must say, but I suppose he enjoyed it. Nobody allowed in his study, either, and so on."

Whitmore drained the potatoes and put butter lavishly in the hot pan. While he sautéed them, he went on talking.

"Your friend, Derrisford, now: his parents tended to smother him, didn't they? I seem to remember they always took up any enthusiasm of his in a big way. Wasn't there a natural history era?"

Bone grinned. "They got him all the books, and took him, and me, to the South Kensington museum four or five times. When they went on holiday they looked up any local zoo or nature reserve. Derry moved on to architecture after a while."

"Your doing?" Whitmore leaned across and adroitly filled Bone's glass. "Come on, man, it's hours before you'll be driving."

"I'm not sure it wasn't my doing, but some of it was his mother's. She'd got him a bit browned off with natural history."

Whitmore laughed. The terrier barked sympathetically.

"It was marvelous from my point of view," Bone said. "All his books, and I went along on their outings to famous houses."

"There was a bet on in the staff room that Derrisford would never manage to leave home. It was thought that if he went to university his parents would move house to be there and join in his reading. Marriage seemed out of the question."

"He got married in the States. He went to Harvard on some exchange or other, and for some reason his parents didn't go along."

"Aha."

"What interested your daughter about Paleys, sir?"

"She had what m'wife called a pash on Kingsley. Poor woman. She was very patient with Vicky, and Vick had to endure long stretches without seeing her when she was off on one of her expeditions. But she was almost as keen on Jake Marsh. We had to make rules about how often Vick might go there when Kingsley was at home; and my word what scenes there were, what accusations of cruelty, of not understanding, of hating her . . . poor Vick. What it is to be an adolescent. She took it into her head that Paradise would be going on one of those expeditions with Kingsley."

Whitmore began to dish up, wearing oven mitts to handle the plates. Bone admired his organization of the business. When he himself gave any of his friends and colleagues dinner he preferred to take them out. His main thoughts, however, pursued Kingsley.

"I don't suppose she got much encouragement to go along, sir. As I understand it, Mrs. Marsh always went alone."

"Oh yes. She struck me as a very detached sort of person. We used to ask them here to lunch or dinner and so on, for Vick's sake and to pay back hospitality; though I'm not sure that Vick enjoyed those occasions. Too anxious in case we disgraced her."

"How did she think you could do that?"

"Heaven knows. Anything from poor cooking to not knowing some fact that anyone who'd spent hours studying Kingsley's reports in *Nature* or the *Geographic* should know."

He picked up the plates and motioned toward the sitting room, where a small table was laid in the window bay overlooking the garden. Bone brought their glasses and the wine, feeling useful, but Whitmore went back anyway into the kitchen and reappeared with a tall jug wrapped in a napkin and steaming, which he put on the table. "Worst thing the world's produced, a gravy boat. Too small, cools the stuff down. Leaves you ladling congealed sludge. How's your steak?"

"Excellent," Bone said sincerely. There was a considerable silence, while the men ate and the terrier sat beside Whitmore edging its bottom closer and looking up with beaming trust. After a while, Whitmore cut off a succulent corner of meat and tossed it dogward. The terrier rose in the air, engulfed it with a snap, swallowed back, and went to stretch out by the small fire that almost slept on its bed of ash.

"You were always good on discipline," Bone observed.

"M'm? Ah—if you're going to enjoy a dog's company you have to make sure it knows what's what. A dog likes to know what's what. And so do children, though they kick up about it."

Bone seized the subject. "Did your daughter kick up about not going along with Kingsley to the far corners of the world?" He wondered what Kingsley had thought of the proposed company of a large enthusiastic young woman on her solitary journeys.

"I told her there was no question of it. Her mother gave her all the reasons, but Vick thought reasons could be reasoned away. I took the easier course, simply adopted a negative attitude, and I really don't know which of us was the least popular. It's a tragic thing to have happened to that poor woman, when one thinks she was able to look after herself in far countries and died at home . . . And Vick hasn't very much to say about it now. She has her own children to say no to; I fear she doesn't, but that's not my problem."

Bone fleetingly wondered how Cha would bring up children, but Whitmore was away telling tales out of school, secrets of the staff room that Bone was amused to hear.

It was not until he was leaving that Whitmore said, "I remember now that when we heard Kingsley Marsh had left—as was thought—Meg said to me, 'I hope she didn't scuttle off to get away from Vicky'; and I did fear that it might have been the case, but Mrs. Marsh told me her daughter-in-law always left without warning. I'm afraid poor Vick had been pestering her. She'd set her heart on it, couldn't see the utter impossibility. Yesterday when we talked on the phone—yesterday, not this afternoon; odd, it's my recent memory that's poor; yesterday she said, 'I can't believe how unimportant it seems now, when it was the one thing in life that mattered then.'"

Bone, getting into his car, waving, driving off, had realized that both Ysobel and Fenny could be telling the truth if Vicky Whitmore, now Vicky Stannard, had come to plead with Kingsley on the night she disappeared. Fenny thought the voice to have been Ysobel's, but we hear what we expect to hear.

He thought: here am I with Mr. Whitmore's good dinner and wine inside me and I'm fitting out his daughter as Suspect Next in Line. I've learned, throughout my years in the business, that there's no such thing as a solution too bizarre. Almost all the murders we're faced with are solved at once, no mystery. The husband, the wife, the business partner, the obvious one is the right one. Just the few are the absorbing ones, the puzzlers. He was not going to lose, ever in his life, the image of Kingsley where she was found. It was volcanic emotion that caused most murders.

A big girl, a not very bright but passionate adolescent; a big girl would have had little trouble in carrying the slight and wiry Kingsley out to her fourteen years' grave.

Friday: the day of Anna Dudley's funeral and of the rock concert. Cha, unconcerned with anything but her own life, ate almost no breakfast but sat hugging Ziggy, somnolent after his own meal, who regarded Bone over the level of the table with eyes that dozed shut. The car to take Bone to London would be calling any minute now; he took his dishes to the sink, ran water into the bowl that had held cereal, and wondered what to say. On the principle that what he might say would no doubt be wrong, he spoke.

"I may not be back until all hours, pet. What are your plans?" Not what *were* your plans, for the consciousness of those was like an ache in the room. Ziggy throbbed softly in the silence before Cha spoke.

"Oh, Grue will be in. She wants us to go to a movie or something. And I've got to finish some course work." Her voice had no energy. She'd talked so when she was recovering from the smash, except, of course, that she couldn't then make words so well. Damn it all, a song and dance about a disappointment. He was right not to let her go, and had to bear her response.

"Fine." The wrong note of false cheer annoyed him. "I expect Mr. Grant will bring you home."

"I expect he will." She bore having the top of her head kissed, and Ziggy purred heartlessly on, laying a silvery arm along the table. A ring at the door meant the driver was here, and Bone told the door-phone that he'd be down, put on his jacket, said goodbye without managing to get Cha to raise her head, and ran down the stairs in a fine mood to start the day.

The M25 was, as ever, thick with vast heavy goods stuff thundering through; cars filled with the debris of August holidays as people returned early to avoid the rush of the weekend. A white-haired man in a very old Mini, his arms straight out in front of him as though he fended off a tiger rather than merely gripped the wheel, overtook Bone's car with great difficulty, driving alongside and slowly edging in forward for the best part of a mile, then cut in ahead, exhausted by the effort. Bone's driver pulled out smoothly to overtake him and Bone glanced at him as they passed; he drove with head thrown back to stare through his spectacles, holding off the tiger for dear life. Some people responded to age as to a challenge; when the glove was thrown down, more supple joints than many possessed were required to pick it up gracefully.

In the next car a small boy, illegally loose in the back, roamed to and fro, a potential flying object. Shay got on the radio to the motoring squad to report the car's number, and Bone thought back. Petra had fastened the baby safely in his carrycot but it had done no good; he would have been four, four in September. How would Petra have coped with her daughter's troubles?

Shay was leaning sideways to fish in a pocket. He produced a tube of Polos and offered it. Bone took one and made himself think about the case. Whitmore's daughter could prove a good source of information, perhaps an important one. At a long chance, she might be the murderer; though had she strangled Kingsley in pique at being refused as a companion up the Amazon, and had then popped her in the wall, Bone doubted that she'd be raring to tell him so after so many years of getting away with it. The trail he followed was not so much cold as entering permafrost.

Raynes Park seemed quite a pleasant little part of Wimbledon suburb once they got off the A3, and they reached the road they wanted not much more than an hour after leaving base. Just time to get heartily tired of peppermint and hopeful of coffee from Vicky Stannard. He had not rung her to ask for an interview; he had merely ascertained, obliquely, from Whitmore that she was usually at home all day. Ignorance of his coming, he held, spared people the bother of inventing stories and thinking up excuses. He preferred them to be under his eye when they were doing that.

As a result, of course, Mrs. Stannard was out. Shay had knocked and rung, Bone had got his hair combed by the honeysuckle that bunched over and inside the open porch as he stood there to peer through the door glass. This had been placed high, so that only a six-foot householder could scan intruders. The mock-antique bottle glass distorted the obscure view. A table opposite the door carried a telephone and a large green plant, and a pair of shoes lay on the stairs. Bone thought of poor Dom and his skateboard. Whitmore's daughter, with three small sons, must take domestic hazards for granted.

"They've had a break-in, sir." Shay's blunt finger indicated the chipped wood, not yet repainted, at the lock edge of the door. The pane nearest to it was opaque reinforced glass replacing the fake Tudor. If the burglar had tried to reach the lock through a shattered pane he would have dislocated his shoulder for nothing, as it was a double-locking Chubb mortice only to be opened with a key.

Shay touched his arm. Mrs. Stannard was wheeling a twin

pushchair over the uneven front path. A baby strapped into one section was so like Winston Churchill in a powder blue tracksuit that the only wonder was the lack of cigar. Beside him rode a child a year older in dirty scarlet rompers, clutching an ice cornet. A boy about four in denim shorts and sagging teeshirt clung whining to the arm that pushed the buggy; deposits around his mouth showed he had been speedier with his ice than his brother was. Mrs. Stannard herself wore a white cotton jersey that gripped her tenaciously around the hips, over a denim skirt. She was indeed a big girl; auditioning as a Valkyrie she'd have left the rest with spears drooping. There was an epic grandeur about her, and a warrior air.

"What do you want? Who are you?"

The baby echoed this with a yell that crumpled his face, Winston Churchill by Francis Bacon.

"We're the police. We'd like to talk to you, Mrs. Stannard."

"Police! Don't say you caught our burglar at last. That'd be the day." She ran the buggy at them, and Shay backed at speed into the honeysuckle. Bone slid to the other side, she leaned over the pram and unlocked the door.

They crowded into the little hall, Bone and Shay crammed against the wall along with a tallcase clock, an oak barometer and a bulging row of hanging coats. While Mrs. Stannard unloaded the pushchair, Number One Son ran yelling down the passage to the back and flung a door wide on the kitchen. Mrs. Stannard carried the shopping and the baby, who stared over her shoulder with congested face, and they followed, Number Two Son fighting past Bone's legs to safety at his mother's side.

"Sit down if you can find a chair," she said with curt hospitality. There were chairs in plenty, but none free. Shay hesitated but Bone removed a blue plastic potty stenciled with Mickey Mouse, and put it on the floor, and from another chair shifted a tattered comic, a pair of socks, a baby's bottle, sweet wrappers and a gnawed biscuit. He and

Shay sat. The oldest boy took the biscuit and, working around the edge of it, also seized a comic and ran from the room.

"Let's see that ID again." Mrs. Stannard, thus showing her familiarity with American police series, gave Shay's warrant card another stare as she fed the baby's legs into its high chair. She stoppered his mouth with a comforter and began unloading carriers. The middle child had found a red fire engine toy which it was running to and fro on the edge of the table, supplying the klaxon noise *forte*.

"I suppose it's about poor Kingsley."

"We were hoping," agreed Bone, pitching his voice to overcome the sound effects, "that you can help us with a fuller picture of events at the time of Mrs. Marsh's disappearance, and of Mrs. Marsh herself. I understand you saw quite a lot of her at that time."

"Coffee?"

Bone's thirst had waned somewhat since he entered Mrs. Stannard's kitchen, in which children's clothes and shoes were on most of the level surfaces along with dishes, jars and now packets of shopping, but she was filling the kettle, calling above the noise of water and the braying of the fire engine, "Was she really murdered? I saw the papers said so but you can't believe *them*."

So much for the press, thought Bone.

Vicky Stannard threw the kettle switch and turned. "I suppose you lot don't say so unless you're sure. It's awful she was found like that." Her large, pale face showed deprecation; being found in a wall seemed to be a social lapse in her book. "I don't see why you think I could remember after all this time. I shouldn't think it could be any use to you." She turned to spoon instant coffee into mugs. The child took its engine to the top of the table and ran the length of it, opposite Bone and Shay, screeling a siren noise against the kettle's whistle. Mrs. Stannard turned with unexpected speed, whipped away the engine toward the end of its run and put it on top of the freezer, where Bone glimpsed the wing of a toy plane and the foot of a stuffed animal. Evidently she set limits on noise pollution.

The child stood open-mouthed, studied his mother's face for a moment, made his decision and ran out of the room. Distant noises of sibling rivalry came from realms of chaos beyond the kitchen.

She pushed mugs of rather milky coffee across to them, and plonked down a sugar bowl in which liquid of some sort had glued the sugar together. She pulled the lid from a tin of chocolate biscuits she had reached from high in a cupboard. Bone was curious as to how she would manage once the children could climb, but he had no doubt she could deal with that. She looked at him now, stirring her coffee, with blue eyes disconcertingly like her father's.

"I always thought Kingsley had been murdered. When she didn't come back, I mean. But not here in England. I thought, by some of those natives she was so fond of, and I'd never see her again. She ought to have taken me with her. I could have protected her . . . Chris said, that's her brother, he said she'd always come through everything, she'd turn up one day. I just *knew* the worst had happened." She took a biscuit. The watching baby made beating, hortatory gestures.

"You didn't think someone here could have done it, someone she knew?"

She considered this, chewing. "You mean did someone here kill her before she went? But that's what happened, isn't it? Oh, you mean did I think of that? No, I didn't. Imagine Jake!" A sudden loud laugh sprayed bits of biscuit onto the table, which she wiped off with her arm. "Jake's all garters and no guts, if you ask me. I mean he's nice but wet. Under everyone's thumb . . . Though if it was anyone else, well, Kingsley could be cruel. She could say terrible things." To Bone's interest, her neck flushed mottled pink. "She could upset people."

"Did she upset you badly?"

"Me? Oh goodness, we were really, really friends. But I

don't see how anyone could get the better of her; she was strong, you know, in spite of being so slight. She told me she could defend herself. She showed me a few things you could do, how to stop people getting hold of you, use their force against them. You know."

Bone's imagination tried out a picture of the slight Kingsley and the not at all slight Vicky practicing wrestling in the kitchen at Paleys fourteen years ago, a hold going fatally wrong, Vicky faced with telling the world that she had killed her idol by mistake, an elephant admitting it had sat on its child. Impossible to plumb the possibilities of adolescent embarrassment; instinct was to hide the accident, cover up the evidence of one's ineptitude.

"Did you see much of the present Mrs. Marsh?"

"Fenny? Couldn't help seeing Fenny." This was not something Vicky had enjoyed. "Always there, hanging around Jake. Don't know how Kingsley stood it. Perhaps that's why she left."

There was a pause while Vicky's bright suggestion turned into an awkward remembering that Kingsley hadn't left of her own accord. She shifted in her chair. "I mean that was why she meant to go. You couldn't get away from Fenny. She didn't like me there, I can tell you. She didn't want anything female in the house with Jake except her. I mean, I really loved Ravenna. I wanted to come and be her nanny and look after her."

The dummy dropped out of the baby's mouth as though in amazement. She retrieved it from the tray of the high chair and pushed it back. Bone thought of Anna, prettier than Fenny, who had lived at Paleys for some years; of Morgan, whom Fenny did not seem to discourage. He caught Shay's eye and weighed up the possibility that Vicky Stannard led a rich fantasy life.

From her father's description of her infatuation with Kingsley, from her own appearance and from his estimate of Kingsley's character, Bone had already judged it unlikely that Kingsley would allow Vicky the intimacy of wrestling holds. In the same line, he could not see Fenny, however

plain herself, envisaging a large plain teenager as a target for
Jake's lust. He could only see that Fenny had tried to protect
Jake against interruption and disconcerting encounters.

"Your impression was that the present Mrs. Marsh was
not on good terms with the first one?"

"Fenny fond of Kingsley? I don't care what she says *now,*
she hated her. Oh, she was smarmy to her. After all, she was
there to help with Ravenna, the poor darling, and she knew
Kingsley could throw her out any time. *Jake* wouldn't have
said a word." She lifted one large shoulder. "I used to think
he was stunning. You know, he would say things in a sort of
way I thought was absolutely glamorous. Only now I look
back I can see what he was really like. And I still do think his
books are great."

"Did Mr. Marsh's mother get on with her?"

"With Kingsley, or with Fenny?" She fixed him with
Whitmore's eyes and said shortly, "Do stop calling them all
Marsh and then we'll know where we are. Jake's mother was
always nice to everybody except about Jake. He used to
work in the sitting room and everyone had to keep away, but
once or twice I'd look through the garden windows and see
he wasn't working, he'd be lying on the sofa or something
and I'd knock on the window and go in and talk to him, and
then Ysobel saw me do it; she was always working in the
garden, she was mad about it, she used to work out there
even when it was dark indoors, she's meant to have strained
her heart digging, I heard. Anyway she absolutely shrieked
at me—she was like somebody quite different, she shrieked
at me, 'Get away from those windows! Never, never go near
my son when he's working.' I told her he wasn't, but she
simply didn't listen. You'd think someone would be glad to
have a bit of conversation when they couldn't write. But he
didn't say a word, he just grinned at me and shrugged.
That's like him, I can see now. He could have said something, told her he didn't mind. Jake was the one person in
Ysobel's life. And Ravenna, I suppose. Ravenna must be—"
her eyes went to the window and for the first time fixed,
working out. Bone glanced out at the garden, or at what he

could see of it for a clothesline on which hung a vast pink-flowered cream nightgown and a row of minute shorts and jeans; a scooter and a slide occupied the background, with some assorted undergrowth—"She must be *seventeen!*" Having accomplished this piece of arithmetic, Vicky sat back. "She was the sweetest child. I'd have looked after her a lot more if they'd let me."

She did not appear to find her own brood the sweetest children. On cue, both the mobile ones burst into the kitchen, saw, demanded and were given biscuits and rushed out again, hitting each other on the way. The baby drummed his heels on the footboard of his chair.

His mother drained her mug and reached behind her to put it in the sink on top of the waiting breakfast dishes.

"Ysobel just doted on Jake. She never wanted Kingsley to go off on her expeditions, deserting him."

Vicky's face took on a heavy sadness. "I wanted to go with her, and when they wouldn't let me I wanted her to stay. I could have gone with her. She wanted me to go. It was Daddy said no. It wouldn't have cost so much and it would have been seeing the world." Again she had been gazing out of the window, seeing perhaps some vision of the rain forest. Suddenly she pushed her chair back.

"I don't know why I'm sitting here talking when I've lunch to get. What else do you want to know?"

"Did you see Kingsley on the day she went?"

"I didn't know she was going! When I called next day they said she had gone." She threw it at him as if she felt again the disappointment of so many years ago. "She'd simply gone, they said, and that was that; and Ysobel said"—Vicky poised her head, suddenly evoking Ysobel's lift of the chin—"'She didn't leave a message, *even for Jake,* so you can hardly expect her to have left *you* one.'"

Kingsley's method of departure was a gift to a murderer; even the birthday card, forwarded by an unknown friend, could not have been better planned to benefit the hiding of her death.

"How did she seem, that day?"

The question puzzled Vicky. "Well, I don't think she'd be different. She wasn't the sort of person who changed from day to day. She was always kind. She never minded me—" and then again the mottling of her neck. "It was Mother who went on about that. And Fenny. She was always trying to put me off."

"You saw her that day. What time was that?"

"What time—goodness, I didn't look at the *clock.*"

"Morning? Evening?"

"In the morning," she said shortly, pushing herself to her feet, and turning to the shelves.

"You didn't call again in the evening?"

She turned back and dumped two tins on the table, Alphabetti Spaghetti and beef dinner. "What makes you think I did? Mother wouldn't let me go in the evenings anyway. Everyone was wrong about Kingsley. She *always* liked my going there."

Mrs. Whitmore had done her best to protect Paleys against constant invasion by her enthusiastic daughter. He did not think there was much more to be gained. Vicky was, he suspected, lying at this point. The eye contact and the challenge of her voice said as much.

"It mattered a great deal to you, your friendship with Kingsley."

She turned aside to take the washing-up sponge and use it to wipe the tops of the cans, an obeisance in the direction of hygiene that left a dabble of greasy wet on them.

"Yes. At the time. One grows out of these things and it's all ages ago, after all. I don't see that you'll ever find out anything." She jammed the tins one after the other under the wall-mounted opener, put the spaghetti in a pan on the cooker and scooping a spoonful of beef dinner presented it to the baby, extracting the dummy with her free hand. It opened its mouth, took the spoonful and, as she turned away, softly expressed it down its chin with a bubbling, interested hum.

"It's a pity you weren't there in the evening," Bone tempted her. "We need to know more about that time."

"Well, you can thank my mother for it," she said, stirring the pan on the stove.

"Thank you, Mrs. Stannard. We'll see ourselves out."

"Just don't let Max out of the front door," she said. "I've enough to do without getting him in for his meal."

Max, whether he were one of the boys or a cat, showed no tendency to rush the front door, and they left without incident.

They sat over ham sandwiches and beer. Their driver, Powers, with a cheese roll and a Coke, sat half turned from them as if in discretion, with them but not of them.

"What's your impression?" Bone asked Shay.

"Why didn't anyone at Paleys mention her?"

"Perhaps she was too large to notice," Bone said unkindly, "like a local mountain."

"I reckon she could've been there that evening, sir—having a go at Kingsley again to take her along. Poor kid, says a lot for Kingsley that the girl never guessed. I mean, can you think for one minute she'd let herself be lumbered with her?"

Suppose Vicky realized it; Bone did not like the thoughts he was entertaining. Kingsley could be cruel. And Vicky had insisted she was always kind, always welcoming. Vicky had suddenly blushed as she said it. Something had come into her mind. Bone had no wish to entertain the idea that Whitmore's daughter could be the one he was looking for, the one who had seized Kingsley by the throat. Could the woman he had just seen be capable of the amount of acting she must have been putting up? Yet he must look at this scenario: Vicky Whitmore, realizing that Kingsley never had any intention of taking her on any expedition, and perhaps hearing it stated cruelly from Kingsley's lips, attacking her idol.

"Very much against Fenny Marsh," Shay was saying. "On the face of it I don't see why."

"Fenny tried to protect not just Jake, I imagine, but Kingsley too. Young Vicky would have interpreted it as she wanted to. How could she face the idea that Kingsley didn't always want to see her?"

She may have been very pathetic, Bone thought. Physical attraction was the devil. Someone, particularly a woman, who lacked it became instantly a figure of fun, their passions grotesque. The Morgan Carradines of this world received an indulgent smile for their trespassings; the Vicky Stannards, a laugh at unrequited love.

13

Locker, across the desk, sorted his report. The day in Kent had heated up since this morning and a standing fan on the side table turned its mild face from Bone to Locker and beyond him toward the window, and back.

"Here's a Mrs. Deal, friend of Fenny Marsh, known the family for years. She mentions the Whitmore girl as always in and out whenever Kingsley was at home. Funny but sad, she says: 'Girls these days fall for pop stars and have boyfriends from primary school age but you still get these teenage crushes.' Mrs. Deal and Fenny have a common interest in this craft sewing as she calls it and they run that shop. She says here, 'Poor Vicky Whitmore was such a pest, but the Marshes and Fenny, she was Fenny Pace then, were good-humored about it. If you talked to the girl it was Kingsley this and Kingsley that, Jake this and Jake that. People tried teasing her out of it but she'd not shut up more than the time it took her to forget.' I've not found any local enemies of Kingsley or the family that anyone can remember, but there's not many people there now that were there then." He looked over his notes in a frustrated fashion, as a dog might look over a field where he knew something was buried if he could only place it. "Here's a Fred Parton lives by the green with his son and daughter-in-law. He has a theory all right, been reading the newspapers, you saw the headline *Wife in Wall,* sir."

"Don't recall that particular bit of gunge."

"'He thought she'd left him,'" quoted Locker, "'but she was *there all the time!*' Old Mr. Parton reckons Jake got the idea for *The Late Lady* from being haunted by knowing his wife was there."

"He won't be the only one to think Jake killed her."

"He hadn't thought through to the implication, sir. He was surprised when I asked him how Marsh knew she was there; but there's talk all right. In general they say, how could Mrs. Kingsley have left without telling anyone? They think it's a cover-up. We've met six or seven who've said it's obvious. I've been asked why Jake isn't in for questioning."

"The household might lie about her habits to protect Jake, but they'd have to take Chris Thorn along with them: he attested to Kingsley's preference for sloping off without a word."

"And as he thinks Jake killed her, he isn't likely to lie for him. But to my mind, sir, that burying her in the wall, that's one person's work. I can't see the lot of them deciding to put her there. They'd make a grave a good way off, more likely; putting her in the wall, that has the look of improvising."

"Yes. One person, having murdered her, has had to live with the knowledge of where she was. Who have we got who's up to that?"

Locker brooded. "Chris wasn't living there; and what about that Vicky Whitmore? She wouldn't be living with it either."

Bone said, "I made a mistake, Steve—should have let you go and see her. I know her father. Have you talked to Shay about his impressions of her?" He sighed. "For what it's worth, and I don't like it, she seemed a cold type. She could be aggressive. I don't know if she could have killed Kingsley out of sheer adoration . . . teenagers can be stark batty."

"You didn't take to her, sir."

"I may have expected to get on with Mr. Whitmore's daughter somewhat better than I did."

"I asked about her at Paleys."

"And?"

"I asked them each separately and what surprised me was I got much the same answer every time." He looked at his notes. "Mrs. Fenny said, 'Heavens, that girl! I'd forgotten all about her. And she was *forever* here. Her mother had issued some sort of command that she mustn't come here more than once a day, so she tended to call in as we were finishing lunch and stay till someone got rid of her—usually me. Kingsley was so good-natured about her. I expect she *was* here that day. I mean, she would be. How could I have forgotten her? I suppose because I wanted to.'" Locker turned a page. "Mrs. Marsh said, 'That appalling child! I'd forgotten her, no doubt because she really was intensely boring. I'm sure she was here that day. It was inevitable.' Jake Marsh said, 'God, yes. Eyes like a fish and all feet and shoulders. Was she here? She *lived* here. Only good thing about Kingsley's journeys was the comparative absence of that hideous pathetic child.' I asked Mr. Marsh if she was in fact there all the time, and he said—" Locker looked up and grinned. "It's interesting, sir, listening to a writer like that. He says it quite differently from what you expect. He said, 'All the time, in fact *no*. In fact she was very sad, she was very thick and the child of intellectuals, and Kingsley was her love object although I would do at a pinch, and she kept seeping into the house to be near her darlings. It is wholly likely that she was here that day. We were all so damned sorry for her and she hadn't the wit to see our rueful efforts at hinting her away. Nothing short of a direct bum's rush would have shifted her. We used to agree we would and then lack the heart. Is she a suspect? God, not unless she bloody tripped over and crushed Kingsley as she fell.' It's taken Mr. Marsh flippantly," he added, unsurprised.

"It's not a bad way of coping," agreed Bone, who had seen most of them. "The only way into this seems to be continued digging. What luck has Fredricks had with the archives?"

"She hasn't reported."

"Let's look at psychology, Steve. *What sort of person* are we looking for?"

"When we've all the facts collated, sir, then I'll get them to Dr. Zeeland; but without waiting for a psychological profile, sir, I'd say we were looking for an actor."

Bone was silent. The person they looked for, man or woman, had fourteen years of perfecting the role, of innocence, of convincing themselves it hadn't happened, that they hadn't done it; that justification such as they had had was as good as innocence. They could act innocence.

Friday's progress conference distracted Bone from his private thoughts. Inspector Blane had been dealing with lager louts and was apt to be sanctimonious. Bone caught himself wishing that Blane could be found d-and-d at some time. Inspector Garron, still on desk duties after an operation for gastric ulcer, was already working himself into line for another. The conference lengthened into tedium. Had Bone been in charge of it he could have cut it off during its first hundred years; so could Blane, nothing if not organized; but they were not.

Bone left, disgruntled. In the lobby, Blane followed and said, "Enough hot air in there to hoist a balloon," and Bone grinned, almost liked him, and went out to find the Chief Constable's car parked so close to his that any move would graze it. Rather than wait while the driver was found, or Sir Grange Gregg disturbed wherever he might be, Bone walked home. He should have walked off his mood, but he was tired, the evening streets were still hot and a cinema crowd was flooding out across his way.

The flat was empty. He came upstairs into its twilit silence and called "Cha?" without expectation, although it was well after her curfew hour of ten. On their noticeboard, the fridge door, a piece of paper was clamped by the cat-shaped magnet. Bone twitched it free and read, with the thought that her excuse had better be a good one:

"Gone to Grue's. Mrs. Shaw here with my boilgy folder says her visitors have gone."

Bone took breath. That was better; and Grizel had been here. He looked around, thinking of her presence, of her seeing the place. Her family had gone, he could call on her in Adlingsden. He read the note again, smiling over the joky misspelling. Still, it was late. He was annoyed now that he hadn't the car and couldn't fetch Cha, but Prue's father should have seen to it that she was back by now. He picked up the phone and tapped out the number. It was all but half a minute before Paul Grant came on the line with his usual hearty "Hallo!"

"My daughter Charlotte."

"Oh—nobody's here. I've been back an hour or so. Aren't they all at this pop thing?"

"I hope not," said Bone, straightening up. He did not say to Grant, "My daughter was forbidden to go." He felt anger, physically a heat in the chest.

"Ah well, they'll be all hours; but when she arrives I'll buzz over with her right away, not to worry," Grant said, radiating cheer.

He was too furious to be civil. The Grants harbored that foul young lout Justin but they kept no track of him. Nichola Grant could not have known Char wasn't supposed to go, for she herself kept other parents' rules, so Cha—Cha had deceived, had disobeyed; would be at that damned place exhausting herself; the ride back . . . he contemplated getting in touch with the Hammersmith police, getting her held till he could fetch her . . . but could they find her in the horde of kids emerging? Suppose she'd collapsed? Bone saw her carried from the crowd, pale and sick. And incoherent —would they think she was drunk? On drugs? He knew what his own reaction would be to an unknown child with slurred speech.

Would she really go? He stood staring at the phone. What didn't match with this scenario were the three words on her note: "Gone to Grue's." She would not lie. If she'd gone to the concert, that's what she would have written, with no equivocation. The subtly different young woman who was emerging might puzzle Bone but still she was Charlotte. She could be trusted.

Petra would have known how to deal with this. A woman . . .

He tapped out the Adlingsden number.

Grizel's voice, simply repeating the number, seemed to bring her presence into the room, her face, the light clear eyes and pale short hair. His hesitant "Hallo" evoked a warm "Robert!"

"Cha left a note to say—"

"Yes, they've gone. The house suddenly feels quite large and beautifully quiet."

"Grizel—"

"What's wrong?"

Her instant awareness was like balm. He said, "I believe Cha's gone off to London to a bloody pop concert I told her she wasn't to go to and she's gone."

"That's not like her," Grizel said. It was what he wanted to think. "When I talked to her she said nothing about going. She'd been crying—but Robert, I don't think she— are you sure she's gone?"

"Paul Grant told me. But damn it, she'd say so. She'd have written 'I've gone to the concert.' It's not like her to prevaricate. She *went* to Prue's and then she went on to Hammersmith."

"Are you sure? Absolutely sure? What did Mr. Grant say?"

"That they'd all gone to the concert. He'd got in an hour ago and nobody was there. Cha's fallen for this pink-haired rat that Nichola Grant's taken in."

"Justin? She told me about him."

"Oh did she."

"Cha said he seemed to see her as a person and not pay any attention to her being lame. He never even looked peculiar when she talked, and she said that with strangers she always talks as if she's got a hamster in her mouth. I thought that was something in the young man's favor. Also he likes her and makes no bones about it, and I didn't mean a pun, but you'll agree that's an attraction."

"I suppose it's irresistible," said Bone bitterly.

"She did not at all sound as if she meant to go to the concert. She talked as if she'd accepted that she couldn't go. It upset her. She said Justin would take some other girl."

"Bloody young oaf," Bone said.

"Be consistent, Robert. You ought to like that idea."

"I shouldn't be bothering you with all this—"

"If you can't bother me with things that bother you, then we've no business together at all. 'Dwell I but in the suburbs of your good pleasure?'—though now I think of it that's not a suitable quotation. Look, Robert. Cha doesn't lie to you. Agreed?"

"She hasn't up to now."

"Then trust her. Don't sound so savage. She's your daughter and you've always trusted her. Haven't you?"

"Yes."

"Then you must. I'd trust her too."

He said nothing, and she waited patiently at the other end of the line. "Then where is she?" he demanded. Outside, a car roared down the street, stopped with a wail of brakes, and reversed. A door slammed, a man's voice called "Goodnight." There was a key in the lock.

"She's here!" Bone said. "That's her. Just coming in."

Grizel said, "Bless you, Robert," warm as a kiss, and rang off.

From the top of the stairs he saw Cha climbing up. She raised an anxious face as she saw his shadow, and began to speak. "I'm sorry. We were at Kat Hazely's and her father didn't come back till just now. I tried to phone you—"

"No sweat," Bone replied, and felt himself smiling. It was about the least truthful thing he had ever said to her.

On the Saturday morning he left Charlotte peacefully busy on the biology coursework, and walked to the station.

He was enlivened by the prospect of seeing Grizel, free of her family and still on holiday. He hadn't arranged a meeting, and intended to ring her when he got to work. Cha had talked to her in a way she could not talk to him. What would Grizel think if she actually met Justin? If Cha went on seeing the young marvel, he had better arrange for Grizel to view him and give her opinion. Also, he wanted to find out why her quotation on the phone last night had been "unsuitable," for he had thought it very apposite.

I don't want, he thought, to have to phone her up when I need to talk to her. I don't want to have to keep away from her relations like a discreditable secret. And Cha likes her, can talk to her . . .

Also in his mind was the irritating reservation he had once woken up with as to a bad dream: How can I ask her to become *Grizel Bone?* It's grotesque, a bad joke, the girls at her school would go to town on it. How could she announce herself in shops, or on the phone?

He was at the station, however. Sir Grange had contrived to drive off with no more than a smear of black rubber from his car's bumper on the Vauxhall's paint. The morning was bright, with a cool wind scudding the clouds. There were solutions to all problems.

Locker waited for him. WDC Fredricks had unearthed a significant item in her search of the archives. Fourteen years ago, the summer of Kingsley's disappearance, a man had killed two women in two successive months and left their bodies, one in a Tonbridge building site in the foundation pit, one in a corporation dump some way out of town.

"Both these places took some getting into. Ingenuity, like. Putting Kingsley in the wall would be peanuts."

"But in Adlingsden?" It was hardly anywhere near Tonbridge.

"He'd been working at Longley." Locker had the map. "It's not so far east of Adlingsden."

"Where's the man now?"

"He should still be inside, sir. Fredricks is tracing him."

"You want to go and interview him."

"I better had, sir."

Bone leafed through the account. "Steve, he knew both these women. This one's a friend of his wife's he'd met at the pub. He killed them for what he called being too familiar with him."

"Well, yes; but suppose with him working at Longley, walking to the bus at Dodd's Corner along the lane, and Kingsley comes out of the house, maybe she passed the time of night, friendly like, and he thought she was giving him a come-on."

"It has to be looked into. Yes. Though these were both premeditated murders, which is why he got such a sentence. She could have met him previously, of course, in her walks around the neighborhood. He might feel that he knew her, and mistake a casual politeness for loose behavior, which seems to have been his way. It never ceases to amaze me, although it should be a cliché by now, that people take it as their right to kill a fellow human being because they think they should."

"This one seems to have thought he was the Sword of the Lord. But they didn't send him to Broadmoor."

"You'll have to see him, but I'm still inclining to think it must be Fenny."

"That lady has something on her mind; and the only thing Mrs. Marsh and Chris Thorn agree about is that she was waiting to step into Kingsley's shoes."

"Good lord, then her feet had been poised over those shoes for seven years. If she did kill Kingsley for that reason, she must have known that marriage wouldn't be anywhere near immediate. In any case Kingsley was going away, she'd have Jake to herself. Yet, I suppose, to wait all serene in the certainty that Kingsley wouldn't ever come back . . ." He hoped it was not Fenny. He had seen that plain, pleasant face in anguish at their first meeting, then in anxiety ever since. He wondered how she would look when she was happy? At no time would she be any competition for the girls who appeared on *The Late Lady*, let alone for Morgan Carradine; yet Kingsley was no looker, either. Her photographs showed strength, intelligence, not beauty. Jake didn't marry beauty, he married affection, strength, competence—and independence.

The phone rang, Bone's outer line that didn't depend on the switchboard. As he picked it up he supposed it would be the pathologist. Cha rarely rang the station. A voice he did not immediately recognize announced, "Monro Walsh speaking from Paleys. There's been another death and I'm not satisfied this time that it's an accident. I'm keeping everyone out of the room where it's happened and I'll be waiting here."

"We're on our way," said Bone, signaling to Locker, who picked up the other phone and started summoning the team. "Who is it who's dead?"

"Mr. Marsh's wife. Fenny."

14

Bone heard the familiar scrunch of gravel as his car edged into the forecourt, the inevitable cry of a peacock like a tormented cat, and climbed from the car. He had been thinking of Fenny, on the swift journey punctuated by the bray of the siren at every hazard or crossroads; this was the third time in a week, he thought as he approached the door, that he had been summoned to Paleys and found death. The front door stood open. He thought, the Figure in the Shroud has taken to visiting here too often; they should shut the door.

He had hardly stepped inside, raising his hand to the knocker, when the woman called Patty, her pug-face showing the mark of tears, the pallor of shock, hurried out from the kitchen at the back.

"The doctor's upstairs. It's so terrible. I can't believe it. Poor Fenny." She was crying again in little snuffles and wiping away tears with the back of a stubby hand.

"And Mr. Marsh?"

"With his mother." She indicated Ysobel's door, for once shut. "Poor lady, she was taken bad again and he's in a terrible way himself." Bone imagined Mrs. Marsh propped on lace pillows, recovering and consoling Jake; there was quite a succession of things to recover from in this house.

PC Gibb, the mobile patrolman, was now looking over the banisters from the landing upstairs, and Monro Walsh's somber face appeared behind him in the shadows. Bone went up the stairs remembering Anna Dudley. Wasn't there an Anna—no, it was an *Amy* Robsart—who had met her death falling downstairs, thanks to her husband's neat way with a piece of tripwire. *He* was a Dudley, the Earl of Leicester, needing his way clear to marry the Virgin Queen for his second wife; but in spite of a general dearth of detectives at the time, Elizabeth had displayed her usual prudence and not married him. Bone had enjoyed the way Whitmore told those stories.

And now Bone was looking at Anna Dudley's death too with a suspicious eye. The most innocent accident in the world would look ominous here, and now.

Husbands were on his mind as he followed Walsh into the big room. Monro Walsh was standing looking down at the body.

"She's been moved already. The whole household has been in here. At least, they did keep the child out."

Bone looked, in silence. He was accustomed to seeing bodies in states of disarray, helpless and exposed in death, but in hardly any cases had he been acquainted with their owners alive. He had liked Fenny, his irrational reason for objecting to her casting as Kingsley's killer. Death was an artist in the grotesque, and had achieved quite an effect here. Fenny lay beside her table. Her feet had pushed a pile of glossy magazines into a crumple against the wall under the window. A thimble glinted by her left hand. Her head was not on the floor but at an angle, propped on a wooden disc and a frill of various-colored papers streaked with brown-red, a Pierrot ruffle askew beneath her cheek. They were letters, with which Fenny would not now ever be dealing, and they were impaled on a spike that was not to be seen, buried in Fenny's cheek. Blood, smeared on her face, came from her mouth and nose, and ran under her chin from the ear; Bone concluded that the spike had entered her brain. At that angle it was to be hoped it had killed her instantly. Her eyes were open in mild astonishment at these men standing over her.

Bone tried at some statement in his usual style. "You believe it was not an accident. She didn't slip on the magazines and fall on the spike."

"Sideways? With that force? It looks very dodgy to me. I'm not a pathologist, certainly not a criminal pathologist, but there are things about this that need looking into. Therefore I rang you at once."

Bone was starting to commend this when Gibb opened the door and Ferdy Foster stood there, bag in hand, surveying the scene.

"Here *is* the pathologist," Bone said. "Dr. Walsh, Dr. Foster."

He saw them size each other up. Ferdy, whose thick hair was now theatrically iron gray, regarded Walsh over his half-moon glasses with peat-brown unfathomable eyes. He said, "As you're trampling all over the scene, Robert, I'm to take it that the world and his wife have already been in here." His voice at the best of times made one suppose his larynx to be lined with sandpaper, and annoyance made him accentuate his drawl.

"You're right, of course," Walsh replied for him, "and the body has been moved."

"I'd be happy—" Ferdy's tone made this a remote contingency—"if someone could tell me how much."

Walsh answered with severity. "The woman who found her told me that she took the body by the shoulders and half-turned her. On seeing the face she screamed. She felt for a pulse. At the wrist. Most of the household then came in. Jake Marsh tried to pull out the spike. That's as much of the disturbance to the body as I could ascertain."

"Ah." Ferdy's gaze became concentrated. "Come on then, Walsh. Let's have a—Robert, shift yourself."

Bone stepped aside. They bent and crouched over the

body in what now seemed amicable conference. Bone heard the word *petechiae*.

He took in the room: shelves with their stacks of cloth arranged by shade, patterned or plain together; ironing board; machine table; a sort of loom on which a quilt was wound; a cabinet full of thread-bobbins arranged by color like the shelves; a pinboard with a half-arranged star in patchwork hanging near the door; on the big table and the little desk, jars of pencils, crayons; a shelf of tall books, art and design; a cabinet with small drawers, a stationery stand. It was a busy, workmanlike place from which those fascinating bright clothes had come. Bone stood looking past Ferdy's shoulder at Fenny with more than his usual sense of sadness at a life ended.

"Not at all a heavy woman," Walsh was saying. "A woman who fell while conscious would have been likely to save herself with her hands, to knock the spike aside in falling. Force would be needed to drive it through the palate and, as would appear, the sinal processes."

A noise of vehicles in the road made Bone duck to look out of the window. Locker was emerging from his car in the forecourt, PC Gibb's colleague was directing the van toward the lane, his gestures indicating the side door. Presently the team came up the back stairs. The photographer reported that they had been warned there was a sick lady in the front room, and so had come around by the side, but this precaution was vitiated by a sudden noise in the hall. Bone looked out into its crescendo, Prints standing back for him, and at the head of the stairs he looked down. The last fight he had witnessed in this house had involved Jake Marsh and Chris Thorn, and here was the return match.

Jake, held at arm's length by the sturdy Locker, was shouting past him at Chris. His articulation was not at its finest but with a fine spray of saliva which must be 70 percent proof came the words "Bastard!" and "Bloody murderer!" His face was crimson. Chris Thorn, holding his jaw, had his back to the stairs and what he was saying did not emerge clearly past his hand. Bone descended the stairs. Ysobel appeared, clinging to her doorpost, her face as white as Jake's was red. From below the gallery came an aghast Patty, a dark young man Bone did not recognize, wearing a happy grin, and a woman he definitely did recognize: Morgan Carradine glowing darkly in midnight blue.

Bone heard feet on the stairs and was passed at a canter by Dr. Walsh.

"Stop that!" Walsh's bellow into Jake's face topped the continuing roar by several decibels and made Locker step aside as though his eardrums had quailed. In the silence Walsh said, "Think of your mother," and pointed a finger past Jake's nose at Ysobel, who took the cue and laid a hand on her breast. Walsh strode over to her and turned her toward her room. Jake was following when Ravenna appeared from the stairs, barefoot and in a black-gray toweling wrap, crossed the hall like all the Furies and shouting "Tell him you didn't, *tell* him you didn't!" seized her father's arm and dragged him around to face her uncle Chris.

Bone, Locker, Jake and Chris all abruptly spoke, if not the same words, to the same purpose. Ravenna, startled to silence, gazed from one to another, her mouth still open.

"Come off it, Tiger," her uncle said. "Be kind to the poor old police. You'll upset their sensibilities." He was on a tight rein, watching Jake, the bruise flaming on his jaw. Jake, it could now be seen, was tear-stained. As Ravenna relinquished his arm he turned mutely toward Ysobel's room and went in.

Ravenna, needing anger, needing a vent for her anger and finding the adult world so united to frustrate her, stalked up to Bone and said, "When are you going to arrest Morgan? *She's* fucking my father."

"Why don't you go and get dressed, Miss Marsh?" Bone could not tell if the dark rings around her eyes were sleeplessness or yesterday's make-up, but their pupils as she stared at Bone were small and made the irises seem luminous.

Ferdy had followed Bone down and she brushed past him

as she made for the stairs. "I suppose I *can* go to *my room,*" she flung at the world in general. "Are you sure a policeman shouldn't watch me dress?"

"We'll want to see everyone shortly," Bone said, "but clothed."

"—and in their right mind," muttered Ferdy, "if possible. What do you suppose *that* young female is on?"

Morgan Carradine's voice, with its curious depth, interrupted. "We'll be in here when you want us," adding a quality of the bizarre by adding, "in the kitchen." One did not associate her with kitchens. Her dark hair, skillfully cut to look untended, gleamed. Patty's, which was untended, did not.

"Where's the little boy?" Bone asked.

"His mother took him over to Beeches yesterday morning because of the funeral," said Patty.

"And they're keeping him," Chris Thorn remarked, going into the drawing room, "until called for. I rang Antonia with the news an hour ago." He cast Morgan Carradine a glance, as he went, and surprisingly it was one of dislike. Bone thought: It's true about the curling lip of disdain. He's doing it.

As both Locker and Ferdy Foster were about to speak to Bone, Jake appeared from his mother's room. Morgan came forward a little way and waited. She wore strap sandals and her toenails, like her fingernails, were painted gold. She was not an actress who was about to relapse into girl-next-door. Jake went toward her, saying, "Bloody medic told Mama not to give me one of her calmers."

"How is she?"

"She's had to take her pill." He looked, now, drained.

"They want to talk to us all soon, Jake. Can we wait in Jake's study, Inspector?"

As Locker concurred, Bone wondered whom Morgan would accuse, given the chance. Jake accused Chris, who accused Jake. Ravenna accused Morgan—who ought, therefore, to accuse Ravenna. The thing was assuming the air of a minor Elizabethan tragedy such as Petra used to delight in.

He retained quotations of hers, lines she declaimed that would always be in his memory.

—life a general maze of error
And Death a hideous storm of terror

He hoped Fenny's death had been instantaneous.

The dark young man who had watched all this and had been ignored by everyone, now came forward as Jake and Morgan disappeared under the gallery.

"I'm Paul Lackland; business partner to—" he hesitated —"poor Fenny. Will you be wanting to see me?"

"You were in the house this morning?"

"Oh yes. Staying the night—my cottage—builders in"— he gave a meaningless gesture—"and Fenny was kind enough to invite me for the weekend. The point is, I'd like to get back and check on what they're doing."

He had a boyish face, the tilted nose and soft contours, the light eyes under dark lashes making you think him younger than he was, but Bone felt a reserve behind the frank manner, saw petulance and obstinacy about the full mouth and the chin. He wore a blue open-necked shirt that echoed the color of his eyes so precisely that Bone was sure it had been carefully chosen. Dark linen trousers were smart compared with the denims everyone was wearing. An awkward touch was added by his indecision over whether a social smile was more appropriate than an air of grief during this discussion.

"I see. Well, Mr. Lackland, I'm sure you can be of help to us if you will wait. We shall see you as soon as we can."

Lowered eyebrows made it plain that Lackland was annoyed at not being allowed to jump the queue as he had expected. As he opened his mouth to object, Bone turned to Locker with an overriding edge to his voice and said, "Mr. Marsh, Inspector?"

He turned his back on Lackland and made for the dining room where Sergeant Shay had been heard testing the tape recorder. He heard Locker suitably delegate the summons to

PC Gibb and then follow Bone. There were olive leather chairs with tall backs around the shining mahogany table. He chose a carver at the head and Locker sat before the tape recorder at his right and opened his notebook. He recorded, while they waited, the place and date and their names, and filled in the same on his notebook.

The room was paneled in light, polished wood. Bone could smell beeswax and candle snuff. Silver twisted candlesticks stood along the table, three of them with two candles in each which had all been burned down a little. A silver bowl of sweet peas was reflected too in the mahogany, and Bone thought that so far the room was more Ysobel's than Fenny's. On the wall opposite the window, however, hung a big roughly knitted landscape with bobbles of green wool for trees, bits of yellow satin for flowers, and crystals sewn on blue wool for a lake; that must have its origin in the brain of the woman who lay upstairs, all such ideas now lost. Bone was conscious of a quite fierce desire to find who had murdered Fenny Marsh.

Her husband came into the room, ushered by Gibb, in a more subdued state than Bone had yet seen him. His pallor and drawn look emphasized the likeness to his mother. How much family devotion could be based on a kind of narcissism? Bone was aware that Charlotte resembled him.

"Would you sit here, Mr. Marsh?" Locker asked. "Have we your permission to record this interview?"

Jake sat down, with a mumble and wave of the hand Locker took to be consent, for he switched-on and said Jake's name and the time. Jake had an air of bafflement at being sent for in his own house and being interrogated at his own table. How much drink had he had time to put away this morning so far? Had he downed one just now, comforted by the gracious Morgan? Would such a mistress—if that's what she was—make a man willing to get rid of his wife? Another question might be why he had ever married the plain Fenny when he could get such creatures as Morgan. Bone deliberately allowed a silence to develop, aware of Locker's attention and Jake fidgeting.

"Well? What do you want to know? If I murdered Fenny? It's always the husband. Husbands kill their wives all the time. I know. I'm a *writer* for Heaven's sake."

It might be supposed he meant that writers had some idea of life. Bone had seen a few episodes of *The Late Lady;* it was based on the story of a woman who had been murdered by her husband and who kept turning up—in various costumes because she could never remember to what period of time she belonged—to meddle charmingly in the affairs of people who lived in and around the old house where she had been killed. Morgan made the sort of ghost a man would give his eye teeth and his bank balance to be haunted by.

It was also quite true what Jake had said. The spouse is the first suspect for sound statistical reasons.

"I've no wish to increase your distress." Bone put Jake in the wrong for any truculent assumption that he was to be harassed. "We must get at the facts, that's all. Did you discover her?" Bone knew Jake had not been the one but it was a way to get the ball rolling.

"No." Jake's mouth drew into a rictus as though his inner eye saw the picture of that room. "Patty did . . . Fen and I both wanted to get on with some work there wouldn't be time for later with a household of bloody guests." He stopped as if thinking that one guest had been bloodier than could be looked for. "We—I went to the study and I suppose she went to her workroom, and I worked for a while. I don't know how long. Patty came in and I was going to bawl her out because nobody's supposed to, but she scuttled out and left the door open and I heard a noise, and Patty having hysterics on the stairs, and I went up. Patty had locked the workroom when she came out, and she was crying about Fenny and how awful. I thought Fenny had locked the door and I banged and shouted until Patty came up. Then, well . . . I went in." He stopped and they waited.

Locker said, "Please take your time, Mr. Marsh."

"I don't know after that. I saw . . . and everyone seemed to come in and be talking. A bad dream. I didn't believe—

you just don't believe it can have happened. God, I don't know what I did. I held her. I wanted to get rid of that horrible thing but—God." His hand made an echo of pulling at the spike's wooden base. "She fell on it, though. Nobody would have killed her? I mean, my God, *Fenny*. No one could want to kill her." His eyes, which had been seeing nothing but that inner vision, saw Bone and he said, "Go on, then: what *terms* were we on, did we *quarrel?*—It's *marriage,* for God's sake."

"No more disagreements than happen every day."

Jake looked at Bone and slowly nodded. His slightly undershot jaw seemed to hang in exhaustion. "It was a good marriage," he insisted. "I can't think all this is happening. Kingsley, Fenny. It's a nightmare. And poor Anna. Look, I loved Kingsley. 'Forty thousand brothers could not with all their quantity of love . . .' Chris can put that in his bloody ethnic pipe and smoke it. I *did*. It suited us. I'd sooner she hadn't taken off every so often for the back of nowhere but she wanted to. That mattered to her. She got Fenny to look after us. I didn't marry Kingsley for a homebody, God knows, and I didn't get one. I didn't like coming second to a rain forest but that was—oh, the deal. I mean that was why that marriage was a good one."

"What makes a good marriage?" Bone asked, as if he wanted to know.

Jake replied slowly, "I thought this out a long time ago and I said it in *Phoenix for Sale;* but no one's heard of that, it's all the bloody series now . . . I said it was working along with the person you've really got, and not the person you'd like them to be. And Fenny, you see, we're—we were happy." He shook his head and suddenly leaned forward. "Make it make sense for me. Chris says Fen killed Kingsley. If Chris killed her for that, and he *could,* believe me he *could*—" But he sat back, staring at the slow turns of the tape reel. "All this can't be happening."

"Tell me about the other people in the house."

Jake took a breath, linked his fingers together, and leaned on the table hunching his shoulders to his ears. "The other people. My mother. My daughter. My son. My brother-in-law. Patty. Morgan. Oh and that Paul bloke, Paul Lackland. Pestering Fenny to run a factory for her work. I don't know him much." The tone said, "and don't want to." "Wished himself on us for the weekend when he knew about Anna's funeral and how things were here, my mother's been ill. And then when Kingsley—you'd think he'd cry off, go to a hotel or stick it out with his bloody builders but no, he lands here, and then starts in on Fenny again, yesterday, the day her friend was buried. Just a visiting shit."

"Thank you, Mr. Marsh." Bone pointed to the recorder, which Locker switched off. Jake had been on the verge of tears and fury, gripping his arms as his voice cracked. He lifted his head.

"Are you sure it's not an accident?"

"Ninety percent sure," Bone said, and was aware of Locker's surprise. Jake heaved himself to his feet and went out, blowing his nose; Bone wondered if he would go to his mother, or to Morgan.

"I thought you'd ask him more than that," Locker said, and his tone sounded reproachful. It was the nearest thing to a criticism he was likely to get out.

"He's not going anywhere," Bone answered, rubbing his chin in thought. "I'd like an overall picture from everyone available before I start looking closer. I'd like to know where the weak spots are. What's your impression of famous author and playwright Jake Marsh?"

"He was a lot more down to earth today than when I talked to him before. A bit shaken out of his fancy phrases."

"We'd better see Patty Bates next and narrow down what the time was; and get her first impressions of how the body looked when she found it."

"If she can remember." Locker was not so much disillusioned as experienced. Shock, he knew, could impress a scene for ever on your brain, or wipe the track entirely. He went to the door to brief Gibb on the next interview, and had to step aside as Dr. Walsh came in.

"Superintendent: Mrs. Marsh is able to talk now."

For a fleeting moment Bone thought he meant the woman upstairs, unable to talk to anyone again; then his mind adjusted to reality, to the invalid downstairs; he stood up, bringing the recorder.

Walsh went on, "She has taken her emergency medication, she tells me, and it's best if you see her now and then she can take a sedative and sleep. Please keep your questions to a minimum. She's had some very bad shocks in these last few days. Not helpful to a woman in her state of health." He frowned at Bone as though holding him personally responsible, and such was the dark severity of his face that Bone fancied a little scene: one of Walsh's patients at Death's door, and Death hesitating to open it if the doctor were around.

As they crossed the hall to Ysobel Marsh's room, a shuffling on the landing betokened the exit of Fenny Marsh, shrouded in plastic, from her house. The men stood back. Bone pulled Ysobel's door shut. The mortuary van had backed up to the door and the sightseers in the road were blocked from what was happening, but Bone heard their murmur, and the sound of cameras; the press here already. The little procession cleared the front door. Van doors were shut. Ferdy nodded to Bone and went out, Gibb shut the big oak door, the van, the cars drove away and there was silence.

When Bone and Locker entered Ysobel's room, she made an effort to raise herself on her pillow and put them at their ease. Bone reflected that the social standards of her age and class were unfairly demanding on the sick and frail. The deep purple blue of her housecoat threw a cruel light up on her face. The long hand, burdened with rings, indicated the sofa and chair, and she said almost in a whisper, "Do sit down." The room glowed with morning light, but no dazzle, the wallpaper's silvery stripes seeming to convert it to moonlight, and green plants in their porcelain pots everywhere gave a feeling of shade. Bone could understand why Jake turned to his mother for protection and comfort, for she could create around herself an atmosphere of peace. What he could not picture was her dealing with a squalling baby, or emptying potties. It seemed gross to have to question her about murder.

"Poor, poor Fenny. I'll do all I can, but I have little to say." She paused, as if to collect herself for more effort, and Locker asked about the use of the tape recorder. She gave silent permission with a hand, and went on, "I woke just as usual, and made myself a cup of tea——"

"At what time would this be, Mrs. Marsh?"

"I wake early, at perhaps half past six. I heard them move about overhead, and I made tea and read for a while, waiting for Patty to bring my breakfast, as I usually do." She glanced at the table by the sofa where Bone was sitting. A copy of *The Warden,* its cloth binding well worn, lay there with an Italian leather spectacle case, a medicine glass, and a small posy of flowers in the iridescent glass globe. "I suppose, people went about the house. I didn't pay any attention, I think I may even have drowsed. Eventually Patty came with my breakfast. I missed Dom, who comes with her as a rule, but he's at Beeches. I could eat very little—but you hardly want to know that—and I had put the tray aside when I heard Patty scream."

She put her handkerchief to her mouth, a small cambric one with white embroidery in the corner. Bone would have expected lace but thought no, that's not her style. "Please take your time," he said.

"I'm sorry to be feeble . . . You must see a good many people in states of distress. Having to be strong for Jake—he's even more troubled if I seem affected . . ." The direct gaze was like Jake's, but not bloodshot. "You know, I think Monro must be wrong. Jake said Fenny's feet had slipped on some papers—magazines, was it?—and Fenny *was* accident prone, you know. Certainly I told Jake that Chris could not be so wicked, no matter what he thought Fenny had done. Jake's wrong, I'm sure. I hope you find it was an accident, as I believe it must be."

"After you heard Mrs. Bates cry out," Locker said, "what happened? What did you do?"

"I? That was so dreadful. I tried to keep quiet in myself,

because when I am unwell, as I was this morning, I can have an attack and upset everyone. It seemed a long time before anyone came to tell me what had happened."

"Who came, Mrs. Marsh?"

She now looked puzzled. "You ask the most peculiar things, Inspector. In fact I was surprised, because Morgan Carradine came in and said that Fenny had had an accident and the doctor had been sent for. I asked how Fenny was, and she told me, she told me really very gently, that she seemed to be dead. She offered to stay with me but I refused, I said she could help Jake, I was sure . . . Jake didn't come until Monro arrived. He came down then. When I saw him I felt the most terrible apprehension. He looked so ill. He came to me and cried." She put the back of her hand to her mouth now and turned her head away. "I'm sorry," she said indistinctly. "Fenny . . . you know . . . I can put up with being ill but not with being a nuisance . . . Fenny was always so good . . . her lovely embroidery . . . and I was able to look after Dom for her. I could still do that, after all. Dom meant so much to them; Fenny wasn't sure she'd be able to have a child after that miscarriage . . ."

"She had miscarried." Bone stated what was in effect a question, and she answered.

"Oh, soon after Kingsley left. And she's had others. Later on, I thought perhaps Kingsley had known there was to be a child and had chosen to go away at that particular time to make it easier for Fenny. I was wrong, of course! Poor Kingsley! And I've been tormented by the thought that perhaps Fenny . . . but I tell myself that it's a morbid imagining. I'm really quite sure Fenny could never have done such a thing," she added emphatically.

Bone was about to speak when he saw that she was going on. "I admit that I'm unable to understand women who put their own interests before their husbands', but then when you actually *know* people like Kingsley, like Fenny, you do see how it is that some women want to—what is it called?— the vogue phrase?—Be their own woman! But getting married means that you are not your own, but sharing; and I never, never could understand any woman putting anything, anything at all before her own child. Not that Ravenna or Dom have ever wanted for anything, unless perhaps their mothers' time, their mothers' attention . . . I've always had all the time in the world for Jake. And Jake, you know, is the most unselfish creature—"

This did not precisely chime with Bone's opinion, but he was silent.

"He's always maintained that we must recognize the importance of Fenny's work and respect it, and we all did. Though I thought it best to have a word with Fenny about Paul Lackland. He's a little too interested in her. She laughed. She said it was her work and not herself—but these situations are dangerous. Here is a personable young man with too much time on his hands, and by this scheme of his they would be seeing much more of each other; and Fenny always insisted that she didn't *like* Paul, so much so that I couldn't help wondering . . . But now this dreadful, horrible accident!"

Her voice was failing.

"But Fenny really had a very happy life. I must help Jake to think of that. She and Jake . . . except for the disappointment about children . . ."

She was plainly very tired. Bone stood up and thanked her and they left.

Back in the dining room, Locker said, "If Mrs. Fenny was expecting, would that be a motive for her getting rid of Kingsley?"

"And someone who thinks that's what she did has now taken revenge? It's a scenario all right."

Gibb, at the door, said, "Mr. Lackland is asking—"

"We'll see Mrs. Bates," Bone said. Gibb grinned and withdrew.

Patty Bates was not in awe of the police, more concerned with whether they would like coffee. Assured that they would, but would prefer to have it after they had talked to her, she was persuaded not to bustle out at once but to perch on one of the tall-backed chairs and peck, like a bird, at the tape recorder as Locker switched on and said her name. It surprised her that they had asked her permission to tape. She looked solemn, an expression not at home on her round features, but the pallor of shock had worn off. Patty Bates was possibly the only person in this house who had had plenty to do since the discovery, attending to the comfort of other people and the running of the place—a smell of baking had wafted in with her.

"Can we start with exactly what happened this morning? Let's start from when you got up, that is unless you heard anyone up before you." Bone had a plan in front of him, of the upper floor of Paleys, showing Patty's room to be above the kitchen within convenient reach of the back stairs. The same small wing housed Dom's room, a bathroom, and the small guest room. In a bracket after "Mrs. Bates" Locker had written "was Anna Dudley's."

"No, I heard nobody before me. I got up about six forty-five, I go in as a rule to see if Dom's all right, he's been having such nightmares since the accident on Monday, and I'd opened his door before I remembered he's at Beeches; thank goodness, too. He likes it there. He's allowed to call old Mr. Thorn 'Grandad' although they aren't related, because he hasn't a grandfather of his own, Mrs. Fenny having lost her parents. Anyway I went down to start breakfast and get the bread in the oven."

"Does everyone have breakfast at a definite time?"

"Fenny told me when I came on Wednesday— Goodness!" The square little hand came up to her mouth. "Think of it, only Wednesday. Fenny told me she and Jake make themselves coffee when they get up, in their room. She likes to get in some work early before the day gets under way—" Patty did not hear her use of the present tense— "and Jake goes to his study to do his writing." In her tone was the suggestion that this was an indulgence to which a man was entitled while the women kept the world going. "And I get Mrs. Marsh's breakfast that she has in her room.

Ravenna doesn't have any. And the guests, Fenny told them they could come and help themselves in the kitchen if I didn't mind."

"And did you?"

She looked surprised again, and two dimples appeared, making the small round face attractive. "Well, I did think it could be difficult if they all came at different times and I wanted to get the casserole for lunch and so on. But of course it didn't happen like that." Her face lost the vivacity. "I did hear people moving about upstairs and so on, but before anyone came down I went to ask Fenny about the lunch, if I shouldn't make a little vegetarian casserole for Ravenna. She doesn't like a fuss made about her being vegetarian, you see, and she generally has a salad."

A salad would be far more trouble, Bone thought. No doubt Ravenna didn't want a fuss made; that young woman preferred any fuss to be her own unaided work.

"So I went up and went in. She hadn't got the door locked—when she's hard at work she locks the door so she can't be interrupted, but if the door opens when you try the handle you can come in." The flow of narrative abruptly died. She had reached the moment, the sight that had been tucked away from view in her mind. She bit her lips, took a breath and said, "There she was on the floor. I thought, fallen and knocked herself out and I went to help, and I saw her eyes were open and I saw that awful—I tried to pick it up, you see, I thought it was under her head, and her head moved too and I saw it was fixed right in her face and I screamed. There was the blood. But I had to pull myself together"—Patty made a little drawing-up and settling movement, but she was trembling—"and I went out and took the key and locked the door, and I went to tell Jake; but he wasn't in the study after all, and I didn't know what to do, I went up the stairs again and I was wondering who I could get hold of, crying and trying to be sensible, and Jake came running up and went to rattle at the workroom door, and he swore because it was locked so I went with the key . . . and Ravenna and Mr. Lackland had heard and they came in too though I tried to keep them out; I mean Ravenna shouldn't see anything like that. Then I heard someone say 'doctor' and though I knew she was dead I went down to the kitchen and telephoned Dr. Walsh; and I had to see to the Aga because of the bread, and people came in from the garden, so I went to warn them, it was Chris and Miss—You see, she said to call her just Morgan but when people are famous you somehow don't like to. Anyway they didn't keep away as I said, they ran upstairs, and then the doctor came, he came through the kitchen because he knew about Mrs. Marsh seeing everyone who comes at the front and it would alarm her; Fenny said that room of Mrs. Marsh's was called the Conning Tower. It isn't a tower at all, of course, but she could see everything from it, and her door was always open so that people can say hallo."

Bone surfaced amid the froth and said, "Think yourself back to when you woke up. People were moving about. What did you hear first?"

But this, Patty was quite unable to do.

When Patty Bates was leaving there was a tangible silence. She was delighted to be at liberty to make them coffee. Locker drew a long breath and said he needed it. As the door shut, he said, "Jake Marsh wasn't in his study, but he knew. He went up and banged on the door."

"Yes. I'm getting the usual superfluity of evidence, Steve. Sorting-time comes later. We're not, it seems, going to have a confession. Shall we see Mr. Lackland next? His wish to go and see what his builders are up to is a little absurd in the context of a murder. Why so anxious to get away? Doesn't like the atmosphere. Making people wait can be useful, Steve. If pressure builds up, interesting things can get said, so I think we'll leave him for a while longer. Let's get a contrast to Mrs. Bates."

As the "contrast" entered, Locker's eyes brightened. He rose with alacrity. Bone too had to keep his hand from the absurdity of straightening his tie. The distant impressions of Morgan Carradine so far, on the screen and in this house,

were not belied. Glamour hung around her like her scent.
There was a perfection about her. The glossy dark brown
hair swept in heavy waves about her face, the eyes, set wide,
seemed a little slanting. She moved easily and offered her
hand, a cool strong clasp. She had social command as well as
beauty. Bone, again astonished that Jake Marsh, evidently
able to attract such a woman, could tie himself to a
Kingsley, a Fenny, rebuked himself for a male chauvinist
pig; yet he could not prevent himself from smiling at
Morgan Carradine as she sat down, a smile that he never
saw in his mirror but that gave warmth to his usually cold
face. Morgan responded with her own, famous smile.

Locker had to be reminded, by a glance and a pointed
finger, to do his act with the tape recorder.

She was asked the same questions the others had been
asked. She had, she said, woken quite early—"I don't sleep
well in a strange bed," and Bone had to turn his imagination
quite deliberately from the image of Morgan restless in a
rumpled bed—and she had decided to get up and work on a
script.

"I'm not a particularly quick study and I didn't think I'd
get much time to myself this weekend." She paused, and
Bone thought of the demands on her attention that might be
made by her host and by the two male guests. Morgan would
never find it easy to get peace and quiet, indeed Bone felt
that disturbance and disquiet were likely to arise from her
presence.

"Did you work in your room?" This was the end room
above the kitchen, looking over the garden but, on the plan,
not one of the larger or better rooms, and he wondered if
Fenny had put her there with a touch of pique.

"No. I went out into the garden. I need a bit of space and
no neighboring ears. I like to act out my lines—give voice a
bit." She waved her hands, parodying the actress. Bone
caught Locker looking fatuous with his head on one side.

"Do you know what time this was?"

"Yes, more or less, because I was thinking about breakfast, so I looked at my watch as I was going out to see how

much time I could take. Fenny's rule is . . . was, to go to the kitchen any time for what breakfast we wanted, but though that was all right with Anna I wasn't so sure about Patty. I didn't want to be too early or too late. It was six fifteen. I was astonished at myself, as I'm not an early riser; but I think it was because people were about early, you see."

What Locker was seeing, Bone did not know. His gaze appeared to be fixed at the level of Morgan's throat, where a fine gold chain glinted with her breathing.

She had seen no one, although she had heard them. She intended to come in at eight for some coffee, "And when we did, there was a commotion going on, Patty came out to tell us not to go upstairs because Fenny was dead. Of course, we did, though." She gave a little shiver.

"We?"

"Oh, Chris had been out somewhere. He looked over the wall when I was working. Just what I hadn't wanted, but I forgot there was a lane the other side of the wall." The husky voice betrayed annoyance. "The wall's quite low there at the end of the garden."

"Had you heard any noise from the house?"

"I don't know. After you've been here or a day or so, you think any ghastly noise is the peacocks."

"How did you get on with Fenny?"

She faintly smiled; the large eyes turned to him. They were beautifully made up with a country-weekend minimum of liner and shadow. It must be routine with a woman who had a public image. He wondered if she had made up before she went into the garden, or after the discovery.

She had paused to consider. The faint smile remained as she said, "We got on very well, Superintendent. We were friends."

Bone's silence may have seemed cynical, for she went on: "In spite of being Jake's lover, yes. Fenny knew if it wasn't me—" she shrugged, and the scent reached Bone again— "it would be someone else. Jake's like that."

Yet it must have caused Fenny some grief, he thought.

"And we're discreet. Jake would loathe to upset Fenny;

and he hates confrontation. He's good at violence on paper but he'll avoid it in real life."

Bone did not say that such people backed into a corner can be frantic and therefore dangerous. He asked, "How much involved are you and Jake Marsh?"

"Involved—" She paused, and the gold glittered on her neck as she took a breath. "I should have expected that, I suppose. Well, we have a long-standing affair. It began in the early days of *The Late Lady* but I can't be exact. He—he is a good lover. And very amusing. He's fun. You aren't likely to see it, as things are, but he is."

"I've seen something of his work."

"Then there it is. And I like him enough to try to arrange to be here for a while. He may need it. We're not, I would say, emotionally involved. You see I'm trying to be as plain and honest as I can about something that hasn't had to be put into words before." She moved in her chair to face Bone, and said with a husky intensity that made him uncomfortable, as when an actress allows her technique to show, "You have to believe that we loved Fenny too much to hurt her in any way."

She seemed to hear the false note she had struck in suggesting that she cared for Fenny as much as Jake did, but she had the wit not to try to retrieve it. Instead, she smiled, rather sadly, and sat back.

When she had taken her disturbing presence out of the room, Locker said, "That sounded straightforward enough."

"Yes," said Bone, "not forgetting that she's in the business of conveying impressions." A ghost of her scent lay on the air.

Patty Bates must have been poised with the coffee, for as Gibb opened the door she hurried in, with a tray before her. There was not only coffee, in big breakfast cups, but beside the milk jug and bowl of light golden sugar was a pretty china boat heaped with biscuits, shortbread, and coconut ice lumps.

"Well, Mrs. Bates," Locker said, "that's certainly welcome; we shall spoil our appetites for lunch."

Bone, who had never known anything to do this for Steve Locker, grinned and thanked her. As she left, Paul Lackland came in, accompanied by a distant long wail like that of a tortured cat. Locker, less used to the Paleys peacocks than was Bone, turned his bulk swiftly to peer out of the window, and missed the look of intense irritation on Lackland's face. Bone did not, nor the speed with which it changed to a bland alertness.

The preliminaries went forward without reference to the time Lackland had been made to wait, or to the problems with monitoring builders. Helpful patient cooperation was Lackland's choice of behavior now. He looked serious, like a good child sent for to tell tales about the rest. Even his face, the rounded forehead below tidy, backswept dark hair, the slightly snub nose and the hint of petulance around the curving mouth, suggested a grown-up boy rather than a man.

He had been woken, he said, by people stirring in the house, going about quite quietly, but he had not roused himself properly until Jake and Fenny, whose bathroom was next to his wall, got up at seven. He heard them talking, their voices; what tone? Oh, Jake grumbling, Fenny just talking. "They went off, I didn't hear any more . . . I got up, ran a cold bath; that bathroom hasn't a shower but a cold bath is as good to start the day. I got in and out of that and went to Fenny's room to see if I could catch her for a good talk about our plans."

"Your plans?"

"We were going to expand the whole crafts business. I've found a brilliant outlet in a whole chain of shops, a smallish but very promising outfit called Rusty Kate. The little rudimentary set-up here has enormous potential. They produce—Fenny's group of local women—some quite good stuff: quilts, clothes, handicrafts, toys and hangings. I've found a site for their workshop. Even Mrs. Marsh agrees that the work is of quality, and she's—well, it's not her style at all. There's none of Fenny's work in *her* room! I told her that Fenny needed somewhere to work where she wouldn't be interrupted with household troubles, and she didn't think it happened; she told me very firmly that Anna Dudley saw to all the household matters . . . this was on Monday." The round forehead creased momentarily in a frown. "Mrs. Marsh could hardly be expected to know how the whole household treated Fenny's workroom as a storehouse for anything they might want to borrow, and her work as so unimportant it could be interrupted any time of day. She couldn't believe that Fenny was going to move her work out. Of course I didn't go into detail with Mrs. Marsh; I mean that Fenny's agreement was still a little—" He tilted one hand to and fro. "That was what I went along to talk about this morning. She'd virtually agreed; a little more persuasion . . . anyway, she'd locked her door; she often did when she was working. I didn't want to wake everyone by knocking. She was in there all right, I heard her move. She dropped something, I think. So I went back and got shaved."

"In the bathroom."

"My bedroom. I've a Braun." Paul put a complacent hand to his chin. "I finished dressing and was nearly ready when I heard a scream. I suppose you want all the detail you can get, but I was hardly paying any attention. I wanted to go and see what the matter was, so apart from hearing people running about I can't say *what* I heard, who was where and so on. When I came out, Jake was banging on Fenny's door, and the housekeeper came up and for some reason *she* had the key. She opened the door and we went in."

"You, Jake Marsh and Mrs. Bates."

"That's right. And Ravenna. She ran out back to her room, and I'm not surprised. It was horrific. I actually was so nauseated . . . I dare say you're accustomed to these things."

Bone made no answer.

"I'd never seen anything like it. Horrific. I had to get to my bathroom in a hurry." He rubbed his diaphragm. "On an empty stomach it's no joke. I sat down on my bed again trying not to think. In the end I went down to the kitchen to see if the housekeeper could give me a settler or something, but no one was there. I had some coffee from the percolator and a crispbread, and presently they all came down."

"They all?"

"Thorn and Morgan and the housekeeper. We all waited. Thorn seemed to have an appetite, I must say. The housekeeper cooked for him, but Morgan had one of those frugal figure-watching breakfasts. We waited till you arrived. I gathered a doctor had come. We were all pretty shocked. And it's an appalling loss. I've got a bit of money tied up in this Crafts and the shop. Fenny was a leading light. She could produce work of a professional standard. I dare say you're looking for motive, though, and I don't see that anyone had one."

"Did you hear anything else in the workroom, sir? Say, when you were getting up and dressing?"

Paul turned to Locker with slight surprise, as if he had not expected him to talk. "No. I was having a quick bath, though; and the razor produces a buzzing noise. I'd have heard if anyone else had cried out."

"You were on good terms with Mrs. Fenny Marsh yourself?"

"Oh, the best. I was very pleased when she first joined the Crafts. And now she'd just come around to agreeing with me about how we should exploit its potential. I've no idea how I'll manage now. It's shattering. All the women relied on her, thought a lot of her. She was really pretty good at managing them. She'll be a loss to the whole community."

Bone thought that if the American fashion of an encomium to the dead were current in this country, Paul could be got to speak it. "Thank you, Mr. Lackland." The tape clicked off under Locker's hand. "You can go and deal with your builders."

"Oh—yes. I will. Right." He stood up.

"We have your address. That's on the Hawkhurst Road, isn't it?"

"That's right." He got up, stood a moment as if undecided about going, and took himself off.

"If there was anything there," Locker said, "I didn't catch it. Pompous piece of work."

"When we hear the tape through we might find something, but whatever it is, it'll have a job to get past that inflated little ego. If he's our murderer, it will be because Fenny punctured his self-image in some way. Shall we see Christopher Columbus Thorn next?"

Locker shook his head, but in wonder, not disagreement. "You'd never credit it, would you, parents calling a child that? It's quite a surprise he didn't use his second name, the way his sister did."

"Perhaps she found 'Mary' too tame; Mary Kingsley was an explorer too, late nineteenth century, I believe; the parents must have named them both in the same line. It sticks in my mind that Mary Kingsley claimed that a good thick skirt was very good protection when she fell into an elephant pit lined with spikes. My bet is that the parents, or one of them perhaps, was an armchair traveler."

"Wheelchair traveler," said Locker, reminding Bone about Lewis Thorn. As he went to the door, he said, "My mother wanted to call me Gideon."

Mr. Thorn arrived bearing a pint beer mug of coffee, which he set down opposite the tray Patty had brought, with its Locker-depleted biscuit dish.

His hair was combed slickly back from the thin brown face. The earring that had come so disastrously adrift the other day in his encounter with Jake had been reinstated. The general effect was of an intellectual gypsy.

He sat down without being asked, folded his arms and looked at Bone down his nose from under hooded lids. He wore black jeans and a scarlet shirt open on a throat as brown as his face but, Bone noted, with no gold chains. The image he was projecting was not macho man, but that of a man who didn't need macho trappings, a free spirit. Bone thought: Here's one native you are not impressing, chum, and because he realized that he was reacting to the implied challenge, he said in his most neutral tone, "Have we your permission to record this interview?"

Chris Thorn gave a short bark of a laugh.

"God, the police have all the nice toys. Pity they don't do you much good. Yes, sure, go ahead. All this is futile, as you well know." His voice, clipped and cool, dismissed them.

Bone thought he would not give Thorn the fun of explaining why "all this" was futile, so he did not ask. Locker clicked on the recorder again and gave Chris Thorn's full name without glancing at his superior, which Bone was sure he was tempted to do.

"What time did you get up this morning, Mr. Thorn?" Bone checked on the house plan that Thorn's room was between Lackland's and Ravenna's, giving on to the gallery facing the front door.

"Time? Six or so. I usually wake at dawn. Habit."

Bone duly received the picture of a man accustomed to being alert, to rising early to start a day full of dangers.

"Did you sleep again, then, between dawn and getting up? Dawn is at roughly four thirty. You may have heard people moving about?"

"I was reading. Going through notes and papers of my sister's. I'm writing an appreciation of her work that I expect the *Geographic* will take. I heard people visiting the lavatories in various bathrooms. No, Inspector, I did not look at my watch to time them. Doors and cisterns were my evidence that this human activity was going on." His mouth twitched in amusement at Locker's meticulousness. "Then I became restless. I had read all the papers I'd brought down. They are kept in the loft here, and I intend to take everything over to Beeches. Father will want to see them too. I could get no more without making an ungodly noise with the loft ladder. Am I explaining sufficiently?"

"Very clearly," Bone said, apparently failing to recognize any sarcasm.

"Splendid. So I went for a walk. I took the footpath almost to Brantley and then branched up through the woods and came back across the fields."

As Brantley was where the now closed railway station used to be, from which Thorn's sister would begin her journeys, Bone wondered if there had been sentiment in his choice of walk. He said, "Did you meet anyone?"

"Not until the last hundred yards of the footpath. I saw Miss Carradine in the garden. Miss Carradine was the first person I had seen, except the unfortunates in cars who must now drive to Staplehurst or Robertsbridge for their trains to jail."

Bone presumed that he was meant to inquire "Jail?" and to have explained to him Thorn's idea of office life. Instead he asked, "Where was Miss Carradine?"

"In the garden. Miss Carradine was in the yew walk, pacing to and fro in the manner of a caged tigress, clasping and twisting her hands and muttering like Lady Macbeth. It would have much amazed you," he assured Bone, with a kindly bend of the head.

"Did you speak to her?"

"I leaned on the wall, and she observed me. She made a swift recovery, with quite a maiden blush, tossing the lovely hair et cetera and spoke of breakfast. We came into the house by the garden door—I jumped the wall from the lane. She was disconcerted at having been surprised—annoyed perhaps—but tried to pass it off with an application of charm. When we entered the house, she declared that something was wrong, and her intuition was vindicated when we met poor Mrs. Bates. She had been weeping, and told us what had occurred, and besought us not to go upstairs, which we instantly did."

"And you saw?" Bone prompted.

"Jake holding Fenny in his arms. La Carradine went and supported him, but we were ousted by the doctor."

"That's very clear, Mr. Thorn. Perhaps you can help us as to the relationships of people in the house."

"You want to understand the relationships of the inhabitants. An anthropological question." It was, Bone decided, the curve of nostril and the lines from nose to mouth that gave him his look of insufferable superiority. He raised his eyebrows as he leaned forward to pick up his coffee, and Bone changed his mind; he recalled that *supercilious* meant the raising of eyebrows.

"Should we start with the presiding genius, my sister's intelligent and courageous mother-in-law? Or her son, whose abilities have received such gross inflation from his success on the box? Not a bad bloke when he married my sister, but his very reasonable doubts of his capabilities have led him to bank on booze." He put down his mug and leaned back with folded arms. "Fenny would go to any lengths for his sake, which must have contributed to his general slacking off."

"The television series doesn't seem to have suffered."

"Once *hoi polloi* take something to their hearts it becomes an institution; they do not notice when the thing's running downhill on impetus rather than steam."

"No doubt you can tell," said Bone. "I haven't been able to view it often enough to judge."

Thorn's heavy eyelids flicked open a little as if he suspected Bone of sarcasm in his turn; but he saw only the studious emptiness of Bone's face and resumed his calm disdain.

"There is the little shopkeeper Lackland, full of shy charm yesterday, silent and palely loitering today. There is my niece, highly adolescent, who hates everybody. There is the voluptuous Morgan, consoling Jake with the skill of long practice."

His mouth twitched. Bone speculated on his reaction should he, Bone, lean over and haul on that earring.

"So what more can I tell you, Superintendent? I've my own theories as to the perpetrator of this latest deed, but I'm sure they would be of no interest to you."

"If they are supported by factual evidence I'd be very interested, Mr. Thorn."

"The policeman plods his weary way. I shall go up to the loft and continue my researches. I gather that your people looked around among my sister's belongings on Wednesday, which would account for the lack of dust. I do not suppose

they were touched, until then, from the day they were put
there to await her return. I wonder how soon after her
departure Fenny put them out of sight."

The hazel eyes opened fully.

"I didn't take to Fenny, Superintendent. We were on civil
terms but we weren't friends. We weren't enemies. I believe
now that she killed my sister, very probably accidentally in a
quarrel over Jake. But I assure you it was not I who filed her
for reference."

15

The minute of speaking silence between Bone and Locker after Thorn's exit was interrupted by a shouting, a trampling, and a flow of soprano bad language upstairs. Bone, instantly at the door, looked and saw Ravenna come backward from her room as if hurled, and her uncle emerge holding, by his elbows, an emaciated youth in black—Justin.

Justin came downstairs almost as rapidly as if Dom's skateboard had been provided, manhandled by Chris Thorn, Ravenna dragging and scratching at her uncle's shoulders and screeching some unpleasant epithets. She and Justin, both flailing about and both dressed in black, looked to Bone like a pair of young rooks disturbed in their nest. A love nest, he supposed, with an inconsistent twinge of anger for Charlotte.

"See what I've—" Thorn clamped a fresh grip to keep Justin in chancery and finished triumphantly "—found!" He was enjoying himself, the victor of a struggle and demonstrating that he was one up on the police. "How is this for a suspect? Bang next to Fenny's room—"

"He was with me *all the time*. Let him *go!*" Ravenna sank

her teeth into her uncle's hand and he did let go, with a yelp. Bone considered recommending an instant tetanus jab. Instead he said to Justin, "I think we had better have a talk, Mr.—?"

"Rafferty," Justin supplied, evidently amused both by the prefix and his recognition of Charlotte's father. He was massaging a wing-like shoulder wrenched by Thorn's grip, and glancing around at the small audience. His black teeshirt bore, surprisingly, a large print of a badger across the narrow curve of his chest. Could this unlikely creature be into conservation?

"Mr. Rafferty, wait here." Bone indicated the bench in the hall with its tapestry seat cushion. Justin grimaced at Ravenna, shrugged and sat down, PC Gibb eyeing him as one would survey a quiescent raptor.

"Miss Marsh, please."

Ravenna, with all her uncle's relish for dramatic situation, tossed her head as she went before them in an invisible tumbril. Once in the dining room she flung herself into Bone's chair at the head of the table, took a piece of shortbread and sprawled, long limbs in black leggings spread out as if to remind them that she was in her father's house and might do as she pleased.

"Sit here, Miss Marsh." Bone put his hand on the back of the interviewee's chair, and waited.

She had not the nerve she would have liked to own. After a sullen, fraught moment she got up and flung into the other chair, saying, "Sit here, sit there; can't you operate unless you're in the big chair?"

"We have your father's permission, Miss Marsh, to ask you some questions and to record this interview," Locker said as WDC Fredricks came silently in and stood by the door.

Ravenna shot her a lowering glare. "Great. Did you get his permission for thumbscrews too?"

Bone did not reply, but spent a little time studying the house plan before him. Ravenna kicked her feet restlessly and turned to look at Fredricks' impression of a kindly horse. Locker waited with his hand over the switch, but he was not the only one to start when Bone suddenly spoke.

"What time did you return from the Hammersmith concert?"

Ravenna opened her eyes. *"Who's* well informed, then? I don't know. Three? Four? Anyway, what's that to do with Fenny being dead?"

Bone ignored that too. "Three or four. Justin Rafferty took you there and back on his motorbike." He did not add, thank God it was you and not my daughter, but he wondered what, if anything, Justin had said to Ravenna about Charlotte or about her father's antique attitudes.

"Yeah. Justin did the transport. Is that criminal?"

Not unless he was drunk, drugged or speeding. In younger days Bone had policed the crowds coming out of such concerts and he knew what it could be like, one of his more potent reasons for not wanting Charlotte to go. It wasn't necessary to be one of the idiot minority to suffer harm, just to be in their company.

"He came in with you?"

"Sure. Whose permission do I have to get for that?"

Evidently not her father's. Would Justin have expected to stay the night if Cha had been his guest at the concert? *Would she have wanted him to?* Without knowing it, he frowned at Ravenna; and saw from a fleeting smirk, very like Chris Thorn's, that she was pleased to think she had provoked his annoyance.

"Did you see anyone on your way to your room?"

She hesitated. "Oh well. Fenny, I suppose."

"You suppose you saw her."

"She came into the kitchen when I was getting something to eat."

"At three in the morning."

"She was mad at me." Ravenna flashed a sudden nervous grin. "It was really funny. Okay it shouldn't be now, but it was. She wanted to shout at me and she had to shout in a whisper because of not waking people."

"There was a row?"

"Oh no." The shrug. "Nothing. I mean she's not—she wasn't my mother so she's not responsible for me."

Where was Justin all this time? Was that sight to make eyes sore also in the kitchen at three in the morning? In the most liberal household, a death's head in black leather would take a heavy slice of toleration. And Kingsley was understood to have had a fatal quarrel in that kitchen by night when this girl before him was a child. Had that quarrel been with Fenny? More to the point, did Ravenna believe it was?

"—Lucky Justin was still putting his bike away in the shed or she'd really have flipped. I kept thinking he'd walk in on us but he's cool. Waited out there till he heard her go. Then we grabbed some stuff and tippytoed up to my room." She grinned openly now, wolfishly, inviting him to think of what had happened there. Locker obliged with waves of disapproval, emanating from him as if he had been a radio beacon.

"Was he in your company the whole time, until now?"

"Yes. And I was in his too. Lucky I did bring him back, right? And I've got my own bathroom, didn't have to sneak about the passages. And he can tell you I never went out. So don't think I did it."

She added with the first faint sigh of feeling she had shown on the subject, "It looked really horrible. Not real, somehow. It's a disgusting way to kill someone, right? Poor old Paul went and threw up."

"Had your stepmother been quarreling with anyone else?"

"Don't know." The idea that she might hold a clue to murder, however, roused Ravenna's interest. "She was in a state yesterday anyway because of Anna. I mean, she minded a lot about her, they were practically lovers. You couldn't help being sorry for her in a way. She was crying when she got back from the funeral and Dad had his arm around her. I don't know who she had rows with." Ravenna brushed shortbread crumbs from her chest. "She might've had a fight with Morgan about Dad. And yes, before I went out last night she was furious with Paul. Could be him." She brightened at the happy thought.

"Were you fond of your stepmother?" Bone asked.

Ravenna was surprised out of her modish calm. "Fond? Did I love her? Well, she was all right when I was a kid. I liked her then. She looked after me. Her and Anna. But I don't see what business it is of yours." She rallied to her challenging tone. "I can't have killed her, Justin was with me. And anyway I didn't. Can I *go* now? Do you want to grill Justin?"

"If you imagine you've had a grilling, Miss Marsh, you're 'way from the facts." Bone put on a genial tone, not without malice; indulgent, adult to child. "Thank you. Yes, that's all for now." Locker switched off, and Fredricks opened the door. Ravenna dragged her feet out of the room, Fredricks followed her and shut the door.

"Reckon they've been a lot too soft with that little madam. It's called abuse if you smack a child these days; but I reckon with Jake Marsh avoiding confrontation and his wife being too nice, they've let that Ravenna get her own way too much for her own good. Boyfriend in her room overnight? And I'll have a word to say to Gibb. He's meant to have checked the whole house for signs of intruders—I'd like to know how he missed Rafferty in her room."

"She'll have popped him in the wardrobe," Bone said.

"M'm. She's not a nice piece of work. You'd think she'd be a bit shaken with all that's happened."

"I wouldn't expect her to show it. Whatever the vogue word is for hip, gear or cool, you can lay your socks on it that showing emotion is out. And it takes time for these things to get through; it's unreal at first, you know that. And who can tell how much of her behavior is whistling in the dark?"

"Maybe it is. She quarreled with Fenny in the early morning. On the face of it that's hardly enough motive for attacking her later on, but with these kids you can't know. And she was acting very odd before."

"She may have taken something."

"Should we search her room?"

"I don't know how Jake Marsh would view that—and if she has half the *nous* I think she has, anything she had will be in the sewage system by now . . . Suppose Fenny went into Ravenna's room early on to talk to her, and found Justin there; she takes Ravenna into the workroom for a word; they have a row, an actual fight perhaps, say it escalates to an attack, particularly if Ravenna's high. And it happens."

Locker slowly nodded.

"I'm not keen on it," Bone said, "but it's there."

"Wouldn't Fenny have made Rafferty leave?"

"She could have told him to go and Ravenna said 'Stay'—all conjecture."

"Do we talk to her again?"

"Let's hear from Rafferty."

Justin sauntered in, hands in his pockets, obliging them with his presence. Charlotte would no doubt have been impressed. Bone told himself sternly that no purpose was to be served by reacting to Justin's manner; why please the boy, anyway?

Sitting readily in the chair indicated, Justin seemed inclined to answer their questions without demur, which made a change from Ravenna. He was at ease, quite interested. This boy, thought Bone, has possibly jeered at the most gruesome deaths that can be faked on video; why should the horror of this death, of a woman he had scarcely met, strike him in the least?

"What time did you arrive here after the concert?"

Justin examined the ceiling momentarily in thought. The eyes were, in this light, greenish—that odd mixture of green and gray. "Don't know." The bony wrist had no watch. "Two? Three? Early. Wasn't dawn."

"You took a long time to get from London. Bike break down?" Locker's voice had an edge on it that Bone had kept out of his, and Justin responded. Hands still in his pockets, he slid down to sit on the end of his spine and stared under his brows at Locker.

"What's that to do with anything? What we did on the

way here's none of your sodding business. And if you think you can fit me up for this because I happen along so handy you've got another fucking thing coming."

"Now then—" but Locker subsided, flushed, as Bone raised a hand.

"You didn't come into the house at the same time as Miss Marsh."

There was a moment's silence as Justin redirected his gaze and considered Bone, perhaps playing back the deliberately cool and reasonable voice. Perhaps he thought they were doing an act of Good Cop and Bad Cop. He thrust his hips forward slightly as if to ease his aggression, and replied without heat.

"I hung about in the back there where I set me bike up. No sense in going in when she was getting a bollocking from some old cow, was there? Make it worse, wouldn't it?"

Had Ravenna told him afterward that it was Fenny? And why should he care? Respect for the dead very likely didn't rate among priorities for him.

"Did you hear what was being said?"

"Didn't put an ear to the keyhole, if that's what you mean. Reckon it was the normal spiel, house like a hotel, and that." The earring slithered over the hunched shoulder. "Don't reckon Ravenna'd listen any more'n I did."

Had Fenny, after that little dust-up, visited Ravenna's room to see if more impression could be made, and walked in on the pair in bed? But had there been a further row, heard by nobody and ending in the workroom, Justin would hardly have hung around to be pounced on by Chris Thorn.

"This morning. What exactly did you see or hear this morning around the house?"

Justin's face was, as Bone had noticed, so thin that his mouth had difficulty closing over his teeth, and it was hard to tell now if he smiled at this tacit ignoring of what had been going on in Ravenna's room. "You mean before someone did in her stepmother?"

Stepmother. Still, in the universal mind, it carried tones of Grimm's fairy tales; of cruelty and terrible fates, both for the children they persecuted and for themselves in retribution. Though Bone was positive that Fenny had not ill-treated Ravenna, the girl might have thought that she did. He nodded, and Justin cast the gray gaze toward the ceiling again. Reflected light from outside trembled on the crystals of Fenny's tapestry and on three gold sleepers now around the rim of Justin's ear.

"I dunno."

"What did you do—from the moment you got out of bed?"

Justin's slow smile now said: Apart from screwing Ravenna, and at Bone's lack of response it widened. "We-ell. I wanted to get away, didn't I? Rave didn't want anyone to see me so I had to watch my chance." He revealed some more teeth. "You wouldn't credit the coming and going. She'd said, 'You can easy slip away in the morning.' Could I *hell*. I only wanted to slope off down the back way out in the garden, get my bike out the shed and bugger off, and I kept looking out and there'd be someone catfootin' it."

This constant activity did not accord with the accounts of others in the house. Perhaps his efforts had been desultory.

"Did you *see* anyone?" Locker was leaning forward with arms on the table, which gave him an air of intense interest; Justin's eyes flickered toward him.

"Only the bloke with the axe just pissing off around the corner, looked like Jack Nicholson."

"Rafferty." Bone injected such force into his voice as almost to spring Justin's hands from his pockets. He tensed, with a brief look of shock, and Bone went on, spacing his words in almost a monotone: "This is not a TV film and it is not a joke. Someone killed a woman, this morning, only a few feet away from where you were; and it's just possible you have a clue which might help nail the killer."

"Okay. *Okay.*" He was resentful, having been got at. "I'll do what I can." He sat up a little and looked suddenly much younger. Bone could almost see back a few years to what might have been a docile little boy. Bone kept in mind that

Justin's father had beaten the boy too; this package was labeled Care In Handling.

"Think of this morning when you were watching for your chance to go. What sounds were there?"

He considered once more, head back. "There was this bath running. And bogs flushing, like. I mean, I don't know what order anything was in."

"Where was the bath sound coming from?"

"Along at the end. Rave's room's on the corner, right, well this was along—" he slid his right hand free and indicated— "and this bloke or woman, whatever, was to and fro, going to the bathroom and back in the end bedroom, didn't have an on-sweet like Rave."

Paul's cold bath, thought Bone, translating on-sweet into en suite. "Fine. And?"

"Well, I thought, now's my chance, everything was dead quiet, not a footstep, no noise bar a peacock or two, so I looked out and shit, there was this woman I hadn't even heard."

"What did she look like?"

"Didn't see her. Just this end of a blue skirt flipping off around the corner."

"The corner."

The left hand indicated with an Olivier gesture, flat with the palm forward, angled at the wrist. "Around to the back stairs."

And the workroom.

"Did you hear anything?"

"I told you. Silent as the grave."

Very likely. "A skirt, that's all?"

"Just this sort of edge of a skirt, low down like, around the corner."

"What was the color again?"

"Blue."

Fenny had been in jeans. Patty wore a print dress. Morgan in dark indigo blue.

"This was while the bath was running?"

175

"No. I *told* you. It was all quiet."

"We go over things to be sure it's exact; to be sure we have the whole picture and every detail."

"Uhuh." Because you're thick, the grunt said. "I mean the *point* was it was quiet. I thought I could blow. Then there was this woman I never even heard, and it put the lid on it. I mean I wasn't going out there to meet people you couldn't hear, was I?"

"Could it have been a man's dressing gown you saw?"

The earring swung to Justin's head-shake. "No. There was this woman smell."

"Did she make no sound at all? Door shutting, floor creaking?"

"Dunno. I shut Rave's door, see, quiet like a flea's whisper. I gave up and stripped off again and had a shower and then I got back in bed again."

Bone inevitably thought of the skeletal young body climbing into bed. Though it might be uncomfortably angular for Ravenna, at close quarters, at least it wouldn't take up much room.

"There was the man then, while I was getting my jeans off. Could be the bathroom man. I heard him at someone's door, tap tap and then he said something like he was afraid to wake people. He gave up after a bit and went back."

"After a bit? A few seconds? Half a minute?"

"Seemed like a long time with me standing bent over." Justin grinned. "Bit like Rave's fight when we got in last night, with her stepmother. Tap tap, then he said something like he was mad and didn't want to wake people. Then he gave up and went back."

"To the room at the right along the landing."

"That way, yeh."

"What did you hear next?"

"I wouldn't hear anything in the shower. I reckoned it didn't matter if anyone heard *me,* they'd think it was Rave. When I came out of the on-sweet she was up and pulling the bed straight, like the sheet underneath had come half off, she was pulling it straight. Then we heard this screech. We piled into bed and under the duvet, Rave said a peacock must have got in, but a bit later, like really soon, there was a noise like hammering on a door and shouting, and Rave sat up and said, 'That's Dad.' She was scared I think. I said, 'It's okay, it's not this door he's at,' but anyway she pushed me under the duvet and got up and put a wrap on and went. I could hear a whole lot of commotion, crying out and talk and running, and after a minute she came back."

"Did she say what had happened?"

"Christ, she couldn't talk right off, she was shaking like a leaf."

This was not in any way the impression Ravenna would have preferred to convey.

"She was really, I mean, seriously upset. She said about her stepmother being dead and this awful thing stuck in her face. We had some drink left and I made her take it. Got her wrapped in the duvet and that. She calmed down a bit. I thought all the kerfuffle had put paid to me getting out easy, too, so I stayed."

"What could you hear then?"

"Oh, dunno. Lots of to and fro and talk and that. Then you lot came."

"And where were you when the constable looked in to check the windows?"

"Rolled up in the duvet against the wall. Rave called out wait a sec she was in the bathroom, and she wrapped a towel around and said, 'Come in.' Your bloke sounded nervous as a cat. Made her laugh, she said he didn't know where to look. Cheered her up a bit. She was getting back to herself, like."

Indeed she was. "Neither of you left the room except when she went to the workroom after her stepmother's death?"

"Right. She's got her own bog and matching avocado bogroll. Great." It may have been amusement, but on that face it resembled a snarl.

"You will be going back to the Grants' house? We need to know where to contact you if any more questions crop up."

"Yeh. There's a little woman asked me if I was here for lunch. Said I don't know."

Bone said frankly, "I'd split if I were you. A death in the family. You'll have to come to the Tunbridge Wells station to read a transcript of this later."

Justin clambered to his feet, like a re-articulation of his bones. "On tape I sound really really villainous," he said. At the door he turned and said with social grace, "Ta-ra, then."

"That's not a nice bit of work," Locker said. "Taking advantage of Miss Marsh. Pity he does seem to have such an alibi. You don't think she'd alibi him if he had slipped out? Or suppose she was asleep?"

"Motive?"

"For kicks. Kids like that don't need a *motive*. They knife strangers in the street for kicks. It's meant to be macho."

"Steve, I didn't think he was right about you."

"Him? About me?"

"You actually are trying to fit him up for it. I don't know if your theories will hold, but don't let your admiration for his manner and appearance blind you to the facts."

Locker shifted and grinned. "Getting far-fetched, was I? But with respect, sir, you talk very soft to these yobs."

"I've met that yob before," Bone said. "He's had good press."

Locker registered mild incredulity, but said, "Oh, well then."

At this point Gibb looked in to say that Mrs. Bates was asking if soup and bread rolls would do for lunch. She appeared beside him in the doorway like a hopeful robin. "Or I could make sandwiches. We've got a ham. Or the Hopsack does a good lunch."

"We won't impose on you, thank you very much," Bone said, smiling.

Her face fell. "I thought you might want to be working. It's no trouble and Mr. Marsh said I could ask you."

"You're very kind," Bone replied. "We've talked to almost everyone, Mrs. Bates, and we're through for the moment. We shall be back later, I expect, but for the moment you are rid of us."

In Bone's mind was the enticing picture of a chance to see Grizel. All morning he had been aware of her house, as if on a map of the village or as if another part of the village was alive for him. He couldn't call on her now, for a talk with Locker was imminent; they must go over what they had heard; but on the way back . . . ? The vision of her face, never matching the reality, swam in his mind's eye.

The two sides of the Pig and Biscuit's hanging sign differed, one showing a blissfully prostrate porker on the "biscuit" mattress, the other a square breakfast biscuit stamped with a smiling pig. Mrs. Burnett remembered them, and when Bone asked if there was a place to hold a private talk while they ate, she ushered them out to "The extension," a side garden only used when a flood of visitors filled the orchard tables. Heat lay on the garden, and they chose a table in the shade. Beyond the trellis, in the orchard, a family party was eating, the children running at large.

The wooden table was crusted with lichen and birdlime, and Mrs. Burnett tutted and said she would bring a brush. Locker removed the birdlime with a tissue and said not to worry, but when she came out with their order she brought out a cherry-patterned plastic tablecloth.

The ham sandwiches proved to be of home-cooked ham although the mustard came in a plastic packet. Locker used both his packet and Bone's. Shay's cheese and lettuce salad came on a vast dish.

There was a pleasant noise of voices from the orchard and the hum of insects in the heights of the great copper beech. Until they had taken the edge from their hunger the men were silent. Locker, finished first to no one's surprise, went for refills, and came back with a tray on which were their glasses golden full and a Chelsea bun of respectable size.

Bone, smelling roses that climbed the trellis behind him, had the thought that a few years ago the three of them would naturally have lit up at this juncture, if indeed they hadn't been smoking all the time. He'd never been a heavy smoker —put off by his father's chain-smoking—but Locker had had a struggle.

"Well then. What are your thoughts, Steve?"

"Taking it as a homicide and ignoring for the moment that it's just possibly accident, we've got several runners." He spread out the notebook in which he had jotted remarks. A corner of the tablecloth, caught by the breeze, rose and caressed his hand.

"Jake Marsh. He was not in his study when Mrs. Bates went to call him. He says he was. He could have gone up through the house not seen by Mrs. Bates earlier. He may want to be free on account of Miss Carradine. Of course if Ferdy Foster gets anything positive off those face bruises it's going to help sort things out. They're faint. It was quick of Dr. Walsh to see them; but they're definitely consistent with her head having been gripped either side from behind, like he showed us."

"The spacing of the marks could be from a man's or a woman's hand," Shay said. "Three on the right side, one on the left."

"When Marsh took hold of her body, it could have been to confuse traces he might have left."

"We're in a lousy business," Bone remarked.

"I do find sometimes I take it home with me," Locker said. "I don't like it—and Cherry gets wild, she says, 'Don't be so cynical.' I got it from the youngster last week: 'I'm not a lager lout, Dad, stop bossing me about.'" Locker drained his glass. "I could have clipped him one, and that'd have proved his point, wouldn't it? But Marsh does write detective stories, so he would know about traces."

"He may not," Shay said. "I've read some of these murder stories. You wouldn't think they'd ever heard of pathology."

"It's all pathology now," Bone said. "Ferdy Foster's the real detective, we're just Plod on the beat. Come on. As against Morgan Carradine for Jake's motive, Fenny Marsh seemed complaisant about the affair, and Morgan does not *seem* to be pressing for marriage."

"Right, sir. Then there's Mrs. Marsh senior. Fenny lived on good terms with her for umpteen years, and that can't be all easy with a mother-in-law. Then, Mrs. Marsh doesn't go upstairs and exertion is bad for her. If you know you've got a dodgy heart you won't go in for violent action, let alone when you've had a nasty shock already that week with the accident on Monday."

"She can take medication and be all right, though I don't know, and nor I suppose does any doctor, what help that would be in real stress. And, as you say, they got on well, for so long. I don't see any motive. How that obsession with Jake crops up, though. Everything is seen as it relates to him. He doesn't strike *me* as a tender lambkin, or a paragon of selflessness either. I'd say he can look out for himself very well. Yet she doesn't seem over-possessive. She got on with Kingsley and Fenny, apparently liked them, was fond of them both."

"Fenny found her something of a nosy parker, watching what went on all the time. That can't have been easy."

"Personally if I'd been Fenny I'd have nailed up that door years ago," Bone said cheerfully. "We've plenty of motive for *Fenny* to murder *Ysobel:* telling Fenny she should give Dom more time, and ever so nicely saying her handiwork wasn't at all her style but no doubt very lovely for people who liked that sort of thing; and giving Jake his tea . . . However, warning her against Lackland doesn't seem to be necessary. Fenny didn't seem in the least keen on that scheme of his."

"But Lackland talked about it as a settled thing."

"*She* didn't. Her annoyance with him seemed to be genuine. I wouldn't say she needed any warning against getting wrapped up in him."

"But Marsh is a difficult character and Lackland's good-looking and persuasive. He certainly thought he'd got his scheme wrapped up."

"You'd say Marsh suspected them together?"

Shay said, "With him carrying on with Carradine, he'd be all the likelier to get possessive over his wife."

"Shrewd psychology," said Bone, and nipped a lettuce leaf from Shay's plate. "I wonder if his mother put such an idea into his head. She'd be a lot faster to get warmed up about his honor than he would. Suppose he listened to her."

"His own bit of how's-your-father with Morgan C. wouldn't stand in his way, like Shay says. It's different when it's a wife. It shouldn't be but it is."

"That's the story for Jake Marsh. What about Morgan Carradine herself?" Locker paused. "Young Rafferty saw, he says, a blue skirt. I don't give much credence to his say-so, it could be another Jack Nicholson with an axe. He'd think nothing of inventing and he's not in a great position himself."

"If she does have a real thing going with our Jake, she might well want to be rid of his wife, no matter what terms she says they were on. We need a bit of corroboration on that—were she and Fenny really such buddies? And one's likely, remember, to be responding to her looks and manner, and lend belief to her because she's attractive. A bit of cynicism about ourselves will do no harm."

"Some might think the opposite, sir. Glamour-puss equals villainess."

"Yeah, my mum used to say, never trust a woman that makes up before breakfast," Shay said. "I tell her it doesn't apply these days."

"Fenny Marsh didn't seem to use make-up at all . . . It seems weird to me, anyone wanting to kill her. She comes out as such a *nice* woman."

"It's no guarantee," said Bone. He felt the same.

"Something *wrong* in that house," Shay said. "First Anna Dudley, then the first wife discovered and now this. Spooky."

Bone too had been feeling a dislike of the place. He said sharply, "Who's the next on the suspect list?"

"Lackland. He was more on the spot than Carradine seems to have been, though we've still to check if she'd be visible down the garden where she says she was. No one says they saw her until Thorn came along the lane. There's the rose arbor hides the last bit near the house."

"So, Lackland; what of our youthful charmer?"

"He says Fenny was convinced she should support his scheme. He even told people so—Mrs. Marsh and Mrs. Bates. Jake says she wasn't going to. Now did Jake Marsh, her husband, not know, or is Lackland lying?"

"She might have been keeping it from her husband for some reason, or on the other hand Lackland may be an optimist."

"It may be he wanted the other woman in the group to believe Mrs. Fenny approved of it."

"But she didn't."

"She can't say so," Bone pointed out grimly.

"He might want her dead so that he could carry out his scheme without her. Though looking at the things she made, it wouldn't be half the scheme, without her."

"What are the main motives for a murder, Steve?"

"Money and love."

"But if it's Christopher Columbus, it's not love, it's revenge. If he's come to believe that Fenny killed his sister, he did it out of hate."

"Love; for his sister."

"What was that Jake Marsh said about forty thousand brothers?" Locker said. "Is that a quote?"

> " 'Forty thousand brothers
> Could not with all their quantity of love
> Make up my score.' "

Bone found the quotation surprisingly complete in his memory. He hadn't known he knew it.

"That's *Hamlet*," Shay informed Locker, who gave him an unimpressed stare. "Well, sir, it is."

"But what about Lackland? To get rid of Fenny is killing the goose that laid the golden eggs. She was the best one he'd got, wasn't she? That's what they say in the village."

"She made the most exquisite stuff," Bone said; he had realized of a sudden that a tunic Grizel had worn to the theater must be Fenny's work.

"I was asking Lady Mary Kentish about the crafts group this morning and she said it'd take three of them to carry out one of Mrs. Fenny's designs, but *she* could work them alone," Shay added. "She's pretty distressed. Lady Mary, I mean."

"It doesn't seem sense to suspect Lackland, though he could have lost his rag when she wouldn't be persuaded. And no one can pretend murder is sense. A murder can be premeditated, worked out rationally with logistics and timing, and be quite senseless."

"Lackland was the one that threw up when he saw the body."

"Means nothing," Bone returned. "You know that. He may not even have seen what he did when he did it."

"Chris Thorn, next?"

"Opportunity: could have spent no time at all wandering around. Brantley may have seen him not, half Kent from dawn onward may have been bereft of his presence while he was at Paleys ridding the world of the woman he thought had killed his sister. And then he could pop down the lane afterward to impress the hell out of La Carradine with his athleticism jumping over walls. He's so snide about her that he must entertain something of a yen."

"Means: he's strong enough. Motive, his sister's death."

"For which there is no evidence that Fenny was responsible."

"Jake Marsh believes Chris killed Fenny," Locker observed.

"Oh, quite. Jake can write a good script but he doesn't come top in my ratiocination league. I think we have to watch out with Chris Thorn as with Rafferty; each in his way making one itch to plant a boot where they would least welcome it."

"Be a pleasure to feel his collar."

Shay looked from one to the other. "What did he *do,* sir?"

"Sarky bugger," Locker said.

"Very likely on his journeys he's been used to police that can be bribed or manipulated; and while I don't hold a brief for the whole of the Force, we are not just the peasants hired by the Establishment to make a show of law and order."

"Wasn't he pleased to find young Rafferty!"

"It didn't much please his niece. I doubt if Uncle is flavor of the month just now."

"By all accounts," Shay said, "she bit a great chunk out of his wrist."

"Where are you placing the said niece in the suspect stakes?"

"This she-was-with-me-all-the-time sounds fine, but when you look at it, One, they could both be lying themselves silly, Two, there is the bathroom—she could have left the room when he was in the shower—"

"Or either of them could have gone out while the other was availing themselves of the avocado lavatory roll."

"So they could. Or, Three, they could be sleeping. Say either of them has a shower, or sleeps, or goes to the toilet, the other could slip out, around the corner to the workroom . . . young Ravenna's got across her stepmother time and again—spoiled her garden, for instance, according to Patty Bates; and she's meant to've undone some pattern that was pinned up in the workroom, and then they had this battle last night; she plays that down, but Rafferty made it sound like quite something. But I was thinking, Rafferty may want to make out it was bad. He's the type for trouble. Did you hear about the knife fight last night in Hammersmith? Couple of lads were chased up Brook Green by a gang and knifed, one's in intensive. That's the sort Rafferty's been around with; he might not think of it much—do it as a favor to Ravenna, like. I know you say you've heard good about the lad, sir, but he wouldn't look like that if he wasn't anti-social. That type's against the world. And he could be on something; her eyes didn't look right this morning earlier. They could have been high as kites first thing in the morning."

Justin had, it was true, got up Bone's nose, but the superior nostril penetration he had achieved on Locker was remarkable. Locker usually evinced an easy tolerance of humanity, but here Bone seemed to see his own reaction magnified like a shadow on a cloud.

Did he believe that Rafferty could so well deceive his own ear for truth? He had thought the boy was, grudgingly and awkwardly, reconstructing the truth as it was in his memory. Yet which of those sitting at the table, in front of Fenny's tapestry, had been lying? Some of them were certainly skilled enough—apart from the common lies with which people bury things they don't want to look at, automatic falsehoods, at which most people are skilled—to deceive a questioner. He did not happen to think that Justin had been trying to; it might be underestimating him severely.

"Have we got anywhere?" he asked.

"Early days," said Locker.

16

He left his car in the pub car park and walked along to the
green. A cricket match was in progress there, white figures
ritually moving, rows of spectators' cars up by the church. A
man was being escorted away from the spectators by a burly
gentleman and a tall boy in white flannels. Bone recognized
a reporter who had been in the crowd on Wednesday.
Nobody seemed to be making trouble and Bone walked on.
Always aware of village gossip when he called on Grizel, he
opened the small gate in the tall hedge and slipped through.
Her house, or rather cottage, was hidden among trees and
shrubs and honeysuckle. He trod the brick path with a sense
of its secrecy. The sunny spot where her sister-in-law had
been basking was the only spot visible from the road.

He had been waiting a long time to see her, and told
himself that anticipation defeats its object, building it up to
impossible mythic dimensions so that fact can only disap-
point. Grizel opened the door as he came to it, and shut it
behind him, and she was there, the myth intact, her light
eyes smiling, amazingly as glad to see him as he was to see
her; she came into his arms and eclipsed her face in his
shoulder, and they stood there for a long moment. He felt so

entirely happy that it seemed enough to stay there enclosed and close for any length of time.

When they let go, she led him to the living room, saying, "It's so good to have you here; there've been too many folk about, who weren't you . . . Robert—" she turned and put a hand on his arm—"is it true about Fenny Marsh? They're saying in the shops—I suppose it must be true if you're here."

"I'm afraid so."

"Of all people. A nicer woman you couldn't meet. And all her lovely work . . . It's horrible. And it's not an accident?"

Bone shook his head.

"You won't want me to talk about it. Mrs. Parton said your house-to-house man had been around while I was out, so he'll be back, I suppose. She said the poor young man had hay fever and was taking tablets . . ."

She was outside the whole business at Paleys. He had been enclosed by the place, and this began to free him.

"Cha hadn't gone to that damn concert at all, of course. Her friend's father had got back late, and was bringing her to the door when we were on the phone."

She sank onto the sofa, sideways, an arm along the back and one foot tucked up. Bone sat beside her, as always unable to believe at first in her presence. She wore charcoal cotton trousers and a light green teeshirt that toned with her eyes, brought out their color without quite matching them. Her short-cut hair glittered in the subdued light, pale, showing the vulnerable shape of her head. The mouth, so composed when shut, now showed its size in a smile. He knew that she was self-conscious about her mouth; she thought it too big. He thought it perfect.

"I'm still here, Robert."

He smiled. "Yes. Was I staring?"

"One of your famous searching looks. They do terrible things to me. It's like romantic fiction. I go gooey inside."

Bone laughed at this unlikelihood. "I shall start seeing myself as—who? Heathcliff? I shall wear a dark wig."

She leaned forward and kissed him, a moth's kiss.

"Do you want coffee? Iced orange?"

"No . . . no thanks. Do you know who young Justin did take to the concert?"

"I can't guess. Prue Grant?"

"No."

"Another of my pupils, then, I take it."

"No."

"Then how could I—? Ah. Ravenna Marsh."

He nodded.

"How did he know her?"

"It seems Cha brought him here, tracking down the craft shop I'd spoken of. I'd seen a sort of waistcoat I thought she'd like . . . I can't get the hang of that young man. Cha likes him, and on the whole I'd trust her judgment. And this morning, he didn't seem obnoxious; but the clothes, and the hair, and the make-up . . ."

"Earrings and attitude?"

"You've seen him."

"No. I generalize about the type . . . Robert: suppose I see a man in a suit, an ordinary dark gray suit, with a pale blue shirt and a dark blue tie. He has polished black shoes and hair that's short back and sides. He's clean-shaven and his hands are clean too. Now, is he a stuffy conventional hidebound timid man? Is he a slick operator, a trickster? A stolid nine-to-fiver? An intuitive bloke with intelligence? An office zombie? He's wearing the uniform. He's wearing the clothes a million men feel comfortable in because they can't be noticed."

"I'm with you."

"Stop smiling. Then there are the jeans and teeshirt and trainers brigade. They're in uniform. The teeshirt may make a statement or it may not. It can be used to state conformity with a group, like Save the Whale or Zap a Pig." Her hand wrote across her bosom, distracting him. "And then there are the leathers brigade. They want to be *that* kind of different, in a uniform they feel at home in. Maybe they are

189

zonked-out tearaways. Maybe they are nice kids who need to express something wild, an image that's not conforming to images. Some of them are looking for trouble and they find it and it's you."

Her finger jabbed at his chest. Her eyes were sparkling, and he smiled again, the rare and genuine smile unlike the stark professional one. "I'm still with you. You're telling me that Justin Rafferty feels at home in the leather image, and I don't find the idea excessively reassuring; suppose his idea of the image leads him to act it out on the motorway at top speed with Cha on the pillion. Or if he feels that his type should treat her in a certain way?"

"From what I know of Charlotte, she would not stand for it. According to her, he's not insensitive. She told me about him when I was around at your place yesterday with her folder. His childhood was a rotten one. His father was on drugs; he sounds to have been a violent psychotic. He terrorized them all, made life a misery. Then Justin was fostered; then sent back to his parents because they were supposed to have got themselves back together, but habit was too strong; and in a way luckily, so was Justin by now, because he sent his father to hospital for eight stitches and was put back in care himself."

Bone did not find this a settling piece of news. Might there be a pattern of violent attack . . . Fenny had berated Ravenna. Would Ravenna cover for Justin if he had murdered her stepmother? Or did she not know?

He returned to his picture of Justin in the Paleys dining room. It was not the picture he had been conjuring just now. There was no match.

Grizel abruptly leaned forward and put her head to his chest. "Lower your blood pressure," she commanded. "Stroke a cat."

He stroked the crisp pale hair; her skin smelled warm, comforting but at the same time stirring. It had associations. He said, "It may be good for my blood pressure but it's hell on the pulse rate."

She laughed. To distract himself he changed the subject.

"Cha seems to have talked at length yesterday. I hope she didn't make a nuisance—"

"No, Robert, she didn't. Indeed she very sweetly said she hoped she wasn't. But her problems are your problems and are therefore mine. And besides—" she raised her head and looked at him, deadpan—"I'm still her form mistress."

"Ah, I forgot that. She's entitled to bother you." He pressed her nose with a gentle forefinger. "I'm grateful. I can't tell you how it's bothered *me* that there hasn't been a woman she can talk to. My sister's not on her wavelength at all."

"Is she the one who calls her Charlie Warlie?"

"When did that come out?"

"In registration once. Did you know Cha has more nicknames than anyone else in the form? . . . Doesn't she talk to Nichola Grant?"

"Prue's mother is so active a social worker that I don't know she has time even for Cha."

"But I gather she's been very good to Justin."

"Justin is Borrioboola-gha," he said, "a heathen, alien and therefore deserving case. I'm the same with my own job. I've tried pretty hard to have time for Cha, but the job—"

"The job is murder," she said elliptically. "In any case, Cha's a remarkable girl."

"Is she really?" Bone asked, doubtful but immensely cheered. "I'm not a fair judge. I merely think she's magnificent. When I look back to the time after the smash, when they told me she might not walk or speak properly again . . . at the best she *might* make a partial recovery."

Grizel made a derisive sound. "How could they know?"

"I suppose what she has achieved is 'partial' recovery. To be fair, she can sound somewhat garbled when she's upset."

"She told the class that the X-ray of her leg looks like a junkyard . . . I don't think you need worry about Charlotte. She has an amount of good sense beyond her years."

"But boys——"

"Boys come and they go. So long as she doesn't begin to feel she has to champion Justin, he'll probably drift out of her life sooner or later."

"M'm. A good warning."

He thought: Let's hope we don't have to arrest him.

17

Bone reached the station refreshed and in a more positive frame of mind. The half hour with Grizel had given him a good deal to think about, but it had also released the concentration on Paleys and its troubles, as if by attaching him again to his own life and the world outside. Parents and children, he thought. I'm apt to be too intense about Cha's disabilities, too protective. I could become possessive; would Cha behave to Grizel as Ravenna did to Fenny, resenting and quarreling? But would Ravenna not have done the same to her own mother?

As a policeman he came into contact with families abruptly and in crises. Their past life might have relevance, in which case he would come to know of it. Normally he knew little.

No sooner had he arrived than Ferdy Foster was on the line. An interesting little item, he told Bone. "We have talcum traces in the hair of the head and on the temples. The marks on the jaw and cheeks and brow are bruises, and the disposal of talcum is consistent with where finger joints would be if the head were gripped either side; the finger joints and hollow of the palm would retain talcum, and transferred it to the hair when the hands were pressed hard to the head. I'm sure you're pleased."

Bone was pleased, but to Ferdy he was not going to admit it.

"How soon can your grossly overpaid department tell me what kind of talcum powder it is?"

"If we had no need to wait our turn at the spectrum analysis you would have it speedily. As it is, Fate has placed you after fifty paint samples. Happy waiting."

Locker, apprised of this, said, "Shay's at Adlingsden. He can collect samples for comparison."

"He can enlist Patty Bates. She could do it without upsetting people."

Things were going forward.

Patty had no trouble getting a shake of powder into the plastic envelopes. She brought each one to Sergeant Shay for him to label so that there could be no mistake. She rather enjoyed the job, which he assured her should eliminate all who were innocent, though he did not explain why. She herself was inclined to think Fenny's death was an accident, because there could be no one who could want to kill her.

Coming out of Mrs. Marsh's bathroom, she remembered there was a talcum flask in the bedroom too, and she took the sample to the sergeant with a request for another little envelope. The house slept in the afternoon, Mrs. Marsh still giving Jake his tea, no one about. It gave her a start, therefore, when she had just finished getting the sample, to see in the dressing-table mirror Mrs. Marsh coming in. She lined up the talcum flask with the hand cream and scent, and turned around to smile at Mrs. Marsh and glance around the room as if she were checking it all. She felt she was quite an actress.

"Did Jake like the honey?" she inquired.

"Yes. He seemed quite pleased with it." Mrs. Marsh suddenly smiled. "You worry too much." She sat down on the little sofa and said, "I told you that you and I can manage very well. You mustn't be so nervous. It's not as if you were a stranger here, or not good at looking after us. We'd never have got dear Anna to take any holidays at all if she had not been so confident that you knew it all; and we are so thankful that you could come in this emergency. My dear, you truly are a godsend to us."

Warmed and relaxed, Patty said, "I wish the police would let up, though. I mean, let us get on with things after such an awful accident."

"It will take Jake quite a time." Mrs. Marsh's face was shadowed.

Patty thought: And you, too. You don't think of yourself, but all these shocks have been bad for you. It's always Jake.

"You need to rest," she said. "It seems to me you and Jake ought to have a holiday. To get away for a while."

The worn look on Mrs. Marsh's face lifted and she gave Patty a wry smile. "Yes. That's exactly what we do need. Well, we'll see. At least *he's* free of suspicion; the police know where he was."

"Oh yes. They can't suspect Jake. Though I had to tell them he wasn't in his study."

"He wasn't? You mean this morning?" she said sharply, sitting up.

Alarmed at Mrs. Marsh's alarm, Patty said, "Well, he wasn't, when I looked in. Perhaps he was in—in the bathroom. I mean, if Mr. Marsh said he was in his study, then he *was.*" She could have bitten her tongue, seeing that anxiety. "They know he wouldn't have hurt her, Mrs. Marsh. You mustn't worry."

She saw Mrs. Marsh regain control of herself, calm down. For not the first time, Patty was glad she hadn't any children herself. They could put you on the rack. She'd seen it, as she saw it now.

"Yes. Thank you, Patty."

Patty took herself off to Sergeant Shay with her little packet of talcum. She would have liked to reassure Mrs.

Marsh, to tell her that she had been collecting evidence herself that would clear everybody, but the sergeant had been so impressive with his "No one—*no one!*"

Ysobel sat still for a moment. Her face showed indecision and pain, but it was the indecision that gave way. She reached out to pick up the phone.

"Those newspaper men! I very nearly didn't answer the bell. Come through, Mr. Bone. We're about to have tea on the terrace."

Bone following, with Locker, Antonia Thorn's upright back as she crossed the parquet of the big, low-ceilinged room, considered the difference in expression that had come over her face when she saw them. She had looked up the slope of the courtyard, her hand shading her eyes, and the severity had quite vanished as she identified them and set out at once for the gate. It was not so often that he was welcomed by those he had to visit, and he felt, as often before, traitorous as she took him by the arm and drew him out through the garden door onto the terrace. It stretched the width of the house and beyond, a paved width bordered by a low parapet and steps down to a grass lawn. Beyond the lawn a long hedge hid the next part of the garden.

He had expected from her words to find both her brother Lewis and her nephew Chris at tea there around the inviting table. Instead, something resembling a wounded crow started up from one of the chairs and went flapping off, down steps and across the grass screeching "Chris! Chris! It's the police!"

"Well, I was in fact going to ask her to tell them you are here." Antonia looked a trifle bemused at such unexpected helpfulness from her great-niece. Ravenna fled on down the grass, black hair tossing, black tunic and leggings giving a bodeful touch to her speed. Antonia, pointing at a spindly iron chair for Locker to fetch from a little further along the terrace, ushered Bone to Ravenna's place. They all watched her hurtle down a hazardous flight of rough stone steps and disappear around the end of the tall hedge. Since they were higher than the third terrace, she came into their view again, gesticulating on the stone border beside a stretch of water that ran, again, the width of the house below. This water so darkly reflected the surrounding hedges and trees that Bone, used to pictures of Mediterranean blue swimming pools, had not realized this was one. Ravenna, agitated on the stone margin, still advertised the presence of the police. Her manner suggested an alarum, not a social invitation to tea.

His gaze, roaming over the dark water, rested appreciatively on two statues poised in gray and graceful contemplation against the dark of the far hedges. In the side hedge near where she danced about, a small classical pavilion, like a summerhouse, made a recess. From this now emerged Chris Thorn, holding his father in his arms, a long bundle of limbs. Bone's mind ran by habit to thoughts of accident; but the accident had occurred to Lewis Thorn a long time ago, and was caused on purpose by an enemy pilot with a thumb on the guns. Chris was talking to Lewis cheerfully as he arranged him, hidden by the hedge. Dom's voice chirped too, and he came toiling to stand on the steps and stare at "the police" heralded so loudly by his sister.

"Lewis loves swimming," Antonia said. "It's one of the things left to him." Bone imagined the freedom of it, water's buoyancy lending a sense of life to heavy limbs. "I'll bring the tea," she said, and left them.

"Wonder how he gets up here?" Locker's question was answered by the whine of the electric wheelchair. Lewis appeared on a path that wound in a great arc among the hidden reaches of the garden to circumvent the steep slope. The chair seemed to belt along. "It wasn't for caution he got his medals in the war," Bone observed. Chris, in a faded green toweling kimono, came up the crooked stone steps with something of his father's speed, tucked Dom under one arm and listened to Ravenna's low urgent talk as they came. She broke off as they reached the terrace and he brought her to the table with an arm about her shoulders. It looked protective.

Dom, set down, ran off barefoot in his bright red shorts,

making an engine noise. Chris stood with his back to the sun and said, "Not given up the case, then, Super?"

He was the man to make everyone feel overdressed when he was in swimming shorts and frayed toweling. He came to stand in front of Bone and looked down at him, bare feet planted on the stone flags, combing his wet hair back with his fingers. Ravenna sat down on the grass verge beside him; both had the inimical stare which in Chris looked arrogant, in Ravenna strangely like apprehension. Neither of them glanced at Antonia coming out of the house with a tray, or at Lewis trundling now more sedately along the terrace toward them.

"I need to have a word with you, Mr. Thorn."

"Oh, but you must have some tea first." Antonia put the tray on the white ironwork table with an admonishing clatter. "It's four o'clock."

There was no argument with that fact. Besides, Bone knew he would be unpopular with Locker if he refused to wait; nor did he wish to imply urgency, and he wanted to know what was upsetting Ravenna about their arrival. It seemed as if she, too, was implicitly accusing Chris by her obvious concern.

Lewis Thorn came up and placed himself at an angle, almost facing the house, his right side to the company. Chris sat, and Antonia's inquiries about milk and a distant engine-noise from Dom were the only interruptions to the poised silence, until Bone spoke. They all looked at him with a sense of *Here it comes.*

"Who designed this garden?"

"My grandfather," said Lewis after a moment. "He had the advice of an American architect with grandiose ideas. Grandpa adopted some, junked some."

Antonia clipped a metal tray to the arm of his chair, and put his teacup and plate upon it. She was offering sandwiches and scones when Chris said curtly: "We'd all be obliged if you'd stop the farcical chit-chat and ask what you came to ask."

"You speak for yourself," his father said as curtly. "Mr.

Bone is polite enough to postpone his inquiries and accept your aunt's invitation to tea."

"He's not *Mister* Bone, he's *Detective-Superintendent* Bone," Ravenna said, shaking her head at Antonia's proffered plates. "He didn't come here for tea and gardens."

"Ravenna, have a scone and shut up," her grandfather advised her.

"I don't want a scone and I'm not going to shut up. I want—"

"I don't know why we have to go through this every generation." Lewis's voice rode down hers with very little increase in force. "Your mother too had spates of retreating into childish bad manners when she was bothered by life."

"Everyone does," Antonia said, as trenchant as anyone. She sat down, unfurled a small rectangular gauze umbrella and fitted it over the plates of food and the milk jug and sugar, and went on, "I don't know how we survived the adolescence of Chris and dear Kingsley, but we did, so I expect we'll survive Ravenna's too."

"My children appeared sometimes to carry their rivalry even into attempts to prove who could be the more brattish." Lewis put his empty teacup onto the table, and Bone passed it to Antonia.

"You've mellowed," Chris said. "You're softer with Ravenna than ever you were with us."

"She's not my responsibility. I can afford to charm her. You and Kingsley were a different matter."

"They couldn't even go swimming without races and contests—who could stay under longer, who could swim more lengths." Antonia sent the filled cup back to her brother.

"I could stay under longer," Chris remarked.

"She could swim longer in winter, though," Antonia countered.

Dom, now an airplane, came banking along the terrace and taxied to the table. "May I have one of those please and a piece of cake and can I eat them by the pool?"

Antonia supplied the scone and the cake and forbade the

pool, and Dom sauntered away to the end of the terrace, to sit on the steps there. She said, "We've told him that his mother has had an accident. The truth will come gradually. Jake agrees we should keep him here for the present. By the time school starts he'll have to know what happened, because the other children will know and talk."

Chris, eating cake, said, "Kingsley could swim through the winter only because of female adipose tissue." Bone was reminded poignantly of Wednesday's discovery, but if Chris remembered it he did not show as much by even a flicker. "She was too pig-headed to lose—couldn't admit when I'd won."

"There I can declare both of you totally equal," said his aunt.

"I don't know how you can *talk* like this . . ."

After a second's silence, in which they contemplated Ravenna's bent head and Bone's mind still explored sibling rivalry, Lewis spoke.

"I'm sorry, Ravenna. It's the way we find it easiest. We'd got used to the idea of her not being alive any more some time ago."

Ravenna scrambled to her feet. "Yes, you can cope with everything so terrifically and you all knew her so much better than I did and you're all so civilized—"

Chris's arched nostril seemed to convey distaste for this drama; he said, "You'd damn well better accept that people do have their own ways of coping. *You* go off to a pop concert, while Aunt Antonia cancels a dinner with friends. And Mr. Bone has no doubt seen every possible permutation of human reactions to loss. He could tell you, but he's not going to. He's going to sit there with a cup of tea and a scone, demonstrating how to behave when you don't want something you're offered. Did the Superintendent brusquely shake his tresses? No, he did not. He took a sip of tea and politely destroyed the scone on his plate to make it look eaten . . ." but his father's snorting laughter stopped him.

"Don't *get* at me," Ravenna grumbled. Chris flung an arm around her, and patted her hipbone. She swung away from him and strode off down the terrace to sit beside Dom. Chris reached for a wedge of walnut cake, and Bone considered the rivalry still. There had been such triumph in that "I stayed under longer"; Kingsley had stayed under for fourteen years. He said, "You're writing an article, you said, about your sister for a geographical journal. Do you write about your own travels?"

"It helps to pay for them," Chris said.

"My son is not unknown in that field," Lewis remarked.

Bone took this as understatement intended to be a small reproof, and was amused at his own irritation. He found himself saying, "Architecture is my interest," as if to assure these people that he was not illiterate. The telephone rang somewhere in the house, and Antonia went in to answer it.

"You wanted a word with me," Chris said. "What about?"

Bone rose, and Lewis said at once, "Give me a decent-sized wedge of that cake and I'll take myself off."

Chris saw to this request, and sat down again, resuming his expression of slight boredom with the methods of the police.

"Your early morning walk, Mr. Thorn," Bone began, as Lewis's chair whined off along the flagstones; but Antonia appeared in the doorway and said, "Oh, those early morning walks. He'll come in soaked to the skin if it's raining. Phone is for you, Chris . . . I'm always relieved, let me tell you, when he has a book in progress so that he's writing instead."

"Or when I'm away and you don't know I'm doing it." Chris gave his aunt a smile of considerable charm in passing her, and disappeared into the dimness of the house.

"Won't you have some more tea? Cake? Good. Mr. Bone? I'm afraid my nephew was right, you weren't hungry . . . I do wish Lewis wouldn't do that. The instructions that came with the chair specifically say you mustn't."

Lewis, with Dom on his lap, was circling Ravenna.

Chris's voice, heard in the house somewhere, now ceased and he came through the sitting room into the sun. "I'll be off to Paleys shortly, Aunt. That was Ysobel; she's located the portrait photograph, the one I wanted; it's in Jake's desk and she doesn't want him to be bothered about it, another bit of cotton wool for Jakie-poo; *so,* she is getting Morgan to distract Jake with a refreshing stroll in the garden. I'm to be there in half an hour."

"Then you've time to take that jam around on your way."

"Is it of the utmost importance that the Westbournes have melon and ginger jam this very evening?"

"I was taking it with me last night, dear, if I'd gone. Of course I can take it tomorrow morning after church. They only want it for tea on Sunday." Antonia was loading the tray.

"On the windowsill, is it?"

"Yes." She picked the tray up and climbed the steps to the house. "Thank you, dear."

They waited while her footsteps retreated, and Chris said, "What about my walk, Superintendent?"

"We were hoping you could pinpoint the time more closely."

"Well, I can't."

"You were absent from the house from about six until eight."

"I was. Walking steadily. If you doubt the time, I could repeat the walk with one of your men, but that would not, naturally, prove I did it this morning."

"Naturally," said Bone. Ysobel's phone call to him had said that she'd seen Chris coming down the stairs "a little after seven," dusting his hands and looking pleased with himself—a not uncharacteristic look, Bone thought. She had been sitting waiting for her breakfast, with her curtains still drawn, "the door a little open as I like it to be." Seeing Chris had startled her because she had not heard him: "He always walks so softly." Bone had noticed this, comparing Antonia's footsteps across the floor. It was not evidence; her having seen him was another matter. Ysobel could not realize the importance of what she had remembered if she was still thinking about Chris's article on Kingsley rather than the possibility opened by his being in the house at seven. Bone had merely cautioned her to say nothing about it to Chris if she saw him.

Conviction was growing in Bone that he needed to be at Paleys. He said to Locker, "We must be off," and Locker got to his feet, thriftily putting all the rest of his piece of cake into his mouth.

Antonia, coming through the sitting room, said, "Oh, have you got to go, Mr. Bone?"

"I'm afraid so."

"I'm sure he's off to arrest the murderer," Chris remarked patronizingly. "Good luck and don't forget the cuffs."

Locker regarded Chris as if he thought cuffs would make an interesting accessory to the earring. Dom, running up at this point, showed every sign of wanting to accompany Antonia as she escorted Bone out, but she firmly redirected him by the shoulders toward Ravenna, who, to Bone's surprise, held out her arms. Dom ran into them and she crouched and hoisted him up. Cuddling Dom, she continued to glare at Bone as if she had rescued her brother from police attack. Bone hoped for Dom's sake that Ravenna would be a help when he heard the horrible news about his mother. What sort of a hand would Jake be at bringing up his son by himself? Ysobel's devotion was a doubtful factor, smothering rather than strengthening, and Morgan Carradine's help was problematic.

Antonia shut the oak front door of Beeches behind her with care, and set off at her slow pace up the gravel, Bone and Locker matching her steps. Arriving at the gate, she turned to Bone and spoke with the same deliberation.

"There is something you must know, Mr. Bone. Something that concerns Fenny."

Bone was silent, but he felt a quickening of the pulse.

"Yesterday, when she came to bring Dom here because of Anna's funeral, she was in a sad state." Antonia paused and looked down at the flakes of rust on her fingers, dislodged in grasping the gate. "Of course I thought it was the dreadful business of the funeral and poor Kingsley, but it was more than that." She raised her eyes, a clear gray under their hooded lids. "She told me she was troubled about Jake."

She paused again, and Bone offered one of his statements intended as a question. "That he was drinking too much."

"Oh, that!" Antonia brushed this aside with a sweep of the hand. "That's nothing new! No, this was about that *Late Lady* woman."

"Morgan Carradine."

"I suppose it's a stage name; rather a good one, if so. But yes, it was about Jake because of Morgan Carradine."

"There was something new to distress her about that situation." He had believed Fenny when she said that she liked Morgan and that, with Jake, there was bound to be somebody. She could live with it, he thought, and he had admired her courage.

"Morgan Carradine had turned up at Paleys yesterday morning quite unexpectedly—Fenny knew she was coming for the weekend but she never thought she would come to Anna's funeral and she was quite touched. Well, she wasn't there for that." A little breeze had got up and teased at some strands of hair around Antonia's cheek. Again she looked straight at Bone. "She was there to ask Fenny to divorce Jake."

Why Morgan should suddenly want something she had seemed content to lack until now, Antonia, in a rigid voice, told him.

"She said to Fenny that she was going to have Jake's baby. It was more of a shock to Fenny than you can imagine: she has had three miscarriages, two since Dom was born. Jake loves children, he would like a houseful—provided," Antonia added with acerbity, "they don't disturb him while he was writing . . . But Fenny was in tears when she told me all this. She adored Jake—you probably saw that—and she would do anything for him except lose him. She said to me that she even offered to that Morgan woman to bring up her child with Dom; but divorce Jake she would not."

The breeze blew the ends of Bone's tie. Happy voices and

the high moan of Lewis's chair sounded somewhere in the garden.

"Does anyone else know about this?"

"I surmise that Jake does. And Ysobel insisted that she did not think it right for her to interfere." Again the edge to Antonia's voice told that she knew what weight Ysobel's words had with her son. She turned the key, and the gate swung to let them out with a creak that grated on the ears.

"I came to the conclusion that I should tell you this, private though it is. If Fenny has indeed been murdered"— and she gripped Bone's arm suddenly, hard enough to hurt—"you must catch whoever did it. Soon."

18

As they climbed into the car, Bone said, "Get on the blower for a WPC to meet us at Paleys, Steve."

"You think it *was* Morgan Carradine, sir? Do we have evidence enough for an arrest?" He relayed Bone's request. The action allocator said at once that a WPC was doing house-to-house at Brantley, which must be about Chris Thorn's early morning walk; she would be directed to go to Paleys.

Bone had not answered; he was staring ahead with his shut-off look. Locker supposed he was operating on "feel." Years of working with his Superintendent had given him respect for this feel. Most successful people in Bone's line of work possessed intuition that could take them to results by paths they themselves could not trace. With some officers it led to abuses, to fixing up a likely candidate as perpetrator, but Bone was among the orthodox who insisted on their intuition's being borne out by facts. Locker thought that Bone, at this stage, did not want discussion; but it was Bone who broke the silence.

"In your opinion, is Jake Marsh capable of killing his wife?"

"He did seem very fond of her. But I suppose you couldn't be positive, with his being so drunk. He could be drinking because he'd killed her. It seemed to me genuine how upset he was over his first wife falling out of the wall like that."

"You've a happy way of putting things, Steve. Was he distressed at her death, or at her appearing? And it can't have failed to cross your mind that he has managed to lose two wives in quite a dramatic way."

"A bit more than bad luck, sir? Just fit two episodes in his *Late Lady*—you reckon we're looking at that sort of imagination?"

"To dump someone as infill behind your garden wall after strangling them, to stick someone's face on a spike instead of a receipt, it's the stuff of horror stories. The Sundays are going to go to town on it in the morning. It would be worse if it were premeditated; but I'm coming more and more to think it's an inspired seizing of opportunity."

Their car had stopped in the middle of Rolvenden to let an old man lead a little boy on a tricycle across the street. Locker glanced at Bone. "You think they are linked, sir? Doesn't that make it unlikely it's Morgan Carradine? Surely she wasn't around in Kingsley's time."

The little boy on the tricycle, having achieved the other side of the street, waved at the car that stopped for him. Bone gravely returned the wave. Locker found himself wondering what age Bone's son, the baby that was killed with his wife, would have been now.

"You think Anna Dudley's death may be linked too, sir? If it was Jake trying to kill Fenny with that skateboard, would he have planned on coming back from the fête and shouting to her, to have her rush out and break her neck in front of her son? Isn't that too heartless?"

"A tricky thing to decide where a murderer will draw the line, or where he or she begins to feel compassion; if Anna Dudley's death was not an accident, someone was willing to put the blame on Dom in any case . . . I'm working on the premise that these murders, of Kingsley, of Fenny, were actually done out of love."

"Love." In his view, Jake did not feel "love" for Morgan, but according to Fenny and Antonia he passionately wanted more children, an incongruous desire in a writer who needed privacy and quiet to work in. Could Morgan Carradine, that cool, elegant woman, care so much about Jake that she would get rid of the wife who did not bear children, and step into her place? Would she have had the nerve? Chris Thorn had testified to her walking to and fro wringing her hands and talking to herself in agitation; easy enough to pretend, when she knew she had been seen, that she was rehearsing a script. Justin Rafferty, if one could trust a single thing that lad said, claimed to have seen a blue skirt go around the corner.

"You notice Morgan went to Ysobel first, Steve. She certainly knew her to be the powerful influence in Jake's life. She's the one we need to question. If we can get her into a corner we ought to hear all that we need."

Locker, who had his doubts as to whether Morgan would have confided any deadly intentions to Ysobel, merely asked, "But a sick woman, sir? She's very brave about it but you can see she's really frail."

Bone, leaning an elbow on the window sill, was smoothing his cheek with his thumb, a habit of his when thinking. "Go back to Anna's death, Steve. You were saying Jake wouldn't want Fenny to break her neck in front of Dom—"

"Mind you, he could have meant to leave Dom at the fête with Morgan and come back on some excuse or other."

"But he would have had to shout very urgently to bring Fenny down at a rate fast enough to cause fatal damage. Who did call out urgently, Steve?"

"Ysobel. But she really was having a heart attack, wasn't she, sir?"

"Oh, no doubt about that. I picked her up. And the doctor and the hospital were convinced too."

The driver swung them crunching over the gravel into the forecourt of Paleys. Locker was starting to speak when they saw the car already there.

"That's Chris Thorn's. He's been pretty quick, sir."

The driver, overhearing, felt himself in some way to blame. "He'll have come by Markham's Lane, sir. That's faster than Rolvenden but they had half of it blocked with roadworks last time I was along, so I came around; they must of cleared the road now. I'm sorry, sir."

"No harm done, Johnstone," said Bone. He was, as it turned out, wrong.

19

Bone, nodding to the constable at the door, which was hospitably ajar as usual, and ignoring the flare of cameras from the street, walked into the hall at Paleys for the fifth time that week. The polished wood floor, the light wood paneling, the sweep of polished stairs, the wall hanging—everything, down to the green fountain of a fern on the stand to the left of the door, was the same, except for one thing. Ysobel's door was shut.

Bone knew again that quickening of the pulse, though with no reason. He hesitated at the closed door, but it was from the back of the house that a shout came, a shout muffled by doors and walls but alarmed and furious. It seemed to be from Jake's study. They ran.

Bone flung open the study door and took in the scene as he advanced. Chris Thorn faced them, backed up against the wall and carrying a chair, its legs outward, as a lion-tamer does. The lion was Ysobel, her back in the indigo silk housecoat still turned toward them. Hearing them, she whirled around and stood for a moment, as Bone now did, staring. Her graying hair was as soigné as always, the neck of her housecoat showed a fall of cream silk ruffles. It was her face that betrayed disturbance. The delicate lines of it were distorted, the eyes wide, and in that second in which she took in their presence all her attention seemed to pass from them, to some inward sensation. She no longer saw them. Something dropped from her hand to the carpet: a knife with a red-smeared blade. Both hands now went to her chest and her throat arched. Bone came forward and Chris shouted, "Watch out. She's faking!"

Bone caught her as she fell. If this is faking, he thought as he took the weight, and looked down into the suddenly waxen face, the empty eyes, even Death is going to be taken in. Slight as she was, she felt unwieldy in his arms in a way he knew; bodies with no life in them appear to have a stronger pull from gravity. He saw the sofa nearby and carried her to it with her feet trailing. As he felt for a pulse, he heard Locker pick up the phone on the desk and dial.

"She had pills in her room." Bone could find no pulse and, laying his head to the cream ruffles, no heartbeat. It was too late for pills. The lavender scent he had disturbed was in his nostrils as he looked up to see Chris Thorn beside him. He had abandoned the chair and was nursing his forearm from which blood flowed, seeping through his fingers rapidly. Indignant and astonished, he said, *"She went for me.* You watch out, she pretended to have an attack. Snatched up that dagger, or she had it in her hand, I don't know, she bloody sliced at me when I went to catch her." He gestured and a gout of blood flew from his arm to land among Ysobel's pure ruffles.

"Is she dead, sir? I've sent for an ambulance."

"She meant to *kill* me! D'you realize that? She damn near got my heart."

"We'd better get that tied up for you, sir."

"She looked like a demon. What in Hell possessed her?"

Another voice tramped in. "My God, what the hell's going on? *Mother!"* Jake, looming in the garden door with Morgan behind him, had taken in the scene sufficiently to stride forward, push Chris aside and drop to his knees beside Ysobel. "Where's her pills? God, she's got to have her *pills.''* He patted her housecoat pocket and then looked up wildly, met Bone's eyes, and saw something in them that made him turn again to Ysobel and, as Bone had done, listen for the vanished heartbeat. He left his head on the ruffles, put his arm across his mother's body and said, "Oh God. Oh dear God."

Chris regarded him as one would watch a man who mourned a cobra. The blood from his arm had blotched his trouser leg and was making quite a mess on the study carpet.

"I'll fetch the first-aid kit from the car, sir," Locker said to Bone.

"She would have bloody killed me if she could. Why? Why on earth?" Chris was examining his arm where a jagged cut ran up from wrist to elbow. Bone's impression was that for possibly the first time in his life Chris had been glad to see the police.

Morgan had joined them. She whispered to Bone, "Is she dead?" It was the penalty of being very beautiful, and an actress, that she did not look quite real in her pity.

"I'm afraid so." It was the correct thing to say, but in this case perfectly untrue. The survival of Ysobel Marsh would have brought considerably more trouble than her demise.

Morgan moved forward to the bookcase where, on a waist-high shelf, a convenient space held a bottle and glasses. She poured, and took the glass to Jake, sank down beside him with an easy grace and touched his arm. Her dress glowed gentian blue in the evening sunlight.

Bone took Chris by the good elbow and steered him out of the room, having a word with Locker as to doctors and the ambulance as he went. In the hall, Chris halted and turned.

"Do you know what the *shit* this is all about?"

Locker sent Fredricks, who was at that moment arriving, out to the car for the first-aid box, and went once more to the telephone. "Come into the kitchen," Bone advised Chris. "You can wash that arm and Miss Fredricks will put a dressing on. Have you had an anti-tet jab recently?"

Chris turned on his heel and charged around the corner

and into the kitchen. It was a big room with bunches of herbs hanging, a red Aga, a long scrubbed table and Windsor chairs. One door led to the lane and one to the garden, or at least to a paved yard trellised off from the garden. Chris had got his sleeve rolled up and was busy at the sink.

"Yes, I've had all the proper injections . . . Was that woman out of her *mind?*"

"Perhaps. Tell me what she did."

"That phone call at Beeches was Ysobel. She knew I was wanting a picture of Kingsley, it's a studio portrait I didn't have, and it was in Jake's desk; so she had to organize Jake out of the way—you know she thought Jake was in the Sèvres or Meissen class and would shatter at sight of the photograph."

Fredricks arrived with the box and undid a dressing packet on the draining board. She got on with first aid while Chris talked.

"Well, Jakie-poo will have to come unstuck from the apron strings at long last. Will he survive, I ask? So when I arrived, Ysobel took me in there—the study—and was ferreting in the desk when she sort of sagged down and gave a moan. I went to help. She was clutching her chest and giving at the knees—I took hold of her arm, holding her up—and the most devilish look came over her face and her eyes came wide open and her arm moved. By that time I'd moved—go easy, girl, I'm not made of tin—and that damn little Damascus dagger sliced my arm. She was bringing it up from under just like a pro."

Ysobel had studied to be a doctor. She would know physiology. "So now you can tell me why. You're the policeman."

"I have conjecture. No proof."

"I suppose she believed I killed Fenny."

Bone's statement in answer did appear to bear this out. "She told me she'd seen you come down the front stairs here at seven this morning." Bone omitted the rest of Ysobel's description.

"Well, I didn't."

Fredricks, straightening up from the finished bandage, signaled to catch Bone's eye.

"Fredricks? Did you have luck?"

"I found a birdwatcher."

"What bird did he see?" Bone asked as Locker came in.

"She described a man who came up to Brantley Old Station, sir. At ten to seven this morning. He was about her husband's height and he's about six foot one. This man had an earring and short dark hair and a suntan." Fredricks had got out her notes. "He had a check shirt, she thought it was greenish."

"From Brantley to here in ten minutes?" Chris said. "Eat your heart out, Mercury." He rolled the bloodstained wreck of his sleeve above the bandage. "Ysobel tried to set me up."

"Evidently."

"She faked the heart thing to get me off my guard. I thought she was faking again when you came in."

"As before, when I came in it was the real thing."

He saw Locker catch on. "You mean on Monday, sir."

"On Monday. Mind you, all this can only for ever be conjecture. The three women who were there are dead."

It seemed a desolate statement.

Chris Thorn sat down at the long table. Fredricks evidently saw more in this move than Bone did, for she brought him a glass of water, saying something to him in a low voice about blood loss. Chris drank it off without remark, put the glass down and said, "To hell with Monday. Why did she go for *me, today?*"

"You were probably the patsy for Fenny's murder, Mr. Thorn. At the moment that's a guess. If she'd succeeded in killing you—if you hadn't been more alert and faster than she expected—" Chris looked down his nose, with a faint smile—"she would most likely have told us that you'd attacked her because she had seen you coming from the workroom this morning. But it's of no use to consider this; it's all guesswork."

A sturdy scrubbing of feet on the mat outside the garden

door heralded Patty, who gazed at the invaders of her kitchen with bewilderment and an effort at a smile.

"Are you back again? I've been shutting up the peafowl. They don't know they're due for sale, but Mrs. Marsh told me this morning that Jake doesn't like them and that they must go. Can I make you all coffee or something? Oh, Mr. Thorn, are you here for dinner?" Chris shook his head. "It does seem a bit soon to talk of getting rid of the peafowl, with Fenny loving them so. She said only a day ago that the peacock was so glorious and she knew exactly how the peahen felt."

She stopped in the middle of taking the kettle to the tap and said, "Is something wrong? Something's wrong, isn't it?"

Locker said, "Yes, Mrs. Bates: I'm sorry. Mrs. Marsh has had another heart attack. It was very violent and she didn't survive it."

She put the kettle down. "Mrs. . . . it'll be because of Fenny."

"I wouldn't be surprised," said Bone. "If the story is as I see it, it's tragedy."

The word hung in the quiet.

Chris said, "Did Ysobel kill my sister?" There was a gasp from Patty.

Bone had begun to hate this house. He said, "She may have done," and went to the garden door. Through the trellis that shielded the garden from the bins and fuel bunker of the kitchen yard he could see the wall. Its gaping hole was shored up with props and plank buttresses.

"Vicky Whitmore knew that Ysobel begged your sister to stay at home. I don't know if it had to do with the independence Kingsley insisted on."

"Jake had agreed to it when they married," Chris said sharply. "I thought he'd gone back on that and killed her. He didn't want her to go."

"I understand that although he hated her going, he was adamant that she should. Your aunt told us that Ysobel had given up a medical career for marriage. Her daughter-in-law would not match up to that; while, waiting in the wings and already deeply attached to Jake, was a woman who would always be at home and who was at that time pregnant."

He turned and said, "I repeat that this is totally conjectural. However, who has always been the strongest force in this house?"

He saw their faces—except for Patty who still stood at the sink, her head down. They watched him, Thorn intently, Fredricks impassive, Locker troubled.

"I don't know why she attacked you."

At this Patty turned, saw that Bone was addressing Chris, and for the first time took in the bandaged arm, and stared.

"Something made her think herself in danger, I suppose; and she believed she could put it all on you. She did not reckon on dealing with a man of quick reactions. She had become very confident. She overestimated her own strength." Here Patty again bent at the sink.

"More likely there was a threat to Jake than to herself," Chris said. Bone gave a slow nod of assent.

"Sergeant Shay was here this afternoon when she rang with her story about you. Mrs. Bates, you helped in collecting the talcum samples, didn't you?"

Patty turned around. She had been crying, and now pulled a piece of kitchen tissue from the roll by the sink and scrubbed her face dry. "Yes I did. But what has that got to do with it? Mrs. Marsh didn't know I was doing it, anyway. I can't believe any of what you're saying. How can you think Mrs. Marsh could do any such thing? How can you talk about her like this? She was gentle and considerate and thought of nothing but other people. She's dead and you're saying all these terrible things about her. She was so ill and frail!"

Chris snorted. "She wasn't too frail to slice my arm open, and she was aiming to get under my ribs at my heart. I've seen a blow like that in a dockside bar and I know what I'm talking about."

"How could she know about a dockside bar—"

"I'm sorry, Mrs. Bates," Bone said. "She had trained to be a doctor; she knew the direction such a blow must take." He could see in his mind's eye Chris fending off the mother tigress. "When you talked to her this afternoon, Mrs. Bates, when you collected the samples, was Jake mentioned?"

"I dare say he was," Patty said, "because Mrs. Marsh liked to talk about him. It *could* have been then when I told her he hadn't been in his study in the morning. You know I said to you I'd gone in and he wasn't there."

"I checked on that," Locker said. "Mr. Marsh said he was just outside lying on the bench. He heard you call him but he was busy working. He didn't want to be disturbed, he was angry but he didn't answer, but then he thought it might be urgent as you'd come in at all."

Chris said, pouncing, "So Ysobel thought Jake would be suspected and she cooked up a story nailing me. And I wasn't going to be able to contradict it. *De mortuis nil nisi bonum,* so let's say—no. I'll say I admire her. I admire her! It's classic."

"Yes," said Bone. "It is."

"I'll bet the Greeks had a prototype. Some lost text by Euripides."

"I *don't* believe it." Patty spoke almost to herself.

"You'd better believe it," Chris Thorn said. "The Super here has got it all worked out." His face was gleeful. "What about Fenny, then, Mr. Superintendent?"

"It was Paul Lackland's plans. He convinced Ysobel that Fenny was really anxious to run this workshop of his. She apparently even thought that Fenny was attracted to Lackland."

"Moonshine," said Thorn. *"Moonshine!* I never thought much of Fenny, and you know it, but she'd got taste. Paul Lackland! Ysobel was away up the wrong river there. But who'd have thought Ysobel could—"

He twisted around and stared at Bone, his face suddenly intent. Here it comes, Bone thought. He's seen it: Kingsley too.

"My sister," Thorn said. "It's a parallel."

Bone did not mention the second parallel, Fenny's pregnancy at the time of Kingsley's death, and Morgan's now, for that was Morgan's affair however much Ysobel might have taken it as hers too.

They were interrupted.

"No!" Patty cried in outrage. "I'm not staying here a moment longer. I'm going home. People can fend for themselves. I'm sorry. I'm not staying here where people are so heartless. If she did do anything terrible you should be sorry for her. You should! She was ill! Too ill to know what she was doing. It's been so terrible here that anyone could lose their mind. Saying you admire her, that's horrible. How you can make fun I don't know."

She was hurrying to the door, and as her footsteps fled up the back stairs Bone and Locker simultaneously signaled to Fredricks, who whipped out after her.

"M'm." Chris grimaced, as Fredricks' soothing tones could be heard overhead. "You must get a lot of incredulity in your line of business. I can't say even I believed it when Ysobel went for me with that dagger. I suppose she'd be counting on that."

The next half hour was busy. Bone sent Chris, in a borrowed Burberry of Jake's to cover his arm and stained clothes from the press vigil outside, home to Beeches driven by Fredricks, Johnstone following to bring her back; dealt, with quiet assistance from Morgan, with Jake's incredulity which was more forceful and a good deal more entrenched than Patty's—in his book, Chris must have inflicted the wound on himself in the course of frightening Ysobel to death; Bone talked to his Chief: Dr. Walsh arrived and, with Locker, carried Ysobel to her bed and called up the district nurse to lay her out; Patty had come down, silent, unreconciled but ready to make coffee and sandwiches; Bone went out and talked to the press. He asked for their sympathy for Jake Marsh whose mother had suffered cardiac arrest.

As he came back into the house, Locker from the dining

room door said, "We're in here again, sir." Patty had made cheese and pickle sandwiches and coffee, and had opened the dining room drinks cupboard. She was trying to be cheerful, and she had not gone home, so Bone accorded yet another good mark to Pat Fredricks.

"How do we deal with this latest turn-up?" Locker asked, pouring coffee. Bone's irrepressible imagination at once equated Locker's phrase with toes turned up and, rejecting the association of this with Ysobel, he thought instead of a marble monument he had seen in which, among the Jacobean, voluminous and convoluted pleatings of skirts and petticoats' hems, the upturned soles of the lady's shoes tidily emerged.

He was saying to Locker, "I talked to the Chief about it," when Sergeant Shay came in.

"It's Dr. Walsh, sir. He'd like to talk to you before he goes."

"Oh yes," Bone said, and Walsh came past him, in dark trousers, a charcoal shirt, and his habitual expression of menace.

"Came to say I've no hesitation in signing the death certificate, unless you think there should be a p.m. You saw it happen, you say. I've been expecting it at any time and when your message reached me I assumed that cardiac arrest had been caused by the shock of Fenny's death."

"Not quite as simple."

"No. I see you have sandwiches, and I've not eaten since breakfast."

Bone moved the plate toward him, and he took two and wandered down the room eating; he paused before Fenny's landscape embroidery and put a hand on it, then turned, swung a chair away from the table to make room and perched himself sideways on the polished mahogany to face them.

Bone said, "I should say it was caused by exertion. Ysobel had just made an attack on somebody with a knife, the one Jake used to keep on his desk as a paperknife."

"On someone?" Walsh raised his eyebrows. "On Morgan Carradine?"

"No, oddly enough." Bone saw that Walsh understood the whole situation at Paleys reasonably thoroughly.

"You didn't attempt resuscitation."

"No. With her heart . . ."

"She was not an old woman, but her heart really was in no condition for her to monkey about. The medication gave her too much confidence, I fear. I'd warned her about stairs, for instance, but she was again and again going up to borrow Fenny's scissors when her own went missing, or glue when hers ran out; but she was so absorbed by those scrapbooks. I suppose every paragraph and every picture that's ever been in the press about Jake is in those books, and it was more important to her to keep them up to date than were my prohibitions. Sometimes she would simply deny that she'd borrowed things—she'd put them in the sitting room, for instance, as Anna Dudley told me, and then she would say it must have been Dom."

"A bit childish," said Locker.

"No. She liked her world to function in a certain way and was quite good at refusing to recognize when it didn't. One problem for her was that she used to be pretty strong—the garden here was all her work originally, did you know? Then she fainted one day when she was lifting Ravenna from her cot."

"How old was Ravenna then?" Bone leaned forward and saw Locker glance at him for this show of interest. Walsh, opening his second sandwich to inspect the pickle, said, "About three, perhaps four."

"At about the time Ravenna's mother died?"

"Soon after that, I think." Walsh raised his eyes to meet Bone's. "I found Ysobel's heart was strained. No more digging, I told her, no more carting stones about. Rest, and you'll recover, I told her."

"I should have had this conversation with you before," Bone said. Walsh had been remarkably unsurprised at hearing of Ysobel's attack on Chris, and it seemed he knew more about Ysobel's mentality than Bone had realized.

"I don't know when we could have talked," Walsh returned. "This is the first time, I think, bar surgery hours, that I've sat down in three days." Taking advantage of this unusual sedentary position, Walsh was reaching out for another sandwich when a tap on the dining room door heralded a minor earthquake.

As Sergeant Shay's face appeared around the door, saying, "Sir, it's—" his announcement of who was there—or possibly *what*—was topped by the sounds of a woman shouting, a baby screaming and something resembling a pair of airplanes taxiing through the hall outside. All three men were on their feet and on course for the hall, and as Bone in the lead passed Shay he caught the words *"—a Mrs. Stannard,"* and saw Vicky with a crying baby in her arms standing in the open doorway of Ysobel's room. Her howling, unlike the baby's, had words.

"She's dead! Come and help! She's dead! Ysobel's dead!"

Bone did not blame Shay for leaving Vicky Stannard alone for a moment in the hall while he came to inform his Super of her arrival; Shay was not to know that Vicky was familiar with this house and had no hesitation in making free of it; that she had come, not to see the police, but to talk to Ysobel. Vicky had never been slow to barge in where she was not wanted, but the poor girl could hardly have looked to interrupt a sort of lying in state. She must have bent over the woman who lay with eyes closed, having a nap presumably, and, in her self-centered way, without compunction tried to wake her. It was a mercy that in discovering she was trying to wake a corpse she had not dropped the baby. It writhed in her arms, its mouth as wide as hers.

"Help! She's dead!"

"We know she is. Stop that, Vicky Whitmore. Give me the baby." Walsh had pushed his way past Bone and took charge of both situation and baby. The latter stopped crying as if he had pressed a STOP button, and squirmed to stare at him, confirming Bone's theory that Walsh's somber expression played a major part in the recovery of his patients.

"I went in there and *touched* her!" Deprived of the baby to hold, Vicky held her cheeks instead as the sobs still issued from her wide mouth. Bone admired the professional speed with which Walsh transferred the baby to his left arm and administered a sharp right-handed slap to Vicky's face, there being luckily plenty of Vicky's cheeks left over even while she was putting her hands to them.

The indrawn whoops she progressed to were echoed eerily at the end of the hall. The origin of the roaring airplanes was made clear as Jake, closely followed by Morgan, came around the corner from his study holding Vicky's two other sons each by an arm. The larger son, Max, now in jeans and a dirty white teeshirt with red spots suggestive of a multiple accident, was dragging his red and blue skateboard and kicking sideways at Jake's shins. Both boys were crying with energy and determination.

"What the bloody hell is going on? Who are these *ghastly kids?* They came right into my study—God! *Vicky!*"

Once seen, never forgotten, thought Bone, as Jake in his shock released the boys. They ran to their mother and butted her skirts hard enough to have toppled any woman of less sturdy construction. "Where have you sprung from?" Jake paused, as though the idea of Vicky doing any springing had its own improbability. Then he recoiled as Vicky, towing her clutching children, made a lunge at him.

"Oh Jake, I'm sorry. Poor, poor Jake."

Morgan could not from where she stood have seen the pure terror in Jake's eyes but all the same she was swift to his rescue. Stepping forward, she seemed to light up the dimness of the hall with that exotic moonshine of glamour that never left her. She drew an arm through Jake's and smiled in a kindly way at Vicky, who stopped dead in her considerable tracks, putting the brakes on her children and causing Max's skateboard to leave his hand and judder across the hall to the stair foot. If I'd been directing this scene in a film, Bone thought, fascinated, I'd do a closing-up shot on that skateboard exactly where it is, to call Anna Dudley to mind. It might be presumed that it did just that for Jake who, with a hoarse moan, snatched his arm free and fled back the way he had come, colliding with Patty who had emerged from the sitting room with a vase of dead flowers. The splash of fountaining water and the slam of his study door were all but simultaneous. In the tiny silence that supervened, the sound of a key turning in a lock could clearly be heard.

"Mrs. Stannard. Do please come in here." Bone gestured at the dining room whose door stood invitingly open. If Vicky was here to see Ysobel, he wanted to know why. Vicky hesitated, seized her baby from Walsh and starting up the crying with an invisible PLAY button, looked at Morgan, flounced (Bone felt he had not until now appreciated the weighty possibilities of this word) and, bearing her squalling baby past Bone and Locker, moved into the dining room and sat down.

The older boys had come adrift from their mother when she changed course to reclaim their brother, and they were now skillfully captured by Fredricks, who must have arrived at the front door in the course of the action. Bone had confidence in her ability to keep them quiet, if not amused, and he followed Locker into the dining room.

The baby, crammed with a sandwich taken instantly from the plate by its mother, offered no comment to what followed apart from a slurred guzzling.

"Do you mind, Mrs. Stannard, if we ask you a few questions?"

"I'd like to ask *you* a few, Mr. Bone. Why was I allowed to go in there and frighten myself silly with finding her dead?"

As he could not allow himself to answer this with the truth—that no one had been on hand to prevent such an uncalled-for move, and that, as for frightening herself silly, perhaps it was rather late in the day—Bone set his face to express, he thought, nothing. The effect was so stern that Vicky Stannard thought better of saying more.

"Oh, well. Anyway." She shifted as though to rid herself of the memory. The baby on her lap revolved its mouthful as a cow chews the cud, a process unfortunately quite visible. "I wanted to ask her something. I had to know, you see, absolutely had to." She stopped to look at Bone as though she appreciated his function for the first time. "You're the police! You should know about this."

Whether she meant to reprove or enlighten, Bone could not be sure but, clearly, she meant to pass on what she knew. She took another sandwich and parted it between herself and the baby, maternal instinct prompting her to this just when it was trying out its mouth for screaming rather than chewing. She put her half to her mouth, but desisted to say, "I've just come from visiting Daddy," before she ate. Bone entertained a brief vision of the Jack Russell terrier lying flattened in the Whitmore hall as in a Tom and Jerry cartoon.

"We were talking about poor Kingsley," she pursued, negligibly hampered by her mouthful. "Daddy was telling me what he'd read in the paper, how she'd been put into the wall: *tipped,* he said. Well, I'd all the time, since it came out, been seeing her as walled up, you know, brick by brick, like they did with nuns in old convents." The baby, chewing away, had been shredding the rest of its half sandwich, and now dropped some pickle from its mouth onto the table. Vicky, with all the professionalism of a mother, wiped it up on a quick finger which she put in her own mouth. "So I suddenly remembered." She halted, looking at Bone as if to impress the significance of this on him. He wondered if memory had never been her strong point, and felt how lowering it must be to find oneself the non-academic daughter of a schoolmaster.

"I remembered what I saw the night Kingsley left."

The baby belched.

"I was going for a walk along the lane. You see Daddy always went on about not bothering Kingsley and Jake. He had this *thing* about it, he never understood they didn't *mind* me being around, Kingsley said I'd made myself quite one of the family; but Daddy said I couldn't call more than once a day or stay more than an hour. It was simply silly but he always asked" (Bone noted that Whitmore's daughter had apparently never thought of lying) "so I'd had my hour or so; but I came out again when I was supposed to be in bed because I was sure Kingsley was going to leave at any time. I thought if I walked up and down I'd see her and I'd somehow thought if she really understood how much I wanted to go then she'd take me with her—" Vicky paused again and looked out of the window, and Bone felt a pang for the vanished impossible hopes of youth, desires for adventure so mangled by the approach of reality. The baby banged the air and stared at the recorder with its faint hum.

"You saw something while you were walking there?"

"While I was . . . ? Oh yes, I was walking back up the lane when I met Ysobel with the wheelbarrow. I was going to look in the kitchen window if they hadn't drawn the blinds, you could see quite well from the lane but now you have to stoop down to look in; but it was really quite darkish and I heard Ysobel before I saw her. We got quite a shock. Ysobel was really rather cross."

If she had done what Bone thought she had, this was not surprising.

"She asked why I wasn't at home and told me I shouldn't be wandering about at night. She made it sound horrid, she said *maundering* about, but she meant wandering. Well, it wasn't really dark, I mean there was a moon, and anyway, *she* was out, wasn't she? She said she'd been getting rid of a load of stones from the garden onto the stones they were putting down in the lane. She was always complaining about how stony the garden was. But you see, after what Daddy said today, I began to put two and two together."

Bone dismissed the unkind thought that this mathematical process was ordinarily a feat beyond her powers. She leaned forward and the baby pushed its fists along the table toward Bone, clearly enjoying the polished surface.

"Do you think it was *Kingsley* she'd had in that wheelbarrow? It could have been, you know. I never thought she *liked* Kingsley. Oh, she was terribly sweet about her but then she was terribly sweet to *me;* so I *knew.*"

Bone, looking at Vicky Stannard nodding at him, was well aware that you did not have to be clever to understand a situation perfectly.

20

Tuesday afternoon was the first moment that Bone was free to visit the small house on Adlingsden Green where Grizel Shaw lived. It was nearly a week after he had caught sight of her across the road from Paleys on the day Kingsley Marsh had come to light. They had briefly met and had telephoned, but every time he visited Paleys he had been aware how near she was; his duties and the loving attention of the press prevented him from seeing her again. She might have glimpsed him on South East Television, offering the usual soporific intelligence that the police were pursuing their inquiries. As he had said it, a vision of the road sign POLICE—SLOW had come into his head. How soon could he expect news from Forensic? The talc traces found in Fenny's hair might or might not be conclusive; he had an indistinct recollection of Fenny herself, in a moment of confusion when he asked her a question on Wednesday, holding her temples in both hands as if to squeeze the answers out. It could well have been a habit of hers when overwrought, and the morning of her murder she had had plenty to worry her brain before Ysobel Marsh drove a spike through it.

Alone for once, and in his own car on the way to

Adlingsden, Bone went over the arguments there had been with Locker over this. It might be a kind of chivalry in Steve that made him reluctant to accept the idea of a frail grandmother padding upstairs in her elegant indigo silk housecoat to murder her daughter-in-law; her *second* daughter-in-law. Locker was inclined to favor Patty Bates' theory that Ysobel, in so delicate a state of health, had lost her wits under the stress of losing her beloved Fenny when she attacked Chris Thorn. She could, Locker insisted, have believed Chris had killed Fenny in revenge for the believed murder of his sister, with or without Jake's help. Bone had answered that even so, she was guilty of trying to knife Chris Thorn, however excusable this might seem to anyone who had met him.

He slowed down as he approached Adlingsden and parked, in a spirit of defiance, not far from Grizel's cottage. It was too bad if her interested neighbor was in the front garden checking up on visitors; it was time he did what he chose to do without so much caution about everything.

Nevertheless, he sat for a moment longer in the car before getting out to cross to the cottage. Two pigeons, one brilliantly white against a dark cloud, cut the air above the green and, with a clatter of wings, landed on a roof that glowed almost coral in the sunlight. A man wheeling a cycle stopped for a chat with a woman in a flowered dress; she put down her shopping bag and eased her back as she talked. A car drew up on the opposite side of the road from him, by the group of shops that included the post office; the driver, unconscious of Bone's gaze, craned to look in the driving mirror, patted her gray curls and, turning, kissed her Alsatian before getting out of the car with her purse and basket. As she walked away, the Alsatian in the car met Bone's eyes with dignity. People are unpredictable, he reflected, in their devotion and how they will demonstrate it.

He was about to do some demonstrating.

Grizel's neighbor was absent from her garden but he thought a head moved behind an upstairs window as he walked down the path to Grizel's door. Her cat, known as The Bruce on account of its interest in spiders, came to meet him from a hiding place in the honeysuckle; he felt the dust from the shrub, and a withered flowerhead, in its fur as he stroked it. The door opened while he was straightening up, and Grizel stood there, smiling. She was wearing navy blue trousers, slippers of navy leather and a loose violet teeshirt with a scrawl of white across as though someone had dashed paint over it. Her eyes, even in the shadow of the porch, were as green as The Bruce's.

"Come in, Robert. I thought you'd come this afternoon. I even made some scones." There was an apparent consensus among Bone's female acquaintances that he was too thin. The Bruce ran ahead, clearly galvanized by the word of scones, and disappeared into the small stone-flagged kitchen at the back. Bone waited until Grizel had shut the front door and then they stood for a long minute, arms around each other, her head on his chest, without saying a word.

When Grizel finally released herself it was with an irrelevance: "I had the term staff meeting this morning. One always starts the year so hopeful . . ." She looked up at him. "You've had a horrible week, Robert. I saw you on the news."

"Cha says I was looking tired and cross. But the tie she gave me for my birthday looked very healthy, in her opinion."

"You did look tired. No surprise, after what you've had to cope with. Poor Fenny Marsh. I only met her once or twice but I liked her a lot. Do you know who did it yet, Robert? Or mayn't I ask?"

He had followed her into the kitchen where, in a warm smell of baking, she was filling the kettle.

"I don't feel that you'll rush out and tell the press anything I have to say."

"The press! The whole village is furious with them and the TV people. Not a single decent picture of the green, and Mr. Fosgrove had his begonias trampled to a mush when they stepped back to get a shot of poor Jake driving off." She opened the pine corner-cupboard and took out pairs of cups, saucers and plates of honey-colored earthenware edged with brown, which she handed to Bone. He picked up the tray to put them on, a tin one decorated with Windsor Castle in sepia, like a Victorian photograph. "You don't think Jake did it, do you? The wretched papers are doing a ghoulish hint at a sort of Bluebeard act. Two wives, one in the wall and the other—I don't think they dared to hazard where he might have stashed poor Fenny, given the chance."

He felt the relief of hearing someone talk who was not concerned with the Marsh family. "No, I don't think Jake did it."

Grizel lifted a hand from loading scones onto a hot plate, to touch affectionate fingers to Bone's face. "Dear Robert. I love you in particular when you're being official."

The Bruce all of a sudden exploded from floor to window sill, neatly landing between two busy-lizzie plants to settle his haunches and supervise the garden. Grizel made tea.

"I'm so sorry for Jake Marsh. First Anna Dudley in that awful accident falling downstairs, then his first wife discovered like that, and then in the same day Fenny and his mother dying. I suppose it was too much for her, only back from hospital on Wednesday. She always struck me, when I saw her in the village, as a very calm woman, very much in control, almost regal. She lived for Jake."

"You might say," Bone remarked, following her into the sitting room with the tray, "that she died for him."

Grizel knelt by the coffee table and began to arrange the cups in their sauces. "You're baffling me, Robert. I decline to play Watson, but tell me, Mr. Holmes, how did Ysobel die for her son?"

Bone at the window listened to the chink of cups behind him and, watching a gold-topped mountain of cloud slip almost imperceptibly behind the church tower at the top of the green, said, "You understand, we have not yet got proof, and for some of it we may never have it. What I'm saying is strictly guesswork."

"I'm prepared to understand anything. Come and get your scone while it's hot."

As he settled into the blue armchair, Grizel poured his tea and put the plate of scones within reach. "Now it's September it's no longer touristy to have scones and cream. That's plum jam, not strawberry. Do you mind?"

Bone's helping showed that he did not. Grizel, drinking her tea, watched him; Charlotte was right, he looked tired. The faint biscuit color he had acquired during the summer had faded to his usual pallor, and the afternoon sunlight picked out the silver in the blond hair. She asked no more questions, knowing how hard it always was for him to talk. Reaching for another scone, he said, "I—and I mean myself, as Steve Locker thinks otherwise—believe Ysobel Marsh killed both her son's wives and was responsible for Anna Dudley's death."

"Good grief!" Grizel set down her cup askew and stared at him. "You must have reasons. What on earth are they?"

Bone told her. She left her tea untouched while she listened and then, when he had done, she fiddled with the jam spoon, thinking.

"So Ysobel murdered Kingsley because she would go off and desert Jake and little Ravenna; and Fenny because she was going in for this sewing and knitting scheme? And she must have got the idea that Fenny had decided to abandon the family and, in a sense, shack up with another man. That Fenny didn't even like Paul had obviously not got through to Ysobel. Or she may have thought Fenny saying so was a blind. People with obsessions see only what they want to see. She truly wanted Fenny to stay and make Jake happy."

"Certainly. She'd planned for that. Graciously allowed first Kingsley and then Fenny a place with her beloved and then believed they despised the privilege. Whatever line she drew, they each stepped over it without knowing."

"Poor Fenny! Then it was all that wretched Paul Lackland's fault really?"

"You could say his conceit killed her, I suppose. Anyway,

after he spoke to Ysobel on Monday morning, I think she planned to get rid of Fenny that afternoon; but she didn't know that Anna had come back from the Bank Holiday Fair for a cardigan."

"Didn't she hear Anna come in?"

"She didn't even see her. Ysobel used to sit with the door of her room open, so she thought she saw everything, but just because of that, people used the back stairs. Anna must have come in that way not to disturb her, because Ysobel had said she wasn't well, not well enough to go to the fête."

"So it was pure bad luck for Ysobel, and a lot worse luck for Anna, that when she called out for help, it was Anna who came running. Why didn't Fenny come?"

"She was using the sewing machine. She heard nothing to interrupt her work for until Anna screamed."

"Why didn't Ysobel hear the machine and think to shout louder?"

"I tried it out. You can't hear the machine much in the hall but it's fairly loud in the workroom. I suppose if Anna hadn't rushed to help, Ysobel would have called louder until Fenny did hear."

Grizel stared at the table. "What a terrible woman . . . Oh, have more cream. I'm neglecting you—if Ysobel were my mother-in-law I'd have reason to be worried."

Bone did not miss that she spoke as though they were already married. Here was the chance he sought, but she went on to speak. "Ysobel was really ill, though. She really had an attack."

"I maintain that she pretended to be in trouble to bring Fenny running down the stairs, and then she got a nearly fatal shock when the wrong woman landed at her feet."

"I can see that talking police shop at meals is going to be a problem for me."

Bone, electrified by the possibilities of this statement, dropped some cream on the rug; Grizel won the race to mop it up, and said, "I dare say Ysobel would have had a genuine attack even if it had been Fenny who died instead of Anna. Success rates as high in stress as failure does. Marriage rates the same as bereavement, did you know?" She looked up at him, folding the messy tissue; her eyes were clearest green.

Bone would have given a lot to know if she were teasing or innocent. All his practice of reading faces failed with her. As he was hesitating for the words to suggest they might try it out, she jumped up to cast away the tissue and take the teapot for refilling. The Bruce, coming calmly in from the kitchen, sat down before the marigolds on the hearth to launder his right hip, paying no attention to the baleful glare Bone absently directed on him.

"Your work," observed Grizel gaily, bearing the teapot back from the kitchen, "especially cases like this, must give you a very jaundiced view of the family. Do you talk to Cha about any of it?"

"I've hardly spoken to Cha, except in passing, for days. The paperwork on all this, not to mention routine bumf, has kept me busy, and Cha's hard at work on that biology folder you brought her on Friday. I fancy she'd meant to do more work before, but now it's term tomorrow and no time left." He sighed. "I don't nag her as I should, I suppose."

"Is she still seeing Justin, do you know?"

"I suppose if he's there at Prue Grant's, she does. Whether she knows I've questioned him over the business at Paleys—whether she knows he was even there—I don't know. He was very useful, too. His remark about a blue skirt whisking around a corner made me think of Ysobel's dressing gown as well as Morgan Carradine's skirt."

Grizel poured fresh tea. "You must see sides of people no one would dream of. I can't get over the thought of that kind, refined woman going upstairs when everyone thought she was too ill to risk such a thing, and—"

"Locking the door and advancing on Fenny. I know. When Paul Lackland knocked and heard someone inside it was very likely Ysobel."

"Why did no one hear Fenny cry out?"

"We don't know if she did. Someone may have heard and thought it was the peacocks; my hope is that she hadn't time—that it was too sudden. Ysobel was very strong for a frail woman; Chris Thorn said as much. People can do amazing things in battle when they're mortally wounded, and she was doing battle for Jake."

Grizel hunched over her knees. "If it wasn't so dreadful it would be very touching; but she never seems to have stopped to consider if Jake would have wanted Fenny dead."

Bone reflected not for the first time on how often people deciding what was best for others could bring misery to the ones they were trying to protect. Would Jake really rather have Morgan's child than the living Fenny at his side? In all this, there was the hidden and smothered jealousy of Ysobel for those who did not give up their freedom; but Jake had married women of that nature.

"And there are parents who commit suicide but are so anxious to spare their children grief that they kill them first. How can any parents bear—" She stopped, and Bone feared she was remembering he had lost his own son. "Robert, I don't know how *you* bear it."

He took the hand she held out to him, in both his.

"Do you think we could manage better together?"

Grizel tilted her head on one side to peer up into his face. She took breath and did not speak, then said, "Is that a proposal?"

"A proposal; whatever; when I look at my life it seems such a bloody selfish thing to ask; but this last week or so has shown me I can't do without you. I could have exterminated all the people who kept stopping me from seeing you."

"And who'd have arrested *you?*" She knelt up to kiss him. "Charlotte will be satisfied at last."

"Cha?" Bone was startled into drawing back from an embrace, and Grizel looked at him wickedly.

"When I saw her on Friday she said she was longing to be a bridesmaid and I was to stick a firework under you. But it's much more environment-friendly to use scones."

21

The wedding went swimmingly—that was Bone's impression. He had left Charlotte, preening herself as the sole bridesmaid, in the porch to wait for the bride, while he went up to the front pew. There were more people than he had expected; Grizel's side he had known would be fairly populous with her colleagues, some older pupils and ex-pupils, people from the village who knew her, and other friends. He could not look around to see who was there. However, quite a few were sitting on his side of the church, and he would have liked to know how there were so many, but powers of observation had deserted him. They were a blur of faces, but surely more than he had invited.

His suit felt stiff with newness. He could smell the rose Cha had threaded so carefully into his buttonhole, smell it above the damp stone and pine and mustiness of the church. He looked back toward the door, where Cha stood in the light, cream roses around the knot of hair on the top of her head, apricot ribbons streaming from this little coronet right down her back. Then she moved out of sight and the organ, that had been tootling pleasant nothings, faded itself out and launched suddenly into festive Vivaldi; the congregation rose, hiding the doorway from him, but a moment later Grizel turned the corner into the nave and came forward on her uncle's arm, smiling at him in the glowing shadow of an apricot straw hat, trim and slender in a cream silk suit he had not been allowed to see until now. The uncle, a tall military sandy-gray Scot, he had met that morning. Cha, pacing after them, was looking at Bone as he glanced, and gave him a tremendous wink. After this moment, he seemed to be concentrating so hard that he took in no detail at all.

Thoughts come pell-mell, faster than words. The vicar of Adlingsden had a good voice; luckily he had proved willing to marry a widower to a divorcee; Grizel had wickedly pouted "Because I am no' an adulter-rous woman . . ." There had been Fenny's funeral here, but this ceremony, equally natural in a church, gave a perspective to that whole bad business. Ravenna at the funeral had been startling among the somber colors in a jacket of flame and violet sewn with gold braid and crystal drops; Bone had recognized what must be Fenny's work, and understood the tribute that was intended. Now here he stood with Grizel at his side, Charlotte competently taking the bride's bouquet to hold beside her own. He was still amazed at his failure to see that she wanted him to marry Grizel. How did parents ever manage to understand their children's real needs?

He made his affirmation clearly, which was a relief as he had feared he would mumble or choke. Her hand lay in his, with a slight pressure. She spoke. They were married. They were in fact actually married.

The day held some small surprises for more than a few; Bone, watching his wife of five minutes sign her name in the vestry, saw that he had taken to himself a Grizelda Kinloch Shaw, and had the grace to murmur in her ear, "In our more tender moments I shall call you *Kinloch.*" His name was no revelation to her; Grizel's surprise he had no inkling of, but it was in seeing how often her husband in happy mood could smile in the way which made people smile in return. She saw that his sister Alison had his features but somehow wrongly arranged so that she appeared discontented and shrewish, not good-looking at all. Her sons, twins a little older than Cha, were fair boys rather pompous about their roles as ushers, though a slight pushing match developed as the bridal procession reformed.

Then outside the church they were all ambushed. A covey of Grizel's school class sprang out and showered them with rose petals, genuine ones, to shrieks of "Hurray Mrs. Bone!" There were also handfuls of corn-grains, flung with glee at this chance of pelting a teacher, however popular. Grizel made a quick decision; she tossed her bouquet—hurled it rather—into the midst of them as they stood clapping and cheering. It may have looked like retaliation, but it left their ringleader, Beverley Braun, chosen by Fate as the one next to marry. As she was built like a center forward and made up like a panda, with a character interestingly balanced between deviousness and determination, the future was full of potential for someone. Bone, with his own future on his arm, walked down the green in the golden sunshine, the great chestnut trees releasing leaves of gold and amber to fall on them like confetti, like blessing, as they made for Grizel's cottage at the foot of the green.

The reception, if such it could be called when it was only a small party for friends, was held at the cottage. She had been anxious about the weather, since they needed to use the garden to take the overflow from the two small ground-floor rooms. She had mustered garden chairs from all the neighborhood, ignoring Bone's suggestion that people could party upstairs in the bathroom and bedrooms just as well.

Beverley seemed to have organized her cohorts out of the way. Bone had feared that they were about to join the party. He and Grizel greeted those who arrived, and soon a happy noise of talk and glasses and cutlery pervaded house and garden. People strange to him, her neighbors, the tall Scots uncle, shook his hand, colleagues of his own were there, surprising him by their evident pleasure in his good luck. Cha, who to him looked enchanting in her apricot frock and crown of roses, moved through it all, talking with gestures and smiles more than with voice; here was Steve Locker with a glass, Inspector Blane, the Chief Superintendent trying to be jovial . . . able to circulate at last, Bone came on his friend Emily Playfair sitting with The Bruce on her knee in the secluded window overlooking the back garden.

"We certainly hope he and Cha's Ziggy will get on," he said. Both cats originated from Emily's household and were, at her suggestion, to have an acclimatizing week there to get used to each other on neutral but familiar ground.

"Leave it to me, Robert." She soothed The Bruce with a brown-speckled hand. "Getting *them* together will be a doddle."

He had smiled and nodded, before it came to him that she was adverting to the difficulty of getting him and Grizel united. He said, "It hasn't been so very long."

Cherry Locker went by with a glass; and Bone's sense of the just and fitting was satisfied at the sight of Cha's and Grizel's headmistress, the stately Miss Mallett, in a long jacket of Welsh tapestry, in converse with Grizel's military uncle.

Grizel's friend Nicola Garland, who taught Domestic Sciences, caught hold of one of the twins, who were now carrying food dishes, and he stood on a footstool to announce with panache, "Ladies and Gentlemen, will you please go into the garden for The Cake." Bone, no admirer of Alison's boys whom he had found crude and bumptious, admitted their social confidence; he must remember to say as much to her. He found Grizel, delightful sight, under the apple tree in the garden, ready to cut Mrs. Garland's fine confection, and he put his hand over her slim warm one on the knife. Cameras clicked. He bent to see under the rim of the apricot hat and was astonished all over again at the clear green of her eyes. He wanted to say a great deal, to say a compliment, to praise his luck. He could only smile.

Her uncle, Colonel Kinloch, proposed their health. Bone said as the glasses were raised, "Thank you," and then, "There'll be no speeches." He was wrong about this, but for the moment everyone laughed, and came to get pieces of cake, and several people seemed to want to kiss Grizel. There was a little flurry and a squeal or two as an apple thudded from the tree missing the table, and Nicola Garland said she would cut up the cake indoors. Most of the guests followed and he was almost alone with Grizel.

"Hallo, you," she said. "We've done it."

"I think we have. I was afraid your whole class was going to join us—or did you want them to? What's become of them?"

"I don't know. Ask Cha. That minx knew it was planned."

Linking fingers they walked toward the house, and stepped inside.

Cleaving the crowd like a Fury, white faced and all in black came Ravenna, fierce eyes fixed on Bone, shouting with distorted mouth.

"How dare you accuse my grandmother?" He saw Locker converging, but Ravenna, hitting aside Alison's restraining hand, came up to Bone and shouted in his face. "You're nothing but pigs! No *surprise* they call you that. Pigs! A helpless ill old lady and now she's dead and can't answer! It's all so *convenient,* isn't it, load it all on her. I know all about police corruption now. You just want your record . . ."

"Better talk in private," Bone said. "Grizel, I'm sorry—"

"Private! Yes, you'd like to talk about it in private! You don't want people to know how you fix things! I won't be intimidated, though. I won't be gagged!"

Locker said, "You don't want to distress yourself like this, Miss Marsh," his voice loud to ride hers down. "Come on now, this isn't the time or the—"

"I'm going to speak out—"

Bone, furious because of the embarrassment to Grizel, the affront at her wedding, said shortly, "Not here. Of course you can speak. But not here and now. Why don't you—"

"Here and now! *Here and now!* I won't let you hush up what you're trying to do."

Locker and Bone walked forward; Grizel slipping aside opened the kitchen door and said, "What about in here?"

and they walked Ravenna, crowding her shouting and protesting, into the little kitchen.

"They're trying to gag me!" she yelled to the guests, craning over their shoulders as they came into the room and Locker shut the door.

"You'd better listen for a moment first," Bone said. "Then if you want to make accusations, your father is sure to have lawyers and you can do it in the proper form." He heard the party noise, which had been hushed by Ravenna's drama, start up louder than before. Nothing like laying on an entertainment at your wedding. He faced Ravenna, who was backed up against the sink which held a huge spray of flowers, brought too late and dumped in a bowl in the sink, propped on the mixer tap. Ravenna's hands were clawed by her sides and there was that in her eyes which reminded Bone vividly of Ysobel when she had turned on him from attacking Chris Thorn.

"What's the point of listening? I'm never going to believe anything you say. How can I, when I *know?*"

"The Superintendent knows what he's doing, miss."

"Oh yes, he knows what he's doing. He wants everything just neatly sewn up and someone to pat his back. Will you get a promotion for this, *Superintendent?*"

Bone put his voice in neutral. "What is it, exactly, that you don't believe, Miss Marsh?" He was sorry for her, trembling and glaring, the pink and yellow of the flowers like a brilliant cockade behind her black hair, trembling as she pressed against them.

"I don't believe *any of it.* I know my grandmother didn't kill my mother. She *loved* her, she wanted us to be a happy family together, I *know* she did. She told me over and over."

But, because your mother wasn't prepared to stay at home and be part of that family, Ysobel killed her. Aloud, Bone said, "Who do you say killed her, then?"

Ravenna shrugged and the flowers behind her quivered. "How do I know? A tramp in the lane. It happens all the time, doesn't it? People come out of nowhere and kill people for no reason. A tramp thought she had money on her. It's your job to find that out."

Bone saw no point in pursuing that any further. He wanted to calm her, as he had no hope of convincing her, to calm her by making her think instead of simply feeling. It was fourteen years ago and he had no proof that Ravenna's theory was not perfectly true. His own certainty about it was quite immaterial.

"What about your uncle? Hasn't he told you how she attacked him?"

Ravenna raised her clenched hands to shoulder level in exasperation. Irrelevantly, Bone saw again that her black nail varnish was chipped and, so far from having talons, she bit her nails. "Oh, Chris is paranoid. He thinks everyone has it in for him. Dad, you, Lewis, everyone. And he got it all wrong. She was *dying,* wasn't she? Of course, she *fell* on him. What did he expect?"

"She went for his heart with a dagger."

"A paperknife, you mean." Ravenna's scorn was triumphant. "That old thing's been on Dad's desk for years. She'd just picked it up—to take my mother's photograph out of the frame."

Bone gave her credit for working it out quite logically. She had not come to confront him without cause. Folding her arms, she leaned back on the sink now and stared defiantly.

"She didn't know what she was doing. You try having a heart attack and see if you know what you're doing with your hands. And you did it to her."

Locker said, "She attacked Mr. Thorn before we came in."

"Attacked! You won't see it, will you? You hounded her to death. She might have got better before, she got better after Monday. But then *you* turn up and give her the fright of her life!"

Without question, Ysobel had not counted on being discovered in the act. Her murders up to then had been private affairs, conducted in the bosom of the family.

Ravenna, though, saw the police, saw him, as responsible for Ysobel's death. No wonder she had turned up to blight his wedding.

"Why do you think my arrival frightened her so?" Still he questioned, to make her think, to make her amenable to reason.

"Because she thought you'd come to arrest Dad, of course. You came to the study."

It made sense. Jake was a perfectly good suspect; even the uninitiated knew that the most likely killer was the spouse. Ravenna was well aware that obsessive devotion to Jake had ruled Ysobel's life. What she could not accept was how far it had taken her.

"Who do you think murdered your stepmother?"

This was the ace question. Ravenna could not claim it was her father or her uncle; here, a convenient tramp was out of the running. That left Morgan Carradine or Paul Lackland; Bone was interested to see which she could choose.

"It was an accident of course. She simply slipped on the magazines. Her feet were on the magazines. I saw. You can skid for yards—" She thrust her hands toward Bone to demonstrate. "You thought it was murder because that's how you see things. Anyone else would have thought it was an accident and there wouldn't have been any of—any of all of this. And my grandmother would be alive!"

She was trembling again and Bone felt renewed pity. When first he had seen her he'd thought she was trouble; what he had not known was how much of it she was heading for in herself. Whatever adolescent quarrels she'd had with Fenny, she knew that she'd been brought up with care and affection; she had worn Fenny's handiwork to the funeral. She loved her grandmother, who had adored her. He debated whether she might not be better off without the truth.

"Wasn't a second accident in one week—"

"You would say that! But accidents happen, they happen all the time. Anna was unlucky. Paleys is unlucky. It's the peacocks, Dad always hated them, it was Fenny who liked

242

them. Fenny just brought the bad luck on herself when she got them."

It was certainly what she wanted to believe, and Bone might have left it there, let her hear more later perhaps, but Locker was moved to defend Fenny, whom he had admired.

"You can't go blaming peacocks, miss, when there's forensic proof it was not an accident."

Ravenna turned her basilisk stare on Locker.

"What proof have you managed to cook up, then? She fell on that spike. Nobody pushed her."

Bone made a gesture that Locker missed. He went on, "Your grandmother did, Miss Marsh. I'm sorry; her finger-prints were lifted off Mrs. Fenny's face and the lab have analyzed the talc in her hair. It's your grandmother's. No one else in the house used that make."

Ravenna's stare glazed, and Bone stepped forward. She might faint, she might attack Locker. Instead, tears seemed to jump from her eyes and she let out a wail, as a child might whose last safety is taken from it.

The door opened suddenly into Bone's back. He moved, and Grizel was there. She put her husband gently aside and took hold of Ravenna who, blinded and howling, allowed herself to be held. Bone and Locker hastily left the kitchen and shut the door firmly.

"Poor girl. I had to tell her, sir. It wasn't fair she should go on thinking like that."

Bone nodded. Ravenna was not going to make the mistake, now or ever, of thinking life was fair. She'd learned that lesson young.

The practical necessity now was to find someone to take her home. If Grizel had to have her arms full this day he preferred it to be with him. Among those whose faces had turned toward him as he appeared again and a slight hush descended, he saw Miss Mallett, and he made for her through the crowd without hesitation. As he had expected, she did not hesitate either, but finished her portion of bridecake and was ready to provide transport to Beeches for Ravenna.

"I know Antonia Thorn well. I shall be delighted to help. The girl must be very upset."

Thank God for headmistresses, Bone thought. Succoring adolescents is their daily chore. Ravenna will be hard put to it to throw Miss Mallett out of her stride. She was already leading the way to her car when Grizel brought Ravenna, with tear-streaked face but no longer howling, through a sympathetic murmur of guests to the front door. She glanced at no one and he thought she was still in shock. He hoped Morgan Carradine would make an understanding stepmother.

Grizel returned, and taking a glass from the tray Bone's nephew offered, she picked up her husband's hand and folded his fingers around the stem. "Poor Robert. Not what you needed today."

They heard Miss Mallett's car start up and drive away. He held the glass to Grizel's lips and she drank. "I'd better not have any more. I'll be driving. Do you want me to get nicked on my wedding day?"

"You would be if this was a sitcom." She drank the champagne, pale gold like her hair. "Your daughter's enjoying herself."

He turned his head to see Cha talking to Justin.

"How the devil did he get in?"

"He brought Ravenna over on his bike, but he said he wasn't going to take her back, not after her making a row at the wedding."

Justin was drinking champagne, a happy skeleton at this feast. Bone could see that Cha was animated, no doubt confident that she looked her best in the apricot dress with her little rosy crown and those ribbons.

"I know why you're marrying me, Robert. You want me to cope with Justin Rafferty."

"The only reason. When Cha is besieged by boyfriends, I shall call on Kinloch."

Later, he drove her past Paleys on their way to stay the weekend at a friend's flat in Hastings. Cha, at present busy clearing up the debris of the party under Nicola Garland's aegis, was to stay with Prue Grant who had also volunteered to help.

No Ancient Mariner had come to stop the car and he felt, as they came to Paleys and drove past, that a cloud was lifting, that something was being exorcised.

"Look, Robert. The peacocks. Aren't they beautiful?"

Fenny's beloved pets were being loaded, protesting, on a van parked in the lane. An iridescent neck protruded from the top of a crate and the peacock gave its baleful scream. Bone, picking up speed, grimaced.

"I'm not sure I don't agree with Ravenna, that they're bad luck."

"Nonsense, Robert." Grizel sounded very Scots and sensible. "The bad luck at Paleys was Ysobel. You know that. I'm not having a superstitious husband, I hope."

Bone, smiling, drove on to Hastings with his good luck at his side.

SUSANNAH STACEY

THE SUPERINTENDENT BONE MYSTERIES

"Unpretentious and credible in the best Agatha
Christie tradition. Very British and very
good...makes you ache for the last page."
—*Yorkshire Post*

GOODBYE, NANNY GRAY

A KNIFE AT THE OPERA

BODY OF OPINION

GRAVE RESPONSIBILITY

THE LATE LADY

**POCKET
BOOKS**

Available from Pocket Books

628-02

ENJOY SOME OF THE MYSTERY POCKET BOOKS HAS TO OFFER!

SAMUEL LLEWELLYN
__BLOOD KNOT 86951-5/$4.99
__DEADEYE 67044-1/$4.99
__DEATH ROLL 67043-2/$3.95

ANN C. FALLON
__DEAD ENDS 75134-4/$4.99
__POTTER'S FIELD 75136-0/$4.99
__WHERE DEATH LIES 70624-1/$4.99

AUDREY PETERSON
__DARTHMOOR BURIAL 72970-5/$4.99
__THE NOCTURNE MURDER 66102-7/$3.50

TAYLOR McCAFFERTY
__BED BUGS 75468-8/$4.99
__PET PEEVES 72802-4/$3.50
__RUFFLED FEATHERS 72803-2/$4.50

JUDITH VAN GIESON
__NORTH OF THE BORDER 76967-7/$4.99
__THE OTHER SIDE OF DEATH 74565-4/$4.99
__RAPTOR 73243-9/$4.99

DALLAS MURPHY
__APPARENT WIND 68554-6/$4.99
__LOVER MAN 66188-4/$4.99
__LUSH LIFE 68556-2/$4.99